Read and Pass On.

P. Coster Aug. 2009 Waukesha
V Heggie 10/2010

SPENCER'S
MOUNTAIN

**Center Point
Large Print**

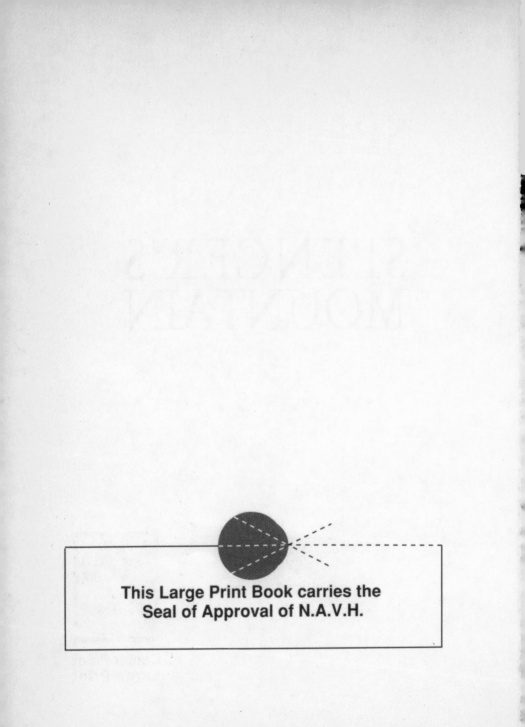

SPENCER'S MOUNTAIN

EARL HAMNER JR.

CENTER POINT PUBLISHING
THORNDIKE, MAINE

With enduring gratitude to my aunts, whose love
and faith and abundant generosity made the writing
of this book possible:
Miss Nora Spencer Hamner
Mrs. Lottie Hamner Dover
Mrs. Julian Myers

This Center Point Large Print edition
is published in the year 2005 by arrangement with
Don Congdon Associates.

The text of this Large Print edition is unabridged. In other
aspects, this book may vary from the original edition. Printed in
Thailand. Set in 16-point Times New Roman type.

ISBN 1-58547-621-8

Library of Congress Cataloging-in-Publication Data

Hamner, Earl.
    Spencer's mountain / Earl Hamner.--Center Point large print ed.
    p. cm.
    ISBN 1-58547-621-8 (lib. bdg. : alk. paper)
    1. Mountain life--Fiction. 2. Rural families--Fiction. 3. Blue Ridge Mountains--Fiction.
  4. Virginia--Fiction. 5. Large type books. I. Title.

PS3558.A456S68 2005
813'.54--dc22

2005001158

CHAPTER 1

ON THE DAY BEFORE Thanksgiving the Spencer clan began to gather. It was a custom that at this time during the year the nine sons would come together in New Dominion. On Thanksgiving Eve they would celebrate their reunion with food and drink and talk. On the day itself the men would leave at dawn to hunt for deer.

All day cars had been arriving at Clay Spencer's house. Each car was greeted by Clay-Boy, a thin boy of fifteen with a serious freckled face topped by an unruly shock of darkening corn-colored hair. Now the day was drawing toward evening, but still the boy lingered at the back gate waiting for the one uncle who had not yet arrived, the one he wanted most to see.

In the west the taller ridges of the Blue Ridge Mountains were rimmed with a fading autumn silver, but in the foothills, in the Spencer's back yard, all was in darkness when the ninth and last car stopped at the back gate. Clay-Boy, waving his flashlight excitedly, directed the car to a parking place.

"That you, Clay-Boy?" shouted the man who stepped out of the car.

"Uncle Virgil?" called Clay-Boy, suddenly shy in front of his city uncle. Virgil Spencer was the one who had gone to Richmond during the Depression when the mill had closed for four years. In Richmond, Virgil had found work as a mechanic and had stayed on there even after the mill had reopened.

5

"We been waiten for you," the boy said.

"Who-all's here?" asked Virgil as he began unloading his gun and shells and hunting coat from the back seat.

"You're the last one," said Clay-Boy.

"Your mama still got that law about no whiskey in the house?" asked Virgil. He reached into the glove compartment and removed a fifth of bourbon.

"There's whiskey there all the same," answered Clay-Boy. "They've been goen back and forth between here and Scottsville all day long." Scottsville was the closest place where store whiskey could be bought.

"What she don't know won't hurt her," laughed Virgil. He concealed the bottle in his hunting coat, and the man and the boy walked toward the crowded little company house where lights beamed cheerfully from each window and the muffled sounds of festive conversation could be heard.

"I'm goen with you-all tomorrow," said Clay-Boy. "On the hunt."

"That's what you said last year," said Virgil.

"Last year I wasn't but fourteen," Clay-Boy objected.

"Last year your mama wouldn't let you," Virgil reminded him.

"This year I'm goen," Clay-Boy said.

Last year's hunt was a shameful memory to Clay-Boy. For as long as he could remember he had wanted to go. Right up until the night before the hunt he had had his father's permission. Then on the eve of the hunt, his mother, learning his plans, had said *no*. He

6

wasn't old enough, Olivia had claimed. Didn't know how to handle a gun. Might not even come back alive with all those men out there crazy with whiskey and shooting at anything that moved. In the end she had won, and he had retired in an agony of frustration and cried silently into the pillow so late that he had not even wakened the next morning and had been deprived of even the pleasure of watching the men depart.

This year Clay-Boy was using a different strategy. He had spoken to his father about going on the hunt and Clay had agreed that it was all right with him as long as Olivia did not object too much. Clay-Boy then decided he just would not mention it to his mother at all and when the time came to go on the hunt he would simply go with the men.

When Clay-Boy and his uncle came to the kitchen door, Virgil threw it open and shouted, "Let's start the party!"

"Well, Lord, look what the wind blew in," exclaimed Olivia. Virgil was one of the youngest of the Spencer men and a great favorite with his brothers' wives. He kissed each of the sisters-in-law in turn, and came at last to his mother, the undisputed ruler of the clan, old but still beautiful, so tiny it seemed incredible she could have mothered such an enormous brood of sons. In her white hair was a jaunty bunch of artificial violets. She had been enthroned in a rocking chair from which she had been directing the cooking, the conversation, and the setting of the table, all the while delivering a lecture on the advantages of a large family; she

7

was far from satisfied with the number of grandchildren her sons' wives had presented to her.

"How you doen, cutie?" Virgil asked.

"Bend down here and give your old mama a kiss," she demanded, laughing happily. Virgil bent forward and her hands came up and held his head while they kissed.

"When you goen to bring a wife home?" she asked, releasing him.

"Mama," he teased, "what do I want with a wife?"

"What you want with a wife is to get some grandchildren like the rest of the boys," she scolded.

"Where is everybody?" Virgil asked, meaning his brothers.

"They're all in there in the liven room, swappen lies. Go on in there. I reckon they're expecten you."

"I'll be a ring-tail ripstaver!" exclaimed Clay Spencer when his brother entered the room. Clay-Boy watched as Virgil was welcomed into the group. The brothers were intensely fond of each other, and there was much clumsy hugging and back-slapping. More often than not their joy in seeing each other was expressed in an oath or a hearty laugh.

Watching his father and his uncles, Clay-Boy was impatient to be one of them. They were tall men. Not one of them was under six feet. They were small-boned but muscular, and each had some different shade of red hair and brown eyes. But it was not only to be like them physically that Clay-Boy yearned. It was his dream that some day he would earn the reputation his father and his uncles already enjoyed, for they were known to be good providers, hearty eaters, prodigious drinkers, courageous fighters, incomparable lovers and honorable in all dealings with their friends and neighbors. It was a proud thing to be a Spencer man, thought Clay-Boy.

Of the nine sons only Virgil had left the community permanently. The others, Matt, John, Rome, Luke, Anse, Ben, Clayton and Ham had left from time to time to look for better jobs, but they were never satisfied away from New Dominion and always came home again. Some of the boys—like John and Ben—drove to jobs in Charlottesville each day, but that was only twenty-eight miles away and they were always home with their families by nightfall.

Clay-Boy's attention was drawn away from his uncles when he suddenly caught sight of his grandfather. His Grandfather Zebulon was a handsome old man. His hair, like his curling handlebar mustache, was white and carefully combed, and even his great age had failed to dim the zest, the merriment, the celebration of life that shone in his clear brown eyes.

The old man sat near the fire. He was not being ignored intentionally. It was simply that he was too old and inactive to rise and push his way into the group. His lips formed words to welcome his son and his hands would rise up to embrace him, but then Virgil's attention would be attracted by one of his brothers.

Clay-Boy slipped over and stood beside his grandfather's chair, and when a lull came in the conversation called, "Uncle Virgil, here's Granddaddy."

Virgil came and hugged the old man.

"Papa," he scolded fondly, "what you doen up so late? I thought you always hit the hay when the sun set."

"Couldn't go to sleep till you got here, boy," said Zebulon.

"How they treaten you, Papa?" asked Virgil.

"I'll tell you the Lord's truth," answered Zebulon in his thin old voice, "these boys have nearly made an old woman out of me. Took my gun away from me, won't let me drive a car from here to the gate, and they hide every drop of whiskey that comes in the house."

"I'll take care of that, Papa," said Virgil. He reached in his pocket and brought out the bottle of whiskey he had hidden away and passed it to his father.

"Now," said Virgil, "let's get caught up on everythen that's been goen on."

Listening to the talk of his father, his grandfather and his uncles, Clay-Boy sat on the floor curled against the edge of a sofa, storing away each word to be remembered and savored long after the reunion was over. Suddenly he heard his name.

"Where is that boy anyway?" It was Clay speaking.

"Right here, Daddy," he said. "I been here all the time."

"Well, come on out here, son," Clay said. "Your Uncle Virgil brought you somethen from Richmond."

Virgil was holding out a long thin package wrapped in brown paper. "I thought it was about time you had one of your own," Virgil said.

Silence fell among the men while Clay-Boy unwrapped the package. He removed the paper and discovered a hunting knife. It was enclosed in a sheath that had slits along the top so it could be attached to his belt. The handle was of beautifully polished wood and when he withdrew the blade from the sheath he found it razor-sharp. Self-consciously Clay-Boy attached the sheath to his belt and returned the blade to its place.

"I sure do thank you, Uncle Virgil," Clay-Boy said. "I been wanten one."

"You know what to do with it, boy?" Clay asked. "Sure," said Clay-Boy. "If the deer ain't dead you jump on him and cut his throat."

"When you goen to take that boy on the hunt, Clay?" asked the old grandfather.

"He says he's goen with us tomorrow," said Clay.

"He's old enough," the old grandfather said. "When I was his age I must of killed me twenty-five deer. It wasn't for sport back in them days. Food. Salt 'em down like you fellers do a pig nowadays. I plan on venison tomorrow night."

"Clay-Boy!" His mother called from the kitchen.

"Yes'm?"

"You plannen on some supper you better put some wood in the box. Nearly empty."

Clay-Boy left the men reluctantly and was going through the kitchen when his mother noticed the hunting knife.

"What are you doen with that thing on your hip?" demanded Olivia.

"Uncle Virgil brought it to me from Richmond," he said.

"You be careful of that thing," she warned. "You're liable to fall down and cut yourself on it."

"Aw, Mama," he objected impatiently. It annoyed him that Olivia always pointed out the most impossible and improbable dangers in any situation. Never had he tried out any new thing without having her warn him that it was too dangerous or that he was not old enough or he was sure to get hurt in the endeavor.

"And if you've got any notions about goen deer-hunten tomorrow you can just put it out of mind right now," Olivia warned as the boy was halfway through the door.

Clay-Boy replied by slamming the door behind him as he went to the woodhouse for fuel to feed the ever-hungry old cooking range.

"Livy, you're goen to turn that boy into a sissy-pants," observed the old grandmother, Elizabeth. "Keepen him here in the house all the time. Never letten him go off and learn men's ways."

"It's just not time for him to go hunten yet," said Olivia. "You start 'em off hunten the next thing you know the old Army or Navy comes in here after 'em and that's just one step away from getten married and leaven home. And where's your child then? Off and gone, that's where."

"Nine of 'em I raised," the old grandmother said. "They all went off and married women, God knows. 'Cept Virgil and God knows what'll come of that boy, breathen city dirt all day and ruinen his eyes with moven-picture shows at night."

"Boys are a heartache," said Olivia.

"God knows," muttered the old grandmother.

When Clay-Boy returned to the house, his arms laden with wood, supper was ready.

The meal was served in shifts, the men served first at the long kitchen table with their women hovering about, refilling each dish as soon as it came near being empty. The table was laden with the good country food that is abundant at that time of the year when all the summer canning is finished, when the hogs have been slaughtered and salted away in the smokehouse, when the fruits of the harvest are gathered, when the safety from hunger through the winter is assured, and a feast can be enjoyed without concern about whether the extra food can be spared.

During the meal the men ate for the most part in silence, but once Virgil looked up, and, spotting Clay-Boy across the table from him, inquired, "When you comen down to Richmond and let me teach you the mechanic's trade?"

Before Clay-Boy could answer, his mother had spoken for him.

"Don't you go enticen that boy out of school, Virgil Spencer," Olivia said. "He's goen to graduate from high school before he goes looken around to learn a trade. And it looks like if he keeps on the way he has been, he's goen to graduate at the head of his class."

"The boy's got a head on him," said Clay. "That's a fact."

The praise made Clay-Boy uncomfortable, and he was glad when his Uncle Virgil buttered his fifth hot biscuit and observed: "I been down yonder with city folks so long I forgot what real food tasted like."

"You can tell that to look at you," said old Elizabeth. "Thin as a rail. What do they feed you in them old lunch counters anyway?"

"Cardboard mostly," Virgil replied. "You order a steak or pork chops or ham and eggs, it don't matter what. Tastes like cardboard all the same."

"That's what comes from goen off so far from home. You ought to be home. Eaten in them old meal-a-minute places all the time. Wonder you ain't dead. When was the last time you been to church?"

"Land of Goshen, Mama!" exclaimed Clay. "Why don't you shut up and let the man eat his supper?"

"You heish your disrespect, Clay," said the old grandmother. "Here, Virgil, try some more of these butter beans. Me and Livy raised 'em last spring and it's about the best batch we put up all summer."

When the men had finished and each had departed, sated and drowsy from so much food, the women removed the dishes, washed them, and reset the table.

As Clay-Boy was leaving the kitchen to follow the men into the living room, his mother called after him, "You better start getten ready for bed, boy."

"I'll go in a little bit, Mama," he promised.

"Don't you try to stay up with them men," she said.

"They're goen to be in there gabben half the night."

"Yes ma'am," said Clay-Boy and slipped into the living room. He sat on the floor at the end of a sofa and watched while the men began to pass a bottle around the room.

The old grandfather had several drinks and the whiskey loosened his tongue.

"There ain't the deer around no more there used to be," he mused. "Nor bear neither for that matter. When I was a young buck look like all you had to do was step out the door and wait for somethen to come along. Bear sometimes, deer sometimes and all the time there was wild turkey. Times is limbered up these days. Ever'thing killed off 'cept some scrawny little old doe that don't know enough to do her grazen while you boys is asleep. That's about all you'll run up on tomorrow."

From the kitchen the old grandmother called, "Don't you-all boys give that old man no more whiskey. You know how he gets."

"Pay no 'tention to her," the old man said. "I been married to that old woman nearly a hundred years and ain't heard a thing from her but belly-achen."

"You see what I mean," from the kitchen. "Not another drop."

"Old woman, you heish your mouth," the old man called. "Any man lived to be a hundred and three on the next Fourth of July got a right."

"Them boys have give that old man too much," Elizabeth grumbled to her daughters-in-law. "Claimen he's a hundred and three! He ain't a day over ninety-five.

Man that old ought to be getten ready to meet Old Master Jesus 'stead of sitten in there drinken whiskey and tellen lies."

"Up on the mountain, when I was a boy," the old man began the story he told each year, "there used to be a big old buck deer that was white all over and had pink eyes. Lots of folks that never laid eyes on him used to claim there wasn't no such thing. Some of them even claimed he was a ghost. I don't say one way or the other, ghost or flesh. All I know is I have laid eyes on him."

Sitting almost at his grandfather's feet, Clay-Boy listened to the telling of the story. He had heard it hundreds of times before, but each new telling would send shivers down his spine, and he knew that tonight when he went to sleep he would dream of the white deer; he always did after he had heard the story.

"I never will forget the day," old Zebulon continued. "It was comen long toward fall of the year and I was out on the mountain cutten some wood against the cold weather. Had my gun along just in case any game come by. Around the middle of the day I took a little rest and was eaten a little lunch the old woman had put in a paper bag, and all of a sudden somethen moved through them woods like a winter wind. Never made no noise, mind, just wind. Well sir, it was that big white deer and I'll tell you the God's truth if I hadn't of reared up right that minute he'd of run over me. I got in two good shots at him. I was a young man in them days, before my eyes turned to water, and I was the best shot in the country. Maybe I missed that deer,

16

maybe he was travelen too fast. Maybe it was like some used to claim, maybe he was a real ghost and buckshot couldn't of done no good even if it went straight through his heart."

"What ever happened to that old buck?" asked Clay, knowing that unless the old man were forced to end the story he might start it somewhere near the beginning and tell the whole thing all over again.

"Nobody killed him yet," the old man said. "The way I figure it he ain't met his match. The way it is, that deer bein' white and all, he stand out where a regular deer don't. He has fought just about ever'thing there is to fight from man to bear and done whopped 'em all. He knows all the tricks there is to know, that deer do."

"Papa," said Virgil, "sometimes I think you made that old white deer up. If he really roams these parts, how come nobody but you ever laid eyes on him?"

"Oh, he's there all right," said the old man. "Maybe the eye sharp enough to see him just ain't come along yet. I've even heard it told that if that deer dies by human hand his spirit will pass into the man that kills him. From that day on that man will be different, marked to follow a path unknown, a man marked for glory!"

The old man's voice had risen so that it could be heard throughout the house, and for a moment after he had uttered his prophecy there was a sober silence.

"That old man is drunk," said Elizabeth from the kitchen. "Them boys is feeden him whiskey just as sure as you're born."

"Clay-Boy!" called Olivia.

"Yes ma'am," the boy answered.

"Bedtime."

"I'm goen, Mama."

Upstairs in the boys' room, Clay-Boy undressed in the darkness so as not to wake his sleeping brothers. As he took off each article of clothing he placed it with care so that he might find it all the easier in the morning. It would still be dark when he dressed again to go on the hunt.

In his bed Clay-Boy sought sleep but it would not come. He was so keyed up that his mind could not hold onto any subject, but kept leaping from one exciting fact to another. Tomorrow he would join the hunters. He owned a knife which was not a secondhand hand-me-down, but a brand-new shining thing that was entirely his own and had come all the way from Richmond. His mother would be angry when she found that he had gone on the hunt, but by then it would be too late. Tomorrow he would become a hunter. So went the thoughts of the boy as he hovered on the brink of sleep.

Finally sleep did overtake him, and as he slept visions of the great white deer came again and again across the fields of his dreams, sometimes distant, a white and marble sculptured ghost at the edge of the forest; another time so close he could hear the swift encounter of its hoofs against the frozen earth before it leapt into the dream sky, so high it would be silhouetted against the moon, white on white; and again so close he could hear the bellowings of its lungs sucking in great gusts of air and exhaling so powerfully that the wind itself changed direction, always its antlers held delicately high above the ensnaring branches of the trees and the bushes. And every time Clay-Boy pulled the trigger he would feel the harsh recoil of the gun against the muscle of his shoulder and wake with the sound of the explosion ringing like a diminishing echo in his ears.

After a while he drifted into a sleep like some gently rocking unguided craft that flowing with the current will drift from shallow into deeper and deeper water, his final coherent thought: Tomorrow *it* will happen. Finally he drifted so deep into oceans of sleep that not even the dream of the great white deer could reach him, and he rested.

CHAPTER 2

IT WAS NOT YET DAWN when Clay-Boy woke to the rich and furtive voices of his father and his uncles that floated up to him from the kitchen. The hours during which he had slept might have been seconds, for he was awake immediately with all the intoxicating thoughts that had been there the moment he had gone to sleep.

He dressed in the darkness. It was no great chore except that he was trembling from the cold and the anticipation of whatever unknown thing lay ahead.

Going down the hall he was careful to tiptoe past the room his mother and father shared. He knew his mother would be awake on account of the noise. Over the years it had become a custom that the men would prepare their own breakfast, and he knew that if he could get safely past his mother's door he would be free to join the men.

"Clay-Boy!" her voice sounded distant behind the closed door and he pretended not to hear. He kept on tiptoeing down the entire stairway until he was at last on the ground floor. He felt his way along the dark downstairs hallway and came suddenly into the light of the kitchen.

Some somber thing had come over the Spencer men during the night. Perhaps it was that they had wakened too soon from sleep or perhaps they felt the effects of the whiskey they had drunk. More probably it was a foreboding about the hunt itself, for no matter who faced the deer that day would be put to a test. Before he came out of the forest, something of his character, his reputation as a marksman, his courage, his stealth, or even his very manhood would be challenged and he would either maintain his position among the men of his clan or he would lose something of himself. There was the feeling that anything could happen and each of the hunters had his own secret intention, hope, and desire that it would be he who would bring back the deer which, even as they gathered to kill it, was waiting somewhere in the darkness on Spencer's Mountain.

At the old cooking range Clay was preparing breakfast. Already there was a huge pile of bacon, and into the bacon grease Clay poured a bowl of eggs for scrambling. Two pots of strong coffee were perking on the back of the stove; the aroma of the coffee and the bacon had a restorative effect on the boy.

"Grab yourself a plate there, son," said Matt.

Clay-Boy went to the kitchen cabinet and took down a plate for himself and placed it with the others heating on the back of the stove.

Before the food was placed on the table and all during breakfast the bottle of bourbon was passed from one man to another. The first time the bottle was passed, Rome automatically handed the bottle around to Clay-Boy's father's place, but since Clay was still at the stove, Clay-Boy took the bottle. Since he had recently wakened from sleep and since in his haste he had not brushed his teeth, the whiskey was the first thing to pass through his throat that morning, and as he swallowed a good slug of the stuff, his first impulse was to vomit it back again. Mercifully, for it would have been unmanly in the eyes of the other men, Clay-Boy was able to hold it down and passed the bottle on to the uncle seated to his right.

"Eat hearty, men," said Clay, placing the platter of scrambled eggs on the table. Clay-Boy, too excited to eat, was glad when the men rose from the table, put on their hunting coats and began gathering their guns.

The old grandfather was not going on the hunt, but as each of his sons filed out of the kitchen door he offered advice and admonitions.

"I'd try that ridge over there right above where the

minnow creek goes under the footbridge. Best place in the world for deer."

Or:

"A deer is a heap smarter than a human man so don't go thinken you can outsmart him."

To Clay-Boy, who was last out of the door, he said, "You know what they'll do to you if you shoot and miss one, don't you, boy?"

"Yes, sir," said Clay-Boy. "They'll cut off my shirt-tail."

And finally, when his sons had reached the back gate, the old man called to them, "Don't nobody shoot each other," but they were gone beyond the hearing of his voice. He closed the door and sat alone in the kitchen and watched through the window as the silhouette of the mountain began to take form out of the darkness.

A light snow had fallen during the night. As Clay-Boy followed along after his father and his uncles, he saw that each of them had stepped in the other's footsteps so that someone coming after them might guess that only one person had made the tracks. Carefully the boy lengthened his stride so that his footsteps coincided with those made by the men he followed.

Ahead of him Spencer's Mountain loomed snow-white, pine-green, arched with the blue of a cold winter morning. The mountain itself housed all those things mysterious to the boy. There were caves there where, long ago, boys had been lost and never found again.

One of the caves had a lake in it, so deep and so hidden that if you dropped a stone from the rim you could count to five before the sound of the splash would travel back to you. The mountain itself he had never explored, being forbidden by his mother; it was said to be the home of the largest rattlesnake ever seen, a snake so outsized and savage that its fame had been carried through several counties by woodsmen who had seen it and had never been able to kill it. The mountain held all that was unexplored for Clay-Boy, but most of all its fascination for him lay in the fact that it was the range of the great white deer imbedded in his memory from the earliest tales he had heard from his grandfather.

The hunting party was about a quarter of the way up the mountain when one of the men called out, "There's a good stand right here."

"Let's give this one to Clay-Boy," Clay suggested, and the other men agreed.

"I'll be right up there where the road turns, son," said Clay. "If one comes 'long I'll let you have first crack at him."

Clay-Boy took up his station just off the roadway. He found an old tree stump, brushed it clear of snow and sat down. For a little while he could hear the distant conversations of the other men as each took his stand, but finally he could hear them no longer and a great stillness settled over the woods.

He was not as cold as he had expected to be. Actually he might have done without one of the extra sweaters he was wearing. After a while he began to feel drowsy. He nodded, catching himself each time before his gradually lowering chin reached his chest. Each time on opening his eyes he would scan all that he could see for deer and, finding none, would begin to nod again.

Something quite suddenly brought him fully awake. It was not a noise, for no sound had come. It was something the boy felt, a presence he sensed, and in the instant his eyes opened he saw standing not more than thirty feet away an enormous deer.

What he saw was fixed forever in his mind, the dull gray sky of the winter morning, the barren limbs of the sleeping trees, the virgin snow and the great deer which stood silent, immobile, and enduring through all of memory.

The deer either did not see him or it had no fear. It stood nearly rigid; only its sides moved as it inhaled gulps of air and exhaled them in small clouds of fog on the frosty air. The animal was a majestic thing. It stood with its proud head high and erect, its many-pointed antlers regally aloft. Its coat was white, and even across the distance that separated him and the deer, Clay-Boy could see that its eyes were pink.

A shocking thing came then into the boy's mind. He had thought so much about the hunt that the whole adventure had been contained in the idea. He had pictured himself coming home triumphantly carrying the greatest deer in the forest, but the actual killing of the deer he had not even imagined. Now it came to him with a terrible knowing that the whole purpose of his being there was that he should kill the live thing that stood before him.

Clay-Boy hesitated. He could feel the small beads of cold perspiration breaking out on his forehead and down his back. He did not want to kill the beast. For one brief moment he wished the deer would leap away and lose itself in the forest, but it stood silent, quivering, waiting.

When Clay-Boy raised his rifle his hands were trembling. Carefully he steadied his aim by laying his head against the butt of the rifle and when he found the heart of the deer he closed his eyes and pulled the trigger. The recoil sent the boy tumbling backward and when he scrambled to his feet he thought for a second the shot had missed its mark. But in that same instant the forelegs gave way and the deer collapsed into a kneeling position. Even when the hind legs folded and the deer's body was entirely on the ground it held its head aloft, as if reluctant to surrender its antlers to the ground.

Clay-Boy had heard enough hunting stories that he knew now what must be done. He ran headlong toward the stricken deer, grasped the antlers, and with all his force twisted them over and rammed them into the ground, thus protecting himself and exposing the deer's throat at the same time.

He reached for the knife, fumbling over the snap at the sheath for a second, and then when he had the knife firmly grasped he plunged the blade into the fur and leather of the animal's throat. A shudder wrenched through the dying deer and when the boy felt the quiver of final strength wane from the antler he held, something seared through his body that filled him with awe and terror.

Clay-Boy turned away, reeled back toward the stump where he had been sitting, and vomited. When his retching stopped he looked up and saw his father crashing through the underbrush.

"I heard a shot," called Clay. "You all right, boy?"

Clay-Boy nodded, and pointed to the body of the deer.

"Oh my God, son," exclaimed Clay. He pointed his gun into the sky and fired three shots, a signal to the other brothers to come in from their positions.

Clay examined the deer wonderingly, and then he looked again to his son.

"You're tremblen," said Clay.

"I was thinking about what Grandpa said," answered Clay-Boy, "about whoever killed the white deer would be marked someway."

"Whatever you're marked for, boy, you'll stand up to it," said Clay.

Someone was approaching down the snowy wood trail; when he turned the bend they saw that it was Virgil. He walked over to the deer, and when he saw that it was the white deer, he turned to Clay and said, "I'm kind of sorry you got him, Clay. It's a burden on a man to be marked."

"The boy got him," said Clay. "Not me."

Virgil went to where Clay-Boy, to hide his trembling, had knelt and was cleaning his knife in the earth and snow. Virgil knelt beside Clay-Boy, and though he spoke to Clay, his eyes were on Clay-Boy's eyes. "It wasn't no boy killed that deer, Clay," he said. "It took a man to do it."

It was a gracious thing for Virgil to say, and the remark had a calming effect on the boy. The trembling began to leave him and he was able now to squat alongside the carcass with his other uncles as they arrived, each one expressing his astonishment and admiration at what he had done, making guesses as to the deer's weight and counting the antlers.

When all the men were gathered they began to prepare the deer for the triumphant march home. Slits were made in the fore and hind legs and then the strong tendon pried through so the carrying pole might be inserted.

Anse, the eldest, and Clay, the strongest, shouldered the carrying pole and led the way out of the forest. When the men had come up the mountain, Clay-Boy had trailed at the end of the line, but now when Clay stepped forward, his uncles motioned for Clay-Boy to step in the line behind his father.

Snow had begun to fall again on Spencer's Mountain, and as it settled thickly over the place where the deer had received its death, the stain of the blood changed from vermilion to red to pink to white, and there was only the white stillness, the falling snow and the quickly vanishing outlines of the steps of men.

CHAPTER 3

AFTER THANKSGIVING the winter turned severe. Snow fell all through Christmas and New Year, blotting out the horizon from the boy who at odd times during the day would stop in his chores and gaze absently off toward the barn where the antlers of the great deer were mounted over the door. As the months passed and nothing extraordinary happened, he became less of a curiosity in the community, and this was a relief to him. But in his own mind he would reconstruct what had happened on the mountain, marvel at the event, and wonder what it could mean.

One day the icicles which had grown on the eaves of the barn began to glisten in the sunlight and melt. Each following day brought some new sign of spring. Olivia's crocuses along the front walk seemed to burst into blossom overnight. The earth began to dry and the only sign of winter that remained was the crusted patches of snow that lingered in shady corners beside the house. Soon, along every path through the hills the redbud and dogwood were in blossom, and the edge of every wood was filigreed with redbud pink and dogwood white.

One Saturday morning Clay-Boy woke at dawn and listened to the sounds of the house as it awakened to morning. The morning was quiet, still bathed in the pale light of dawn, broken only by the abrasive cry of some wakeful rooster. The only sound from inside the house was the regular, terrible rise and fall of his grandfather's snore. It came from the room downstairs which the two old people shared. Clay-Boy wondered if his grandmother was awake; she frequently complained that she had not slept a wink all night on account of the old man's snoring.

At five o'clock, Clay-Boy heard the alarm from the clock his father kept beside his bed. It sounded for a moment, then was silent as Clay wakened and turned it off. Clay-Boy listened now to his father's long deep yawn, smothered so as not to wake the children, and then after a moment the tortuous screech of bedsprings as his father raised himself in the bed and put his feet on the floor. Clay usually muttered to no one in particular a four-or-five-word weather forecast. This morning he said, "Goen to be a beaut."

Then there was silence again while Clay got into his work clothes, broken at last when he made his way down the stairs, through the living room and into the kitchen. Once in the kitchen Clay set about building the fire in the old wood cooking range, drenching each stick of wood with kerosene to make the fire start quicker. Then when the fire roared up the chimney he dressed in a heavier coat to go out and milk the cow and feed the pigs.

With the milk pail in his hand Clay tiptoed back to the foot of the stairs and called softly, "Sweetheart." It was his name for Olivia and the only thing he ever called her at that hour. And she whispered, "All right. I'm awake."

By the time Olivia reached the kitchen, Clay had gone to the barn. Soon the aroma of strong black coffee drifted up the stairway to where Clay-Boy lay, and the tantalizing smell of fried lean bacon, the bubbling, spattering, hissing sound of fried eggs, and all the warm rich sunny smells of biscuits baking.

Clay announced his return from the barn by placing the pail loudly on the kitchen table. Then Olivia strained the warm foamy milk into Mason jars, placed them in the refrigerator and sat down to breakfast with Clay.

While they ate they talked quietly and the sound of their voices floated up to Clay-Boy.

"Clay-Boy's goen to need money for his class ring soon," his mother said. "I put a downpayment of three dollars on it when they ordered them, but there's twelve more has to be paid when the rings come."

"I'm senden that boy through high school to get an education," said Clay. "What the Sam Hill does he need a ring for?"

"It's like a sign," explained Olivia, "something to show he graduated."

"What does he need a sign for?"

"Well, he can walk in some place and ask for a job and the minute the man sees that ring on his finger, he'll know he's a high school graduate and that'll put him ahead of the ones that aren't wearen one."

"A ring is somethen pretty to go on a woman's hand is my way of looken at it," said Clay. "Clay-Boy don't need any ring to show he's graduated from high

30

school. It's what they put in his head that counts."

"He's goen to be the only one in the class that won't get a ring, then. You want him to be different from the others?"

"You're A-1 right I want him to be different. I want him to make somethen of himself. The rest of 'em ain't goen to amount to a hill of beans. But Clay-Boy's goen somewhere in this world."

A man who had been to school only a few days in his life, Clay had an incredible respect for learning. In New Dominion it was a rare thing for a boy to graduate from high school because extreme youth was no barrier to finding a job with the company. Most boys dropped out of school once they passed the seventh grade to take a job, either to earn their independence or to help with the support of the numerous brothers and sisters. Long ago Clay Spencer had ruled out this possibility for his own sons and daughters. "I'll give 'em what I was too big a fool to get," he would declare. "Them babies of mine will get a high school education."

Now the first installment of his dream was drawing near. Clay-Boy, the only boy in a class of thirteen seniors, was due to graduate on the first of May.

"I know it's sinful to wish for somethen that just can't be," said Olivia, "but it would be my heart's craven to see that boy go on to college."

"He's got the brains for it," Clay nodded.

"No use daydreamen," said Olivia as she rose from the table to begin preparing the children's breakfast.

31

"Goen to be a nice day, looks like," said Clay. "There's the sun comen up."

A ray of sun sent a pencil of light into the room where the boys slept. Clay-Boy, careful not to wake his brother Matt, who slept beside him, rose from the bed and went to the window to watch the sun come up.

His window overlooked an orchard of crab apple trees. Clay-Boy pretended to himself that they had been planted by Johnny Appleseed, and there was no reason why they could not have been. Now in the first light of a spring morning a curtain of light fog was lifting from the orchard. Already the tender green leaves were glistening on the trees, disguising the heavy gnarled old trunks and branches with their color and shape.

Suddenly a flock of goldfinches flew into the orchard, thousands of little golden bundles that might have been flung from the morning sun into the pale green fog-damp orchard. They would cling to the young branches, fill the air with their canary-like warblings long enough to announce the new day and then disperse to their separate chores of eating or singing or courting. Each spring they came to the orchard and some mornings they came in such number that the pale green leaves would be concealed and the trees would become a swaying mass of gold and singing.

Clay-Boy watched the gold-green singing morning until he heard his mother's voice calling from the foot of the stairs. "Breakfast, everybody! Breakfast!"

Clay went to the center of the room and pulled the

cord that turned on the single electric bulb hanging from the ceiling. The glare of the bulb revealed two beds in the room. The one in which Clay-Boy had slept contained his next oldest brother, Matt. In the other bed, huddled together in a single blanket-covered lump were his next three brothers, Mark, Luke, and John. Clay-Boy gave each sleeping form a nudge, then crossed the hall, went into the girls' room and switched on the light. There, in two more beds, were Becky, Shirley and Pattie-Cake. There was another child, but he slept in a baby bed in the room with his father and mother. His name was Donnie; he had not grown old enough to have much impact on the family and was referred to mostly as the baby. When he was satisfied that the girls were awake Clay-Boy went down to the kitchen. One after another the brood followed.

"Lord God Almighty!" said Clay as he sat at the head of the table and looked at his assembled offspring, "I never saw so many beautiful babies in my life."

There were nine of them in all. Each one had red hair, but on each head the shade was a little different. Clay-Boy's hair was the color of dry corn shucks. Matt's was the red of the clay hills. Becky's long curls were the pink of a sunset; Shirley's plaits were auburn. Luke's hair was the russet of autumn leaves. Mark's was reddish-blond. John's ringlets were a golden red and Pattie-Cake's little ponytail was an orange red and the baby had so little hair it was hard to tell what shade it might become. The shade could be from dark to light, the color was predictable.

Each of the children was small of bone and lean. Some of them were freckled and some were not and some had the brown eyes of their father and some had their mother's green eyes, but on each of them there was some stamp of grace of build and movement, and it was this Clay voiced when he said, as he often did, "Every one of my babies is a thoroughbred."

They were assembled at a table nine feet long. Clay had built it himself, and it was flanked on each side by wooden benches. There was ample room at the table for all the children and even room left over; friends or relatives who happened to drop in around mealtime were sincerely welcomed. During the summer hardly a meal went by when, squeezed in among the Spencer children, there weren't two or three of the neighboring children taking advantage of the Spencers' sprawling hospitality, however frugal their means.

"Look at them babies," said Clay. "You ever in your life see anything prettier than that?"

Olivia looked up from the pan where she was frying eggs to each individual's liking and said, "I wish I could keep 'em that way. If I had my wish in this world my children would never grow up. I'd just keep 'em little the rest of their lives."

"I remember one time when I was a little old tadpole boy," said Clay, "I had this little baby duck. Mama's got a picture of me somewhere holden that duck. I used to think that little web-toed quacker was the prettiest thing I ever laid eyes on. Just hated the day to come for that duck to grow up. One day I got the fool idea that if I'd squeeze that duck hard enough every day I could keep him from growen, so every mornen I'd nearly squeeze the tar out of him. One mornen I squeezed him too hard I reckon, because he up and died, but it taught me somethen. You try to keep a thing from growen and it'll die on you."

"Still I hate to see my children grow up and leave me," said Olivia. "You just never know what's goen to become of 'em."

"My babies will turn out all right," said Clay. "They're thoroughbreds." He looked over his brood fondly and when his eyes met Clay-Boy's, he said, "I'm goen to work on the house this mornen, son. I want you to help me."

"All right, Daddy," replied Clay-Boy.

The house was not really a house but a dream Clay had. It was his dream to build a house with his own hands, a house his wife and children could see being constructed, a house that would give strength and love to their own lives because they had seen the strength and love with which it was built. He had promised the house to Olivia on their wedding night and had shown her where he would build it, on the summit of Spencer's Mountain in the same spot where his mother and father's old cabin had long since rotted away.

The site was important because it had a history. In 1650 two gentlemen of the Tidewater, Abraham Wood and Edward Bland, seeking a new fur-trading field, had made a journey of exploration into the western mountains. A member of the party, Benjamin Clayton

Spencer, came upon a mountain where the earth teemed with richness and which was filled with all manner of game. On the summit he built a small lean-to and returned there the following spring with his wife and children to make it his home. From that time the mountain had been family property and was known as Spencer's Mountain.

Clay's father, Zebulon, had brought his bride, Elizabeth, to the mountain when they were married, and there they raised their family and tended their crops as generations of their people had before them. Zebulon and Elizabeth were people of the mountains, and events in the outside world mattered little to them. They received little news or none at all unless an itinerant preacher stumbled into the settlement, exchanging sermons for food, or performing a wedding for a couple down in the hills whose oldest child might be two or three years old. Sometimes they would hear of the outside world from a passing peddler who had lost his way. The peddler would sleep in the barn and go on his way quickly, knowing he was among frugal people who felt no need for his bright tin pans or gaily patterned dress fabrics. Elizabeth used the iron skillets her mother had given her when she was married, and her dresses she made from wool she carded herself.

So it was that when a stranger came into the mountains he told his stories to a polite audience. And Zebulon and Elizabeth in those early times, when they heard of the death of kings, the rise and fall of some country across the sea, victories in war, discoveries in medicine, the election of presidents, received these tidings the way they had as children listened to stories told by the old, only half believing and not caring in the least.

They lived in a small pocket of civilization. Time flowed by them and made little difference to them. Zebulon raised his own corn and sweet potatoes, onions and turnips, and supplemented them with game. He made his own whiskey, and Elizabeth brought forth her young with the help of a sister who had come to be with her or a hastily summoned neighbor from down in the hills if Zebulon could find one in time.

On a morning before the century had turned, a stranger made his way up the mountain and spoke of a curious kind of stone Zebulon had noticed all through the mountain and down in the hills.

"It's called soapstone," the stranger had said. "It's impervious to acid, which simply means that acid can't eat through it. That makes it ideal for laboratory sinks, kitchen and laundry sinks. It can also be used architecturally as flagstone or even in the construction of buildings. We plan to quarry the stuff and came to see if you would sell your land."

Zebulon had refused to sell the mountain even though his neighbors down in the hills sold their farms one after the other. The people were promised that once the company could get them built they would move into fine new homes, at only token rents where they could enjoy—many of them for the first time in their lives—such conveniences as plaster walls, central heating and indoor plumbing.

Eventually Spencer's Mountain became an island of privately owned land surrounded completely by company land. In the shadow of the mountain a stone quarry was opened and the settlement which grew up around it was given the name New Dominion.

Then the people who had sold their land came down from the surrounding hills. First came the lean tall men, their worn overalls faded a light blue from many washings in strong homemade soap. Then came their women, stringy, silent, and reserved, cautious in their speech, bringing with them flocks of children, shy at first, clinging to their mothers' dresses, but curiosity winning over their reserve.

All around them were the nail-and-hammer sounds of building, the smell of fresh lumber, the churning of mud as more horses came into the busy area. Sometimes a lone horse carried a woman and three or four children while the husband walked alongside. Others pulled buggies or, more frequently, wagons laden down with entire families and with their possessions.

The little village took shape according to no organized plan. The houses were built on company land as the land was acquired and any cleared space served as a homesite. Each of the houses was uniformly ugly, three rooms downstairs and three rooms upstairs. Their roofs were covered with galvanized tin, and while every room of each house received one coat of white paint the outsides of the houses were left natural raw clapboard which over the years turned a soft worn gray that was oddly beautiful and warm.

With the company commissary as its nucleus a small business community began to develop—a livery stable, a barber shop; a long two-story building with living quarters upstairs and a room downstairs lined with stools and counters became the New Dominion Hotel and Restaurant. Because beer was served in The Restaurant it became an unspoken law that no *good* woman ever went there. In a room next door a billiard table was installed and it became forevermore known as The Pool Hall, the first place a woman sent her oldest child to look for her man if he did not return by a reasonable hour on payday night.

So there came into existence an odd little pocket of humanity clustered together in the rolling hills that led up to the Blue Ridge Mountains. It remained a small and isolated hamlet inhabited by hill people who brought their hill ways with them. The first thing a man did once he was settled with his family in his new house was to build a barn, a chicken house and a pigpen in his back yard; behind that or on some nearby slope he would plant a vegetable garden each spring. Rather than reaching out to the larger communities of Charlottesville, Lynchburg or Richmond for entertainment they enjoyed themselves with square dances on Saturday night and Sunday school and preaching on Sunday. Rather than shopping for clothing in the cities that were within reach they bought through the local commissary or ordered from

Sears, Roebuck and Montgomery Ward.

For a while the Spencer family remained aloof and apart from the little village, but gradually they became dependent upon it and a part of it. At first the boys would come, all nine of them, drunk and shooting their guns like cowboys and scaring people out of their wits at night. Sometimes the boys would appear and stand silently against the wall of The Dance Hall and, until one of them decided he wanted to dance, there would be a nervous and apprehensive feeling in the room because they might just as easily decide they wanted to fight. They did both with equal joy and vigor.

As each of his sons became twenty-one Zebulon would give him his choice of land so that by the time Clay, the youngest, was twenty-one years old the mountain had been divided into nine plots and Clay fell heir to the original cabin and lived on there with his father and mother. Virgil was the first to sell his land to the company, put the money in his pocket and go off to see the world. Rome married a girl from the village who was never happy on the mountain, and at her urging he took a job with the company, sold his land and moved into a company-owned house. The other boys followed suit, and when Clay came down from the mountain to a company house and a job in the quarry he brought with him his mother and father. Only he of all the boys held onto his share of the mountain.

As the years went by, the vision of the house he would some day build never left Clay's mind. Every time he passed the site he would imagine the house. In his dreams it was always painted white, the windows trimmed with green shutters and a wisp of smoke trailing from the chimney into the blue sky. The vision was so real to him that he could almost hear the children's voices inside or see Olivia's face at the window.

Yet, as strong as this vision was, he had never gotten beyond excavating the basement; this he accomplished every summer, only to have it fill in again during the fall and winter rains. Each summer he would attack the hole again with the intention that this year he would at least get the foundation laid during the week ends when he did not have to work at the mill.

Clay would have accomplished a good deal more on the house had he not been such a good-hearted man. Often he would plan to spend a day working on the house but pass it instead repairing a washing machine for a neighbor or helping a friend saw wood or slaughter hogs. Clay was good with mechanical things. There was nothing he could not repair. Since appliances were hard to come by for most of the New Dominion folk, they were held together by bobby pins and glue, spit and imagination until the absolute end of their usefulness was reached and even Clay Spencer could no longer make them work again.

Even though the demands on Clay's time were heavy, eventually a day came when he would announce to the family that he was getting back to work on the house. The news always brought pleasure to Olivia and the children because it marked for them a new season of hope, an assurance that everything might improve magically, for if Clay's faith that the house would be built was so strong, then it was possible that other dreams might come true too.

Now at the breakfast table the announcement had been made and the day took on new meaning.

"I reckon spring really is here if you're goen to start work on the house," said Olivia.

"I may finish that house this year," boasted Clay. "It's spring all right," said Olivia dryly.

"You'd better fix us up a little lunch to take up on the mountain," said Clay. "You bring it on when it's ready, son. I'm goen on to the barn to put a rope on Chance."

Chance was the family cow. She had received her name when Old Mrs. Frank Holloway had sold her to Clay on the strength that "she give a good chance of butter." Old Mrs. Frank Holloway used the word *chance* in its ancient English sense of a sizable amount.

"Why are you putten a rope on Chance?" asked Olivia.

"I'm taken her down to Percy Cook's bull. I'm goen right past his place and I'll just drop her off," said Clay.

"I don't see why you got to take Chance today," said Olivia.

"Because I'm goen right past Percy's place."

"Then Clay-Boy can just stay home. I don't want him seein' things like that."

"What are you talken about, woman?"

"You know what I'm talken about. Clay-Boy's too young."

"If this boy don't know what a cow and a bull does by this time it's time he's finden out."

"There's plenty of time for finden out about such things when he grows up."

"Livy, this boy has killed the biggest deer ever seen in this part of the country. He's a man now. It's time he's finden out what a man needs to know."

"Killen things don't make a man out of a boy," objected Olivia.

"Sweet merciful Moses! How do you talk sense to a woman! Fix us some lunch, woman, and when it's ready, boy, bring it on up to the stable."

"All right, Daddy."

Clay left the house and Olivia began to prepare sandwiches for lunch. She looked at Clay-Boy uncomfortably once or twice but said nothing. When she handed the lunch to him in a brown paper bag she said, "Down there at Percy Cook's when you see what happens you remember that there's a difference in what happens between cows and bulls and two human beings."

"Yes'm," he said.

"What cows and bulls do has got nothing to do with love. You remember that," she said, and then Clay-Boy fled to the barn where his father was waiting.

Most of the time Chance was a good-natured beast who grazed quietly in the crab apple orchard. Today she was fractious and full of devilment. When Clay-Boy approached she lowered her horns menacingly at him until Clay tugged her by the rope attached to her halter.

"Come on, you swaybacked old hellion!" shouted Clay, "You won't be half so frisky comen home."

The cow seemed to know where they were headed, and in her eagerness to get there ran, trotted, galloped and sprinted so that they covered the five miles to Percy Cook's in near-record speed.

Percy Cook was a farmer who had a mania for building small sheds on his land. The house he and his wife Ottalie and their countless children lived in was hardly more than a shack; surrounding it there were other shacks built of boxes, tarpaper, sticks and boards.

There was a shack for the chickens, another for a tool shed, another for a spring house, another for the cows, another for the pigs, another for feed, one for the sheep, one for the goats and still another for the dogs. If Percy Cook was fond of building shacks, his wife's hobby was having children. They lived on an untraveled road and never left the farm. Once, some years before, a hunter had driven a car back along the old river to Percy Cook's place, and the car had so frightened the hoard of children that all the driver had seen as he drove up into the back yard were countless little naked behinds disappearing under the porch where they had remained until they were overcome by their curiosity; later the whole army of little white-headed, buck-naked children had poked their heads out from under the house and remained there until they were sure it was safe to come out again.

As Chance, Clay and Clay-Boy came to the Cook place, Percy had just finished milking his own cows and was carrying the milk toward the house. He was a lean, tanned, wrinkled, shriveled little old man with a high, carrying voice.

"Lord God Almighty, if it ain't Clay Spencer. Howdy there, Clay!" he called.

"Percy," called Clay as he struggled to hold onto Chance, "this bowlegged old butter churn has pulled me all the way from New Dominion. Which way you got Methuselah?"

" 'Thusela's down yonder by the creek last time I laid eyes on him. He goen to be powerful glad to see that little heifer. Turn her loose. She'll find him."

Clay loosened the rope he had attached to the cow's halter while Clay-Boy ran over to open the gate that led to the bull's pasture. Freed of the rope, Chance trotted about uncertainly for a few minutes, then ran into the pasture. When Clay-Boy closed the gate behind her she turned and looked at him hatefully.

"Lemme take this milk to the house, and then I'll be back in case they need any help," said Percy.

"They don't need no help from us, Percy," said Clay. "They'll find each other."

"How do you know they'll find each other, Daddy?" asked Clay-Boy.

"It's nature, son," answered Clay.

"I reckon you're right, Daddy," said Clay-Boy. "There comes Methuselah now."

Methuselah, a magnificent old black warrior, had

already sensed the presence of the cow and had come halfway up the field in search of her. Now that she was in sight of the object of her desire Chance pretended he was nowhere in sight. She seemed to have decided to ignore him and began calmly grazing in the short grass.

"If that cow don't beat all," said Clay-Boy. "Pulled us all the way down here to get to that bull and now she won't pay him any attention."

"She's bein' a lady," chuckled Clay.

Percy returned and joined them at the fence. Chance continued to graze in the grass, apparently indifferent to the performance Methuselah was putting on for her benefit.

When he had first observed her he had come toward her in a trot, but now he stopped almost three hundred feet away, lowered his head almost to the ground and gazed at her in an appraising way. Next Methuselah moved about Chance in a circle, occasionally trotting off the way a dog will which wants to be chased.

"He sure is acting silly," laughed Clay-Boy.

"You'll act silly too when the love bug bites you, boy," said Percy.

Methuselah looked back and saw that he had not aroused any interest on Chance's part. Now he drew himself up, gave a bellow that shattered the air and began an aggressive, belligerent stiff-legged march toward the cow.

"He's ready," chuckled Percy Cook. "He's tired of footen around."

Chance grazed on, seemingly unaware of Methuselah's attentions, but when he had advanced within about twelve feet of her she reared up and shook her horns at him. When Methuselah ignored her protestations she began to back away and suddenly broke into a run. As suddenly as the running began she stopped and waited. When the bull reached her he mounted her with one awkward attempt and they remained locked together, wild-eyed. To Clay-Boy what then transpired appeared not merely outlandish, but most uncomfortable.

"I don't think they're goen to need any help, Percy," said Clay turning away.

"'Thusela never did," said Percy, with one backward look at the communion of the two animals.

"You just goen to leave 'em like that, Daddy?" asked Clay-Boy.

"Sure, son. They'll know when to stop," replied Clay.

"What's the matter with you, boy?" asked Percy Cook. "Didn't you ever see a cow and a bull before?"

"No, sir," said Clay-Boy. "I never saw anything like that before at all."

Percy winked at Clay. "Son," he said, "the best part of liven is all ahead of you," and then he grasped Clay by the arm and said, "I declare I'm glad to see you, Clay Spencer. Why don't you and your boy come on up to the house and enjoy a cup of coffee with us?"

"Thank you all the same, Percy," answered Clay, "but me and this boy are doen some work on my house up there on the mountain. I'll pick up Chance on the way home."

"Tell me somethen, Clay," said Percy. "You know we don't get no news down here in the sticks. What's goen on in the world?"

"Well," said Clay, "them Huns is at it again."

"What they up to this time?"

"Some bohunk named Hitler has took over the country and is raisen Cain. Them fellers that talk about the news on the radio seem to think he goen to cause trouble."

"What kind of trouble?"

"War maybe."

"I don't know," said Percy. "I wouldn't worry about it. Them old Bolsheviks is always fighten amongst themselves."

They parted from Percy at the roadway; Clay promised to pick up Chance that evening, then he and Clay-Boy continued on toward the mountain.

The boy and his father walked for some time in silence. Clay had observed his son from time to time but the boy was lost in deep thought.

"Is somethen botheren your mind, boy?" Clay asked.

"No, sir," replied Clay-Boy. "I've just been thinken."

"You want to talk about anythin'?"

"Well, sir, yes sir. I've been puzzlen about Chance and that bull."

"Ain't nothen puzzlen about it, boy. That bull just naturally needed that cow and she naturally needed him. That's all there was to it."

"What I mean is he didn't appear to be having a very good time."

"Honey," said Clay, "you don't know much about the subject, do you?"

"I don't know a thing about it, Daddy," said Clay-Boy regretfully.

"Well, son, it's time you did."

Clay walked over to the grass beside the road and sat down. "Come here, boy," he said. "I'm goen to tell you everythin' about it you'll ever know."

Clay-Boy sat down and waited while his father assembled his thoughts.

"Now in nature," Clay began, "everythin's either male or female. It's that way with cows and turtles and flowers and chickens, same as it is with people. Now the male has got male seed in him and the female has got female seed in her and it takes both kind to start out a new life.

"Ever' so often male and female things get a loven feelen for each other. They want to get close to each other. The old male he'll strut up and down a-flappen his wings or throwen out his chest like old 'Thusela did, and the female will run six miles to meet him and then pretend the thought never crossed her mind, just like old Chance did. But somehow they get together so the seed can go from him to her, and if you'll take notice sometime of the way male and female things is built, that is about the closest two bodies can be to each other.

"You'll know what it's like one day and when you

49

do, remember that you ain't any bull and that little girl ain't any cow. You be easy and gentle with her, and if she loves you a little bit before, she'll love you a lot more when it's over. And don't get the notion there's anythin' lowdown about it, because the Lord Himself thought it up and made us the way He did. That's how He figured out to get new life on this old earth and this old world would just dry up and blow away if it wasn't for what I just explained to you. You understand what I'm tellen you, boy?"

"I reckon I do, Daddy," said Clay-Boy.

"Not by a long sight you do," said Clay with a grin. "You won't ever understand it."

"Why not, Daddy?"

"There ain't nobody that understands it."

And that was the end of the matter.

When they arrived at the site where Clay planned to build the house Clay looked ruefully down into the muddy hole which only last autumn he had referred to as "the cellar."

"Love of mud!" he grumbled. "Seems like I waste half my time diggen this cellar all over every spring."

He walked around and around the hole finally squatting beside the boy.

"Son," he said, "I'm tired of throwen the same dirt out of this hole every year. This time we're goen to shore up the walls so they'll stay. Now there's a rock pile over at the edge of the field near the foot of that big pine tree. Start toten that rock over here while I

50

get this dirt out of my cellar."

Clay took a shovel from underneath a tarpaulin where he stored some tools, jumped into the hole and began throwing shovelsful of earth up out of the hole.

Clay-Boy found the rock pile where his father had told him it would be. All morning the boy carried the rocks from the pile to the edge of the hole. He worked diligently, carrying as many rocks as he could, but on his return trip, empty-handed, he could look around him and enjoy the warmth of the sun, watch the slow majestic flight of a buzzard gliding high off in the sky or the scurrying flight of a field mouse he frightened in the fresh new broom sage that covered most of the field.

Clay worked briskly. It was such a joy to be at work on the house again he was tempted to overdo himself, but he had done hard labor for long hours before and knew he had to slow down his pace or else he would not last out the day. He fell into a rhythm, sinking the shovel into the yielding earth with his hands, tamping it with his foot and lifting it up and out of the hole and flinging its load of earth to one side. He interrupted his rhythm only once; that was when he found an arrow-head and bent over to pick it up to save for Clay-Boy, who had a collection of Indian relics.

Once Clay caught sight of his son as Clay-Boy came to the edge of the hole to drop his load of rocks.

"How we doen, boy?" Clay shouted.

"Right fine, I reckon, Daddy," the boy answered, a smile lighting his thin freckled face.

"You're damned tootin'," his father shouted.

"Damned tootin'," the boy echoed gleefully under his breath and they fell again to their work.

The sun was setting behind the mountains, sending up splendid shafts of light against the western sky when Clay and the boy quit work. The basement was almost rectangular again and Clay looked down into it with satisfaction. Tomorrow they would come back and start shoring up the walls with the rock Clay-Boy had carried from the field.

Clay returned his shovel under the tarpaulin and they walked a little way down the hill. Once Clay stopped and turned to look back.

"I can see it now," he said. "Your mama sitting up there on the front porch resten of a Sunday. It'll be pretty, boy, you know that? Your mama will plant flowers comen down the walk on either side and I'll put in a bed of grass where my babies can play."

"It's getten dark, Daddy," the boy reminded him.

"We'll be getten along in a minute, son. We got till Monday mornen in front of us. Can you see the house, son, the way it'll be and all?"

"I got an idea what it'll look like," said Clay-Boy, impatient for home and supper.

"It ain't the looks, son. It's a feelen I want you to have about this house. First place, it's goen to be yours one of these days. And it won't be none of them thrown-together company houses either. This will be your own house that belongs to you and can't no land-lord ever tell you to move or get off the place because

52

you'll be standen on your own ground. You understand, son?"

"Yes sir," replied the boy.

"You'll sit up in that house one day with all your babies playen around you and you can tell 'em you helped build it. You can tell 'em you helped lay the foundation, and helped nail every two-by-four together. You tell 'em that and it'll be a thing to be proud of and glory in. Along with that you'll see the sweat and the work and the know-how that goes into a house, and what makes a house strong, one that won't fall down in a million years. You'll tell that to your babies, son, and they'll feel proud and safe because they'll know the house they live in is good and solid."

"Aw, Daddy, I haven't even got a girl yet," the boy said sheepishly.

"You'll be getten one," said Clay. "Let's go home to supper."

They picked up Chance at Percy Cook's farm and the man and the boy and the cow plodded home together. It would be hard to say which of them was the most tired.

By some magic Olivia always had supper ready when Clay arrived home. The table was set, the children and the two grandparents were already assembled at the table when Clay and Clay-Boy walked in the door.

"Y'all get washed up and come on to supper," said the old grandmother. "Livy's fixed up a meal here that's too good for poor folks."

That they were poor had never really occurred to any of the Spencers. They were familiar with the absence of money, but this was the common condition of all the people in the village, so they were not only ignorant of their condition but even managed to be happy in it.

This very lack of material things created often a curious paradox. Once in a while they could not afford such luxury items as toothpaste, yet they fed on quail, pheasant, wild turkey and duck and venison. Once Clay had brought home a possum, the trophy of a night's wild scramble through gullies and pine forest, over creeks and swampland after the hounds. Protesting, Olivia had cooked the thing, but everyone agreed the meat was fatty, too gamy and disagreeable. From the summer garden Clay brought home sweet young ears of corn, great beefsteak tomatoes, mealy butter beans, snap beans, peas, squash. All summer long, at least once a week Olivia spent a day canning vegetables from the garden, blackberries, dewberries and wild strawberries the children would pick by the gallon. If the frost came early and killed the tomato plants she would gather bushels of green tomatoes and fill the kitchen with the vinegary aroma of green-tomato relish.

"Don't tell me nothen about bein' poor," said Clay, sitting down to the supper table. "When I was a little old shirttail boy we used to go sometimes all week long on nothen but what we could shoot or steal."

"Oh now you heish tellen them children that, Clay," protested the old grandmother. "You know I never taught one of you children to steal, and your daddy would have thrashed you within an inch of your life if he ever caught you doen such a thing."

The old grandfather was too busy eating his pork chop to comment, but he knew the story Clay was leading up to and he gave his son a wink.

"Yes sir," Clay continued. "We used to be hungry half the time. I remember one winter we was so poor we didn't have nothen to eat but a slice of bacon. Mama was good at maken out, though. I'll hand that to her. She sure made that piece of bacon last a long time. What she done was tie a string to it and let each one of us chew on it for a while. If one of us swallowed it she'd pull it back and hand it to the next one."

"Aw, Daddy!" the children cried, half-believing him.

"Don't you pay no 'tention to that crazy man," the old grandmother cried. "He's maken them stories up."

"Mama," Clay teased. "You're just sayen that because you're so old you've forgot what it was like."

"I never forgot a thing in my life," the old woman insisted. "I fed you children good and didn't have to know no science or biography or any of them courses they teach up there at the school these days. I knew what to give my family and don't you tell me any different."

"Sorghum molasses and black-eyed peas," Clay commented. "That's what we got most of the time."

"That's a fact," the old woman agreed. "I fed you plenty of black-strap molasses, but I never to this day found anything half as good-tasten and half as good for you. The world would be a heap healthier place if everybody would eat more black-strap molasses."

When Clay had finished his supper he leaned back in his chair and said, "Man, oh man, them was prime pork chops."

"Have another one, Clay," urged Olivia. "There's plenty."

"Can't do it, woman," he said. "Thanks all the same. A meal like that always puts me in mind of that nat-ural-born homen pig I run up against one time. I ever tell you babies that story?"

"No Daddy, you never did," a chorus of voices answered. It was one of their favorite stories and he never tired of telling it.

"Aw, I think I told y'all that story," he said, remembering the exact moment and time of the last telling.

"I don't remember the way you told it," Clay-Boy said. "Please tell it again."

"Well," Clay began, "it happened the year I was eleven years old and bought me a bicycle. Earned the money setten out tobacco plants for Old Man Godsey, lived over yonder in the Glades. Pap had come down with that trouble he had and took to bed and everybody pitched in to help Mama bring us kids up.

"One day word come from Mama's brother Uncle Benny Tucker, lived over yonder in Buckingham County, for her to send one of us boys over there and pick up a shoat-pig he wanted to give us.

"Mama wanted that shoat powerful bad and me and

Brother Anse wanted a trip to Buckingham County just as bad so nothen would do but we take off one day about four in the mornen to go after that pig.

"Buckingham County is a long sight of a way from here, but Anse and me made it on that bicycle by about the middle of the day. Found Uncle Benny Tucker plowen his winter wheat, but he knew us boys was anxious to start back home again so he came in out of the field and took us down to the pigpen and said, 'Y'all boys go out in the pen there and pick out a nice-sized shoat. Don't catch one so big you can't lug him home on that bicycle,' Uncle Benny said. So me and Anse got out there in the pen and wasn't long before we had us a nice-sized shoat. Uncle Benny said come on by the house and have dinner with them, but Anse and me wanted to get back home before fall of night so we said we'd better start on home.

"Well, I was bigger than Anse so I did all the foot-work on that bicycle, but Anse didn't have it no easier than I did 'cause he had to sit on the handlebars and hold that pig at the same time, and if you haven't ever tried to do a thing like that it's kind of hard to get it in your mind. We got him home though and gave him a name which was Jabez. Mama was powerful glad to get the pig and said it was one of the finest she'd ever seen and she was sure she could get him up to three hundred pounds by killen time. Anse and me turned him loose in the pen and we was two tuckered-out boys that night, I'll tell you.

"Well, the next mornen I come to the breakfast table

and Mama said, 'Son, go out yonder and feed that pig and I'll have your breakfast ready time you get back.' I went out to the pen, but I didn't see sign one of Jabez. I figured maybe he was inside the little shed so I poured his slop in the trough and hollered, 'Soueeeeeeee! Souoo Pig,' but no Mr. Pig. Finally I got tired of foolen around with him so I didn't do nothen but jump over in the pen and looked in the shed where I figured he was sleepen. He was gone. I looked around a little more and then I found out what happened. There was a hole underneath the fence, just big enough for Jabez to slip through—and that's what he'd done. Well, we looked for that pig for a week without finden so much as a pound of lard.

"One day about a week later, who should turn up at the house but Uncle Benny Tucker and what was he carryen in a bag but Old Jabez! Don't ask me how Jabez did it, but he'd found his way forty miles back to Uncle Benny's farm. Uncle Benny gave him to us again, and I fixed that pen air tight. Couldn't hardly a mosquito squeeze out of that pen once I finished with it, but I'll tell you somethen hard to believe. Next mornen when I went out to slop Jabez, he was gone again. This time we didn't bother to look for him. I got on my bicycle and went on over to Uncle Benny's. I told him what'd happened and we went down to the pigpen. Jabez wasn't there. We started back for the house and hadn't got more than halfway across the field when I spotted somethen comen towards us lickety-split. He was muddy and briar-scratched and lean as sin, but that was one happy pig.

"Uncle Benny didn't have the heart to send him off again so he give me one in place of Jabez and we didn't have no trouble with the new one to the day we ground him up for sausage. And Uncle Benny never slaughtered Jabez. He kept him around till he just plain died of old age. I never knew to this day whether that shoat just plain loved Uncle Benny Tucker or whether he was a natural-born homen pig."

"Lord-a-Mercy, Clay," said Olivia, "you and your long-winded stories. Look at Pattie-Cake fast asleep. I've got to get these children to bed."

Olivia organized her forces to cope with the complicated process of seeing that everybody got his Saturday-night bath and was put to bed.

"Becky, you wash the baby and put him to bed. Shirley, you take care of Pattie-Cake. Matt, you keep the fire goen so there'll be plenty of hot water and Luke, Mark and John will keep the woodbox full."

"What can I do for you, Livy?" asked the old woman. "Anything you feel like doen, Grandma," replied Olivia. "I'd appreciate a helpen hand with the dishes."

Clay-Boy had no assigned task; it was understood that he would operate as a kind of flying squad to pitch in wherever trouble developed, to prod the boys along with their bringing in the firewood, to rescue the baby if he should slip in the bathtub, to help along the assembly line that began at the bathtub and ended with each child in clean pajamas and in bed.

Finally when they were alone Clay and Olivia sat together in the living room to get caught up on what had happened to them while they were away from each other during the day.

"Colonel Coleman stopped by," said Olivia.

"What did he want?" asked Clay.

Colonel Coleman was the general manager of the stone company, but in spite of the difference in their economic and social levels he and Clay were friends who shared a common interest in hunting and fishing. The Colonel would never buy a hunting dog without asking Clay's advice and seldom went hunting without asking Clay to accompany him.

"He said he had to spend tomorrow in Washington and he wondered if you'd stop by over there and feed his dogs for him sometime duren the day," answered Olivia.

"You told him I'd do it," asked Clay.

"I said I was sure you'd be glad to do it for him," said Olivia. "I thought at first he'd come over to make you another offer for that land on the mountain."

"He knows I'm never goen to sell that little piece of land," said Clay. "I took him by there once on a hunt and showed him where I'm putten up the house and he even said he'd try to see to it that no quarries ever got opened up over that way."

"I reckon he's a good-hearted man after all," said Olivia.

"The salt of the earth," said Clay.

After a little while Clay and Olivia too went to their

60

room, and once the lights were out and everyone was in bed, all the people in the house began to call good night to one another. From the girls' room Becky called, "Good night, Luke," and Luke answered, "Good night Becky, good night Pattie-Cake," and Pattie-Cake called, "Good night Luke, good night Mama," and Olivia answered, "Good night, Pattie-Cake, good night, Shirley." Other voices would join in a round song of good nights until all thirteen people in the house had said so many good nights that they could not remember who they had said good night to and who they had not and the whole goodnight chorus might start all over again unless Clay would finally give the long sleepy yawn which was a signal that everyone had been bidden a proper good night. After that a tentative good night or two might rise from a couple of the younger children and then they would fall silent too.

Clay slept and dreamed of his house. It was a proud thing to have a house a man had built with his own hands, a place to call his own. He saw it in his mind, white and shining in the sunlight, Olivia planting petunias along the front walk and the children playing about her in the grass.

Outside, the night was filled with sound. The high mechanical screech of the cicadas was a metallic din which gradually whined into silence. A turtle dove called. His mate answered, far off, and then her voice sounded again and his voice cried out, closer now. In the distance, flowing over the pine trees, from the swamp, over the pond, came the thousand-voice choir of frogs. Once only came the saddest sound in the world, the single unanswered voice of a whippoorwill, but there was no one to hear it. Everyone in the house was asleep.

CHAPTER 4

THE WHOLE WEEK went by without Clay's being able to do any work on the house on the mountain. Three nights he worked late at the mill, and while he regretted the time lost on building his house he welcomed the extra money he got from working overtime for the company. One night there had been rain and the other night he might have worked on the house he had spent helping his father-in-law, Homer Italiano, saw stovewood.

At breakfast that Saturday morning, Clay-Boy asked, "You goen to need me to work on the house today. Daddy?"

"You got somethen you got to do?" asked Clay.

"I got exams comen up," said Clay-Boy. "I thought maybe I'd do some studyen if you didn't need me."

"You had better study then," said Clay. His mind was on a pile of fieldstones he had noticed at the foot of the mountain, and he was eager to collect it with the idea that one day they might become the fireplace and chimney of the house.

But after breakfast, as he stepped out of the back

door and looked up at the sky, his mind was filled with the vision of a certain fishing hole he frequented on Rockfish River. He could see the slow strong movement of the deep slate-colored water, dappled with sun and shadow and fairly jumping with carp and bass and catfish. The fact that he had announced that he would work on the house nagged him for a moment, but then he answered the voice of his conscience with the excuse that a nice mess of bass for the supper table would please Olivia. Besides, he had worked hard all week and deserved a few hours of peace and rest in some quiet place.

In the end he compromised and decided that he would take his rod and reel and stop by the river until he had rested and then continue on to the foot of the mountain and the fieldstone.

On the back porch he went to the shelf where he kept his fishing equipment and took down his rod and reel.

"You are the first man I ever saw build a house with fishen tackle," teased Olivia through the screen door.

"What do you know about builden a house, woman?" Clay laughed.

"I don't know much." replied Olivia, "but every one I ever saw built was put up with hammer and nails. This must he a right funny house you're slappen together up there on the mountain. I've never seen you carry hammer or nails away from here yet."

"There ain't a thing to nail together yet, old woman," he said. "I been spenden all my time on the basement.

You want a place to keep your canned goods, don't you?"

"I got me a place to store my canned goods, and sometimes I think you'd be smarter to work on this place than spenden all your time on that castle up there."

"That's what it's goen to be all right," he retorted. "A castle fit for a royal-butted king. And you'll change your tune once you see it."

"You watch how you talk, Clay Spencer. There's innocent young children around this place, and I'm doen my best to make Christians out of them."

"Nobody ever made me into a Christian, and look what a tall dog I turned out to be," Clay teased her.

"Humphf!" she said with pretended disgust and turned into the house. Clay laid down his fishing tackle, eased the kitchen door open and grabbed Olivia up in his arms. She struggled with pretended anger, but he held her so her feet could not reach the floor. Her cries of outrage mingled with the children's howls of delight as Clay danced Olivia around and around the room, alternately kissing and tickling her. Finally, out of breath, he put her on the floor again and she rearranged her clothing and her hair.

"You old fool," she cried.

"That woman is plumb crazy about me," Clay laughed. "I wish I had twenty more just like her."

"Pick her up again, Daddy," the children cried.

Clay started after her, but Olivia ran out of the room.

"Y'all be good babies," Clay called to the children.

He kissed them all and went up through the back gate. As he came out on the road, he met his mother-in-law, Ida Italiano.

"Where you gallivanten off to, Miss Ida?" he called.

"Up to the Baptist parsonage, Clay," she replied. "The Ladies Aid Society is cleanen it up for the new preacher."

"That's a fact?" said Clay, falling in step with Ida. "Livy did mention there's a new preacher comen in."

"They tell me he's a powerful good speaker," said Ida. "You ought to come down to church in the mornen and listen to his sermon."

"Lord, Miss Ida," laughed Clay. "The roof would fall in if I ever walked in that Baptist church."

"Don't joke about it, Clay," admonished Ida. "Don't you want to save your soul so you can go to Heaven and be with all decent folks when you die?"

"Miss Ida," said Clay, "the Baptists have got one idea of Heaven and the Methodists have got another idea and the Holy Rollers have got still another idea what it's like. I've got my opinion too."

"I can just imagine what your idea of Heaven is," sniffed Ida. "A fishen pole and a river bank."

"That's part of it, yes ma'am," agreed Clay. "I use up a little bit of Heaven every day. Maybe it's just haulen off and kissen the old woman, or haven one of my babies come and crawl in bed with me at night and snuggle up against my back, or a good day's work on my house up on the mountain. I don't have to wait to die for it, Miss Ida. I got Heaven right here."

"That's not Bible Heaven," said Ida.

"It's the only one I ever expect to see," said Clay.

"I'll pray for your soul anyway, Clay, if you don't mind," said Ida.

"Appreciate the favor, Miss Ida," replied Clay sincerely.

They parted at the Baptist parsonage and Clay continued on down the road toward Rockfish River.

When Clay reached the bank above his favorite fishing hole he set down the box he carried his fishing tackle in. Looking for a lead sinker, he pushed back one of the upper trays and found—forgotten but happily nearly full—a quart of whiskey. He remembered now he had hidden it there the last time he had been drinking.

He pulled the cork out of the bottle, sniffed the contents. This was a habit he had acquired after Olivia once found a hidden bottle and diluted its contents with castor oil. Satisfied that the bottle held what it was supposed to, he lifted it to his lips, tilted it back and took a long gurgling throat-searing drink.

"That's prime whiskey," he said to the world.

He searched around in the tackle box, found the sinker he had originally been looking for and attached it to his line. Then out of the minnow bucket he lifted a large black chub, saucy and active, hooked it through the flesh beneath the dorsal fin and dropped it into the water to recover from the shock of the hook. The minnow shook itself fiercely. Satisfied that it was an inviting bait, Clay cast into the river in a little eddy just above an outcropping of stone.

Clay lay back on the bank and there began in his mind a fantasy he often enjoyed after throwing a particularly inviting minnow into a particularly productive-looking pool. "That looks like a place where the grandaddy of all the bass in the river lives. That old ripstaver is layen down there against that rock hopen some June bug is goen to come floaten past him and when he sees that minnow I got on my line he ain't goen to believe it. He'll just sit there for a while and stew about it, but after a while that minnow is goen to make him so hungry he's goen to priss over there and see if he's real or not. Then he's goen to open that big old mouth of his and chomp down on that minnow and that'll be the last of you, Mr. Bass. Come on, you slippery monster! Bite."

Clay's daydream was interrupted when a car came to a stop on the highway above the bank. Presently Clay heard the car door open and slam shut, and a head appeared above him. The face was a friendly one and though the man had a city look to him—he was dressed casually in a sport shirt and slacks—Clay liked him immediately.

"Howdy, stranger," called Clay.

"How's the fishing?" the man asked.

Clay could tell at once if a question of this kind was mere curiosity or if the inquirer honestly wanted to know. He gave the stranger a swift glance of appraisal and decided he was a man who knew a mullet from a mud cat.

"Biten," Clay replied.

The stranger's face lighted up with an eagerness Clay recognized immediately.

"I've got some tackle in the car. Where's the closest place I can get some minnows?"

"Right here," said Clay and motioned toward his minnow bucket.

The stranger went back to his car and in a few minutes returned with fishing equipment that Clay noted with approval was well oiled and cared for. Nothing else was said between the two men, but Clay watched as closely as he could without staring directly at the stranger while he made his way quietly down the side of the bank, lifted the minnow bucket just high enough out of the water to select a minnow without injuring the others, closed the clanking tin top with a minimum of noise and plunged the hook through the meaty back of the minnow, then dropped it in the water for a moment so it might recover before he cast it into the deeper water. The minnow swam listlessly for a moment, then with a promising spurt of energy plunged forward and down, making the red-and-white cork bob frantically up and down on the surface. Carefully the stranger lifted the minnow out of the shallow water and cast expertly into a quiet deep-looking pool just beyond the swirling eddy where the water fell over a rock formation. He laid the rod against a fallen log where it would be secure and sat down.

"The name's Goodson," the stranger said and held out his hand to Clay. "Thank you for your hospitality."

"Spencer's mine," said Clay, "and don't mention it."

A comfortable fisherman's silence fell between them. Each, absorbed in his own particular bobbing cork, waited patiently and silently for a bite.

It was Clay who hauled in the first fish, a fierce and outraged six-pound bass that continued to fight even after Clay had taken him from the water and had secured him with a small chain through his gills.

To celebrate, Clay took a nip from his bottle; Mr. Goodson, elated by Clay's catch and encouraged by it, joined him.

At the Baptist parsonage a group of ladies was busy preparing the house for the arrival of their new minister. The parsonage itself was a white frame house that had been built along a pleasant road about a mile from where the Spencers lived. It contained six square rooms and faced squarely on the highway in much the same manner the Baptists faced their God. The grass of the front lawn was quite green, clipped and proper and kept healthy, if not from God's good rain at least from frequent baptisms by hose. There were no frivolous zinnias or nasturtiums to mar its green expanse, although some white snowball bushes bloomed on the lawn in early August. In the back were some hollyhocks along the path that went to the henhouse, but that was all the frivolity there was about the house. All told, it was a very Baptist establishment.

On this particular Saturday afternoon, the Baptist Ladies Aid Society had summoned its members to prepare the parsonage for the new parson's arrival. If the number of ladies present exceeded the membership of the Ladies Aid Society it could perhaps have been due to the fact that every woman who had a daughter of marriageable age had brought her along, since the one thing they knew for certain about the new minister was that he was not married.

Mrs. Lucy Godlove, along with her daughter Barbie-Glo, and Mrs. Tillie Witt, along with her daughter Honey-Glo, had drawn the chore of cleaning the kitchen. Neither of the girls had much enthusiasm for their task. It was by no coincidence that both of their minds were on the same thing. They were both thinking about the square dance at Buckingham County Courthouse that was held every Saturday night. Each of them was devising in her mind some way she might sneak away from home and attend the festivities, sneaking away being a necessity since neither of their mothers, being Baptists, condoned the sin of dancing.

Lucy Godlove talked a great deal, which was unfortunate because half the time she did not say what she thought she was saying. Speaking of Frances Paine, who was taking a course in beauty culture, Lucy had reported that Frances was taking a beauty vulture course. The influenza academic had taken Lucy's father in 1917, and she never let Barbie-Glo go to Charlottesville without warning her not to speak to any of the University of Virginia students because it was a well-known fact that all they thought of was hauling young country girls off to their maternity houses and raping them.

While the girls devoted their minds to their plans for evading their mothers that night, the two women chatted about the new preacher.

"Be nice if he was young," sighed Lucy Godlove.

"Be nice if he knew some new sermons," observed Tillie Witt. "That's all I ask. It had got so with old Preacher Goolsby that I knew what he was goen to say before he could open his mouth."

"I didn't mind Brother Goolsby so bad," said Lucy Godlove, "except once in a while his stutteren used to get on my nervous. I still can't say the Lord's Prayer without stutteren, but I'm hopen that'll clear up now he's gone, bless his soul."

"I just can't stand hearen the same old sermon, over and over. I never did do half the things Preacher Goolsby used to preach against anyway, that old adult'ry and idolizing gold. Come to think of it, I don't think I ever had any gold to idolize," said Tillie Witt.

"What I'm hopen this new preacher will do," said Lucy Godlove, "is put some life back in the church. Church is all I got in my life, God knows."

Church indeed was Lucy's life. Her husband Craig was the night watchman at the mill and since he had left her bed and taken up with a girl named Alabama Sweetzer, Lucy had turned completely to the church. She went to Sunday School, the Sunday Morning Sermon, the Sunday Night Sermon, Wednesday Night

Prayer Meeting, the Ladies Aid Society every Thursday afternoon and she even attended the Friday-night meeting of the BYPU, the Baptist Young People's Union. Every year at the Annual Baptism over at Witt's Creek she got herself baptized, went down with her eyes screwed tight together and her hands clenched together and came up screaming that she had seen Jesus and sputtering muddy water, her drowned hair in long wet coils down her shoulders. Afterward she would walk around telling everyone that she felt as clean as the day she was born.

Each year as Christmas approached Lucy would take charge of Christmas Tree Night. This was the program that was presented each Christmas Eve at the Baptist church. On this one night of the year the church lost its chilly barren look and was gaily decorated in pine wreaths tied with gay Christmas red bows and fes-tooned with streamers of crepe paper and creeping cedar. Nervous children dressed as shepherds and angels recited poems that Lucy would make up in her head. Always some little boy forgot the poem he had worked on since Thanksgiving until he found his mother's face in the audience, mouthing the searched-for word, and then was able to continue. Afterward Mr. Willie Simpson, who sang so loud in the choir, would arrive all dressed up in a Santa Claus suit and there would be presents for everybody.

One year after Lucy's Christmas presentation half the congregation stopped speaking to her because she had given all the principal parts in the pageant to her own children, ugly little skinflinty things; they all looked like cats, and since it was the year Barbie-Glo was taking that mail-order course in toe dancing, Lucy had worked in a toe dance for Barbie-Glo who was playing the part of Mary the Mother of Jesus, and her little brother Woodrow, who was supposed to be Joseph but forgot all his lines and turned the whole thing into an awful mess.

There were even those in the Baptist church who hoped now that a new minister was coming he might appoint someone else, more capable if somewhat less dedicated than Lucy, to conduct the annual celebration which had become such an ordeal.

In the living room of the parsonage, Ida Italiano and Eunice Crittenbarger were waxing furniture. Eunice was a snoop and a gossip and turned every social encounter into an opportunity to find out anything she could about other people's business. Since prying into other people's affairs came naturally to Eunice it was inevitable that she become the local correspondent for The Charlottesville *Citizen* and submit to the newspaper each week an account of what she considered newsworthy in New Dominion, some of which was published and which earned her the sum of three dollars a week. For this sum she would submit from ten to fifteen pages of single-spaced, badly typed copy from which the editors had to delete such items as:

Hiram Motherwell's old sow pig, Petunia, had fourteen babies Thursday night. Mother and children all doing just fine except for the one that was eaten.

Franklin Bibb is laid up with intestinal trouble again. This is the same old trouble Franklin has had for years and his sister, Wanda, died of. Dr. Campbell says Franklin had better do something about himself or he won't live to tell the tale.

There was a fight down at The Pool Hall last Friday night but nobody was hurt. This isn't much news as there is a fight down there most every Friday night. They ought to close it.

"I wonder what old Preacher Goolsby really did die of," Eunice remarked to Ida.

"I think it was just old age," replied Ida. "He'd been feeble for years and he was way up in his eighties."

"I don't know," said Eunice. "Once they get sick people over there in that old University of Virginia Hospital you're just as good as dead. All they do is let them young students cut people open and study what's inside 'em."

"I've heard that," said Ida, "but they sure were nice to me over there that time I broke my hip. The nurses took real good care of me and never a day went by the doctor didn't come in and look at me. He was an Episcopalian, that doctor, but he was just as nice as he could be."

"Anyway, I'll bet we never do find out exactly what Preacher Goolsby passed on with. Miss Ida, didn't you and Preacher Goolsby have a fallen-out one time?"

"It wasn't what you would call a fallen-out. No," said Ida.

"Seems like I heard y'all had a fuss or somethen."

"What you're thinken about was when Preacher Goolsby married Clay and Livy. But it wasn't any fuss and never a harsh word passed between us. He come to me the very next day and told me he'd married 'em, said he turned 'em down at first, but they would have found another preacher somewhere, and they would of. But there never was any hard feelens between the preacher and me."

"What did you have against Clay Spencer marryen Livy?"

"Clay was a wild boy. I don't reckon I would of carried on so if I'd known then how he'd settle down. He's been a good husband to Livy and I love him now just like one of my own. You won't find a more good-hearted man than Clay Spencer.

"I love to hear Clay tell a joke. I'll be feelen just as blue as I can be, real down in the dumps, and I'll run into Clay Spencer and he'll have me laughen in no time.

"Clay drinks and he takes the Lord's name in vain, but he's a good provider for Livy and he's a good father to them children. Lord, how he loves them children. I reckon you just have to take the good and the bad in this world. We better do some work, Eunice, or that preacher's goen to walk in here and find us gabben our heads off."

As the late evening sun shifted into the west it cast a

pool of light into a particularly fruitful fishing hole on the Rockfish River. It illuminated for a moment an empty whiskey bottle, an enormous string of sizable bass and two drunken men.

"There was something I stopped here to ask you," Mr. Goodson said. "I can't for the life of me remember what it was." He baited his hook and cast with an elaborate gesture, but the bait fell into the water directly in front of him while he searched with unsteady eyes across the river where the bait should have gone.

"Maybe you just stopped to do some fishen," suggested Clay. He lay in the grass squinting up at the falling sun, his hands crossed over his belly. His hook had long since been swept downstream and into an overhanging willow tree where it was hopelessly entangled.

"I can't remember why I stopped at all," said Mr. Goodson, and he started to sit back in the grass. When he was halfway down there came a sudden whirring from his reel, a big fish from the sound of it.

"Jesus Christ!" shouted Clay.

"That's it!" said Mr. Goodson.

"Grab that fishen pole, man," shouted Clay. "You have done snagged yourself a sea monster."

"That's what I stopped to ask. Which way is New Dominion?"

"The hell with New Dominion," cried Clay. "Bring in that fish, son."

The entire length of cord had unwound from the reel and the rod was bent in a taut oval and the line was tearing through the water so fast it made .a sizzling sound. There was so much tension on the line that the rod was beginning to slide gradually into the river.

Mr. Goodson caught up with the reel at the river's edge. When he held the rod securely he gave a slight jerk to set the hook in the mouth of whatever behemoth had taken his bait. Slowly, torturously, he began to reel in. Beside him, Clay interrupted his prayer only to shout some unintelligible direction for landing the fish.

Neither of them was ever to know what was at the other end of the line. With a stinging zip the line snapped and the bent rod snapped straight.

"Great Jumpin' Jesus!" shouted Clay. "Damn to hell that black-souled fish and Jonah's black-bellied whale!" Mr. Goodson blinked.

"You shouldn't talk that way in front of me," he said.

"Why not?"

"Because I am a minister of God," Mr. Goodson said. "I may even be your minister."

"I ain't got no minister except the sun of the sky and the dirt of the earth," said Clay.

"I am the new minister of New Dominion," insisted Mr. Goodson.

"You're lyen," said Clay.

"No sir," said Mr. Goodson and hiccoughed.

Clay began to laugh. Almost immediately his laughter got out of hand and the great gulping *wah wah wah* sounds that were coming out of him were too strong to take standing up. He fell to the ground in a paroxysm of gleeful suffering, rolling over and over in the weeds, the mud and the pebbles along the side of the river. It was only when he rolled into the river itself, immersing himself completely, that the sound of his spasm of laughter fell still.

The sheepish grin on the minister's face turned to a look of concern as Clay disappeared beneath the water. But as quickly as he went down Clay was on the surface again. Making a great splash and cry he paddled about in the river and when he had refreshed himself he headed in to the shore. He crawled out onto the bank and lay there for a moment to catch his breath.

Mr. Goodson staggered down to where Clay lay inhaling and exhaling vigorously. He bent unsteadily over Clay and inquired, "You didn't see anything of that fish I lost down there, did you?"

Clay rose up and threw his soaking wet arm around his new-found friend.

"Son," he said, "you're too good to lose. Come on, I'm goen to escort you to the Baptist parsonage myself."

The parsonage had been spotless since four in the afternoon. Now it was close to six o'clock and the ladies were more than anxious to go home and prepare supper for their men, but not one of them was of a mind to leave without greeting the new preacher when he arrived.

There were several conjectures about what might have happened to him, but not one of the ladies had the ingenuity to guess that the fault was Clay Spencer's.

When the sound of a car approached they would look up eagerly; when one finally stopped in front of the parsonage the entire membership of the Ladies Aid Society rushed up to the window and concealed themselves behind one of the white lacy window curtains they had installed that afternoon.

The arrival of the new minister would have been dramatic enough had he merely stepped out of the car and walked up to the front door. But the way in which he was to arrive was to furnish conversation for the next ten to fifteen years. In the first place, the ladies were astonished to see Clay Spencer step out of the car. Walking almost as if he were sober, which he nearly was by this time, Clay made his way around to the other side of the car. He opened the door, eased something out that had been slouched against it and threw it over his shoulder. Unaware that any eyes rested on him, Clay started for the parsonage carrying the inert body of the new Baptist minister. When he opened the front door he found himself staring into a circle of female faces.

"Good Lord, Clay, what's happened?" cried Lucy Godlove.

"He's all right," said Clay. "He's just . . ." He had started to tell them the preacher's real condition, but he realized that he must not. "He's all right," he said. "He just run into somethen."

A chorus of sympathetic voices offered suggestions that somebody go after the doctor, that the preacher be put in bed, and that he ought to be kept warm. As the ladies pressed closer to offer aid they realized that Clay had been drinking.

"Clay," said Lucy, "you are in no condition to take care of him. Put him down here and we'll do for him."

"I'll just take him up to his bed if you'll show me the way, Miss Lucy," said Clay, backing away.

"That preacher is liable to have infernal injuries," declared Lucy. "You can't tell what's broke inside him there and you ought not to be moven him around."

"He'll be all right. All he needs is a little sleep," insisted Clay, practically dancing around the room to keep the persistent Lucy from detecting the liquor on the preacher's breath. The activity began to rouse the preacher. He struggled up out of Clay's arms and assumed an unsteady upright position on the floor. Silence had fallen in the room which was broken only when one of the women sneezed.

"Bless you," said the minister with a friendly smile.

Lucy Godlove's suspicion had become aroused and she stepped forward, put her face up close to the preacher's face and drew in a deep breath. She turned to the other members of the Ladies Aid Society and announced in a whisper of disbelief, "He's dead drunk."

The ladies withdrew like a flock of hens discovering a rattlesnake in their midst. They reassembled on the road in front of the house and stood looking back at the parsonage in outrage.

Gradually it dawned on the preacher what had happened. "God in Heaven," he exclaimed.

"It's a good thing for you He's on your side," observed Clay, "You're goen to need Him."

The regular Sunday morning service at the Baptist church was not held the following morning. Mr. Goodson arrived a full hour before the meeting was scheduled but he was the first and only soul to arrive. For a long time he waited at the door for someone to come, and he was almost relieved that no one did appear. He was badly hung over. Further up the road the service at the Methodist church had gotten under way and it did not help his spirits any to hear them singing:

Yes, we'll gather at the river,
The beautiful, beautiful river;
Gather with the saints at the river
That flows by the throne of God.

Mr. Goodson wished he had never seen a river. He wished he had never seen New Dominion and he especially wished he had never seen Clay Spencer. His career as a minister in New Dominion had been cut short even before it had begun and perhaps his entire ministry was doomed. He remained at the church until noon and then returned to the spic-and-span parsonage and sat trying to map out some campaign to win back his lost flock.

It was noon before Clay heard the outcome of his encounter with the new minister the day before. He had fished since early morning and returned home for Sunday dinner in the middle of the day. Olivia's mother and father had stopped by, as they always did after church on Sunday, and the entire family was sitting on the front porch. From the way his mother-in-law was rocking in her rocking chair, Clay could tell that she was furious.

"Miss Ida, I want you to know I'm sorry for getten that preacher tight yesterday," he said.

"Huh," said Ida without so much as a look in his direction. "I didn't know he was a preacher until it was too late," said Clay.

"What makes me so mad is that just yesterday I was tellen somebody what a good man you were, Clay Spencer," said Ida grimly. "I could bite my tongue off today. You've ruined the Baptists, you're a shame to the community, and it's a wonder the Good Lord don't strike you dead in your tracks."

"Aw now, Miss Ida," said Clay, "it don't do a man no harm to take a drop once in a while. Even a preacher. And it wouldn't surprise me if that fellow didn't do a lot of good for this community. How powerful is he in the pulpit? Did he preach a good sermon?"

"I wouldn't know about that," said Ida. "I went to the Methodists."

"That's right, Clay," said Olivia in a somber voice. "Nobody went to the Baptist church this morning, not a soul."

"Why not?" demanded Clay.

"Would you want your children goen down there to

listen to a drunkard preach?" cried Ida.

"You mean to tell me not one single hymn-shouten, foot-washen hypocrite showed up?"

"Clay!" admonished Olivia. "You be careful how you talk."

"I just wish I'd known," said Clay, "I'd have gone down there myself to church."

"Yes," said Ida bitterly, "And just like you said the roof would probably have fallen in."

By the middle of the week the Ladies Aid Society had organized itself, and it was decided that they would transfer en masse to the Methodist Church. Olivia told Clay about their decision that night when he came home from work and he was furious.

"Why that prissy-butted old hymn-shouten bunch of hypocrites!" he roared.

"Clay!" remonstrated Olivia.

All through supper Clay was thoughtful, and later in the evening, after he had milked Chance and brought the milk to the house, he set the pail on the kitchen table, and said,

"I'll be back around bedtime, honey."

"Where are you goen?" asked Olivia.

"I got some business to attend to," he said.

"What kind of business?"

"Honey, I got that preacher in this mess. I'm goen to get him out of it."

For the rest of the week, instead of going up on the mountain to work on his house during the evenings, Clay would leave the supper table and go calling on his friends and neighbors.

"Miss Lucy," he said to Lucy Godlove, "I am not a man that keeps records, but just looken back I can count eleven times I've been over here to get your washen machine goen in the last two or three years."

"At least that many times if not more," agreed Lucy.

"And in all that time I never charged you a penny nor sent you a bill, ain't that a fact?"

"Yes, indeed," nodded Lucy.

"Well, I'm senden you a bill right now," said Clay. "I'd appreciate it if you'd go back to the Baptist Church next Sunday mornen."

"They'd expel me from the Ladies Aid, Clay," said Lucy.

"Don't you worry about the Ladies Aid," said Clay. "I've fixed enough washen machines and iceboxes and electric-iron cords for the ladies of this town without ever asken for a penny. Now I'm collecten in full and any lady that don't show up next Sunday at the Baptist Church is goen to get a sizable repair bill from me on Monday."

Knowing that his mother-in-law Ida would be a more difficult case, Clay did not go to her at all but instead approached his father-in-law down at the mill.

"Son," said Homer, "I'd like to help you out, but I doubt if Ida ever sets foot in the Baptist church again. You know how dead set she is against drinken."

"I know," said Clay, "but I was thinken maybe if you switched back to the Baptists, Miss Ida might feel like she ought to come with you."

"I'll tell you the God's truth, Clay," said Homer, "I don't set too much store in a preacher that drinks liquor myself."

"Mr. Homer, that preacher had never touched a drop of liquor in his life before he met me that day," said Clay, and then compounded his lie by adding, "Another reason I wanted you to get to know Preacher Goodson is he's part Italian like yourself."

"I vow now," said Homer, who was especially proud of his Italian ancestry; his forebears had indeed been brought to America by Thomas Jefferson, who had hoped with their help to start a wine industry in Virginia. It was one of Mr. Jefferson's experiments that failed, but several of the Italians he had invited to Monticello stayed on.

"It was on his mother's side," lied Clay, "but he tells me he's just as much Italian as you are."

"I never heard an Italian preach, that's a fact," mused Homer. "I ain't promisen you a thing, Clay, but I'll have a little talk with Ida when I get home tonight."

On the following Sunday morning Clay stationed himself on the front porch where he was able to see the little road that led off to the Baptist church.

When Olivia had herself and all the children ready for Sunday school she herded them all out onto the front porch, where she found Clay grinning happily.

"What are you laughen about, you old possum?" asked Olivia.

"From the crowd I've seen goen by, the Baptist church is goen to have an overflow this mornen," said Clay.

"Well, I'm not taken my children down there to hear a drunkard preach," declared Olivia. "We're goen to the Methodists."

"Honey, I can save you a long walk up to that Methodist church," said Clay.

"What are you talken about?"

"There ain't goen to be any service at the Methodist this mornen," said Clay.

"How would you know?"

"Well, I just happened to run into the Methodist preacher the other day and I remarked to him that it would be kind of neighborly if he'd come over and hear the Baptist preacher's sermon this mornen."

"And he's goen to do it?" asked Olivia disbelievingly.

"At first he didn't think much of the idea, but then I started tellen him about a nest of skunks I've had my eye on right there behind his church and how I'd been plannen to clean 'em out one of these days and I thought maybe I'd do the job as a favor to him this mornen."

"Clay, I don't know how I can hold my head up in this community. Now you've gone and turned the church into a regular circus."

"You better get started, honey," said Clay, "if you're goen to get there anyways on time."

Olivia rounded up the children who had scattered all

over the yard and with them in tow hurried toward the Baptist church.

Shortly Clay heard the strains of the opening hymn floating from the Baptist church across the quiet morning up to his front porch. He wondered if Preacher Goodson had chosen the hymn knowing he would be listening.

Shall we gather at the river,
Where bright angel feet have trod;
With its crystal tide forever
Flowing by the throne of God?

In harmony with the voices that drifted up across the hill, Clay's voice joined in:

Yes, we'll gather at the river,
The beautiful, the beautiful river;
Gather with the saints at the river
That flows by the throne of God.

When the hymn was finished, Clay smiled with quiet satisfaction, rose from his rocking chair and went to the barn to get some tools. He was still humming happily to himself as he walked along the road toward Spencer's Mountain and the house where at long last he would be able to put in a full day's work.

CHAPTER 5

THE DUSK OF EVENING seeped down from the mountains over the meadows of spring and through the blossoming crab apple orchard. The trees were in full blossom and their light perfume was carried on the wind all over New Dominion. The air was cool but, sitting at the base of one of the old trees, Clay-Boy Spencer felt the warmth of excitement and expectation. He felt more than saw the change as the sun slipped away beyond the horizon and left the orchard in the cool blue light of fading day.

Clay-Boy had come to the orchard to think. Something had happened during the day so unbelievable and so nearly impossible that he needed to be alone somewhere to let his mind absorb the thing gradually.

In an hour Miss Parker, his high school teacher, and Mr. Goodson, the new Baptist minister, would be coming to the house and the thing would be made known to his parents and then to the community and it would become everybody's property. But now for the moment it was a secret, a dream that he had never even dreamed before, and suddenly he was standing on the threshold of its coming true.

Yet much depended on what would happen that evening, and the boy had some misgivings. In the first place it was Friday, and on Fridays his father often stopped at The Pool Hall for a few bottles of beer before coming home. In the second place it was Pay

Day and on Pay Day his father always stopped for a beer or two before coming home. It was not that his father ever became mean or ugly when he drank. Some of the men came home in rages, broke all the furniture, beat their wives and chased their children out of the house.

When Clay drank it only magnified whatever mood he might have been in when he started drinking. If he had been a little sad he would become sadder, cry a bit and hug all the children close and tell them that the world is a cold and bitter place, that a man could work day and night and still never get the time and money to build a house for his babies. If he were affectionate he would hug them all the harder and tell them how much he loved them. If he were feeling jolly he would tell them long ridiculous stories about his boyhood and his adventures in the world.

No matter what his mood, Olivia would disapprove of his drinking and tell him so with her silence and her look the minute he entered the house. But he knew how to win her over. He would pick her up and waltz her around the kitchen in his arms, tickling her and kissing her until she would shriek, "Put me down, you old fool," and then he would put her down and shortly she would have his supper ready and lots of steaming black coffee to go with it.

The sun shifted somewhere out of sight and the light faded again, leaving the crab apple orchard in near-darkness. Clay-Boy rose from his seat against the trunk of the tree and walked out into a little clearing. From this point he could see the center of New Dominion, a small cluster of buildings in a little cup of land between several hills. The commissary, the post office at which his Aunt Frances officiated and the barber shop were dark, but light and movement came from The Pool Hall and the mill where the night shift was at work. Around the core of the village at intervals were the great gaping quarries, pockmarked on every hill and in every meadow.

Physically it was an ugly place, but the boy had never seen anything to compare it with and he did not know that it was ugly. Yet in his imagination, out of what he had read, from the pictures he had seen in books, he knew that there were other worlds, many places beyond the rim of the mountains and that people lived differently in those worlds and that now by incredible chance a door was opening for him into a different world.

"I'm going away from here," he said aloud, and his voice to him seemed as filled with sadness as with victory.

Faintly the boy heard his name called, but he was not ready to go and he ignored his mother's summons. He spent a while looking at the schoolhouse where a single light beamed from the seniors' home room. Miss Parker would still be there, correcting papers or preparing lessons for tomorrow. Again anticipation flooded his mind, his thoughts turned to what would happen that night and he turned homeward.

He came out of the orchard, crossed the road and,

standing under a wisteria-covered arch that covered the front gate, he looked up at his home. It was the same house his father and mother had moved into when they were married. At first Clay had objected to doing anything to improve the place because they would only be there long enough for him to build his own home on Spencer's Mountain. But then as the children came along and the house on the mountain was slow in materializing, Clay and Olivia had done their best to make the company-owned house into a home. Clay had painted the house and laid a flagstone walk from the front steps down to the front gate. He had put up a fence of sturdy locust posts and heavy wire to keep the children from running into the road that ran in front of the house. He had gone into the woods and brought back young maple trees which now had grown to thirty- and forty-foot shade trees. To the practical improvements Clay made, Olivia added beauty. Bordering the entire yard were her flowers—iris, petunias, daffodils, crocuses, black-eyed Susans. All along the fence ran roses which Olivia had raised from cuttings she had gotten from her neighbors. Over the arch Clay had built for her she trained a wisteria vine that was filled each spring with heavy scented clusters of purple blossoms.

The thought of leaving saddened the boy. He stood looking up at his home and he felt as if a curtain were being drawn across the scene, cutting him away from his family and separating them from him.

"You-all come in now, children," Olivia called. "It's

dark, and in the dark you're liable to get hurt. Snakes out there this time of night and Lord knows what else you'll step on in the dark. Come on in now."

A screen door slammed shut. His mother's voice carried on the spring air to the boy and he noticed that her voice was higher than usual, tinged with some vague worry.

"I'm not goen to call you-all again. Hurry on in, now."

Somewhere a baby cried. Somewhere, far off, a dog bayed at the awakening moon. Inside the house he could hear his mother talking to the other children.

"Everybody sit down now. Supper's on the table."

The boy walked up the flagstone walk toward the house. So far he had not heard his father's voice and that could mean either that his father had already gone to bed or that he was not yet home.

"Where have you been?" his mother asked as Clay-Boy walked into the kitchen.

"I went for a little walk," he said, taking his seat on the bench.

"This was sure some time to take a walk," said Olivia. "Them people comen here tonight and your Daddy off Lord knows where."

"I was hopen maybe Daddy would be home," Clay-Boy said.

"You better eat your supper in a hurry and go look for him," said Olivia.

"All right, Mama," Clay-Boy said and picked up his knife and fork.

"Wait a minute," said Olivia. "We don't ever get in such a hurry around here that we forget to say the blessen. Whose turn is it?"

"It's my turn," four-year-old John said proudly. His eyes were big and grave and he turned them now on each person to see if all had assumed the proper air of reverence. Satisfied that he had everybody's attention and that each child had his hands folded and placed under his chin, he recited in a sing-song:

Thank you for the food we eat,
Thank you for the world so sweet,
Thank you for the birds that sing,
Thank you, God, for everything.
Amen.

A chorus of *Amens* joined John's, followed by a clatter as knives and forks were picked up and each child assaulted the plate in front of him.

"Becky didn't say *Amen*," tattled Shirley. Shirley was the extremely pretty one. Her long auburn curls fell almost to her waist and even at nine it was plain that some day she would be beautiful.

"I did too say *Amen*," said Becky, the smart one. Her face was thin and her hair bright red. One of her eyes had been blackened recently at school when she had been involved in a fight. The black eye was a great pride to her because she won it protecting Luke from some boys who were bullying him.

"You did not say *Amen*," insisted Shirley. "If you

did nobody heard you."

"The reason you didn't hear me was because I whispered it," replied Becky.

"Why did you whisper *Amen,* Becky?" asked Luke. Luke was the musical one. At eight he could already play the piano. The Spencers did not own a piano, but one day at school Luke had climbed up on the piano bench and simply begun to play a tune. The tune was "You Are My Sunshine," and of course he had not played it perfectly, but still it was recognizable. It had amazed everybody but Olivia who, when told, simply stated, "Oh, he's always been musical."

"I whispered it to see if God could hear me," replied Becky.

"Did He hear you?" asked Luke.

"I don't know," answered Becky. "I'm testing Him."

"Of course He heard you," said Olivia. "God hears everything."

"I hope He didn't hear Matt today," said Becky.

Matt had been bent over his soup. Hearing Becky's comment he raised his head and looked at her fiercely.

"You better shut your yap if you know what's good for you," he said.

"That's no way to talk to your sister, Matt," admonished Olivia, who was trying to eat her supper with one hand while she fed the baby with the other.

"Matt's goen to hell," continued Becky. "Today he mashed his finger and he said somethen bad."

"What did he say?" asked Olivia.

"He said 'Damn, damn, double damn, triple damn,

hell!' " answered Becky with some satisfaction.

"Did you, Matt?" asked Olivia.

Matt pretended he had not heard his mother and continued to eat his soup.

"Did you say what Becky said you did?" asked Olivia.

"Daddy says it all the time," answered Matt.

"That is no excuse for you to say it," said Olivia. "If I ever hear you say such a thing again I'm goen to wash your mouth out with Octagon soap."

"Why is Matt goen away?" asked three-year-old Pattie-Cake, who was struggling with some food in front of her. Pattie-Cake waged a constant fight with gravity, and most of the time she was so busy keeping things from falling down that she did not often have time to enter a conversation. Sometimes her milk fell over. Usually the floor around her was littered with meat that started for her mouth and had fallen to the floor in transit. She even had trouble keeping her pants on; those too kept falling down and half the time she ran around with her chubby little rear bouncing in the wind. "I don't want Matt to go away," she said through the hamburger she had somehow safely managed to get to her mouth.

"Matt's not going anywhere," said Olivia. "Now you eat your supper and watch what you're doen."

"Where's he goen?" demanded Pattie-Cake loudly.

"He's goen to hell," said Becky. "For sayen bad words."

"I want to go too!" said Pattie-Cake. "I want to go with Matt!" Her eyes filled with tears at the thought she might be left behind. Suddenly she burst into loud angry screams. "Now, see what you've done," said Shirley.

"Donnie, you sit!" said Olivia to the baby, who somehow found it impossible to remain seated in his high chair but much preferred to stand and reach for everything within the radius of his arms. Olivia stuffed him down in his high chair, went around the table, picked up Pattie-Cake and attempted to quiet her.

Mark, the quiet seven-year-old, remained oblivious of the activity going on around him. Paying not the slightest attention to the hubbub on all sides, he reached quietly for a second biscuit, buttered it and went on eating. Mark was the businessman of the family. During the summer months he spent all his time collecting junk, pieces of iron from discarded automobiles, old aluminum pails, mountains of news-papers, magazines, wrapping paper, string, balls of yarn, strips of cloth and metal. All these he sold to the junkman who made a stop in the village once a month. When he wasn't collecting junk Mark was selling pig-weed to the neighbors, all of whom kept at least one pig, or in season he would pick berries and sell them. None of the rest of the family knew exactly how much Mark was worth except Olivia, who had discovered his hoard one day underneath the mattress in a Sir Walter Raleigh tobacco container. She had counted five dollars and eighty cents, his life's earnings and savings. Olivia worried about him. She could never figure out what was going on in his head.

By now Olivia had quieted Pattie-Cake, who was satisfied that Matt would not go to hell and leave her behind. Olivia was starting back to her place at the foot of the table just as Donnie leapt headlong from his high chair. Olivia shrieked at the top of her lungs and so did the children as they all rushed to the spot where Donnie lay quiet, white and unmoving.

Olivia seized the baby and held him in her arms but he did not respond. His little head lolled drunkenly to one side. "Oh God!" screamed Olivia. "He's broke his neck."

All the children burst into tears and milled around the room screaming and crying.

"Run for the doctor, Clay-Boy," shouted Olivia. Clay-Boy scrambled over the weeping children, the benches, the table and out the screen door. Going up through the back yard he fell over an exposed root of an old oak tree and cut his hand on a bed of white flintrock. Across the hill he could see the light of the doctor's house, and he decided to take a short cut through Luke Snead's pasture even though Luke kept a vicious horse pastured there. Clay sprinted through the high broomsage and through little clusters of Scotch pine, tearing his clothes and his skin on barbed wire and cornstalks and blackberry vines.

The local doctor, maintained by the company, was Dr. Amos Campbell. He was a kind, able gentleman as well as an excellent doctor. He had come to the village from Amherst County, where his family had been original settlers. He was greatly respected by the men of the village, and the women held him in such esteem that they would do everything humanly possible to hold onto their babies until he returned from vacation rather than allow someone else to deliver them.

Reaching the house the company maintained for the doctor, Clay-Boy found it empty. On a note pad which hung outside the main door Clay found penciled, "Am delivering the Bibb baby. Leave word if you need me and what the trouble is."

His hands were trembling but Clay-Boy managed to write: "Please come to Clay Spencer's. Donnie has broke his neck." He dropped the pencil and ran back along the path he had come by. His anxiety increased with every churning step and by the time he reached the kitchen door he was sure the baby would be dead and that he would find the house in a frenzy of grief.

The kitchen was empty of people and the house completely quiet as Clay-Boy opened the screeching old screen door and walked in. All the supper dishes had been washed and put away and the kitchen was spotless.

As the screen door slammed shut he heard his mother's voice from the living room, "That you, Clay-Boy?"

"Yes ma'am," he answered. He walked into the living room and there sitting in a rocking chair was his mother holding Donnie, who was wide awake and, from the way he was holding his head up, showed no signs of a broken neck. The baby's face broke into a grin as Clay-Boy walked in.

"Looks like I sent you on a wild goose chase, boy," said Olivia. "You hadn't been gone two minutes when Donnie came to. All he had was a bad knock on the head. I tried to call you but I reckon you didn't hear me."

Relief flooded the boy's face for a moment, then it changed to anger. His face and hands and clothes were torn from the briers and barbed wire he had run through. His breath was still coming in long panting gulps, and seeing the cause of his condition he walked over to the grinning baby and said, "You scrawny little pup, what do you mean by scaring me that way?"

"Clay-Boy!" Olivia exclaimed, "Don't you ever let me hear you talk like that in this house again."

"Mama, I'm just tired of it," Clay-Boy complained. "All I do around here is run for the doctor and go to the store and wash the dishes and dress the children and churn the butter and do a little homework after everybody else is in bed."

"You're the oldest, son," said Olivia.

"I'm tired of being the oldest," he replied.

"I can't help that," said Olivia. "What you get in life is what you're stuck with and you're stuck with being the oldest. You had just better make the most of it."

"I'm goen away from here, Mama," the boy said with a sober voice.

"What are you talken about?" demanded Olivia.

"I'm goen away. That's why Miss Parker and Mr. Goodson are comen here tonight. To ask you and Daddy to let me go."

"Go where?"

"To Richmond."

"I didn't have my babies to send them off to all corners of the world. What do they think they're doen putten ideas like that into your head?"

"They think they can get me a college education, Mama. They think they can get me a scholarship at the University of Richmond. I wasn't supposed to tell you but that's what they're coming here tonight to talk about."

"I vow," said Olivia wonderingly. "Sometimes I think educated people have got less brains than us fools."

"Wouldn't you like to see me go to college, Mama?"

"Clay-Boy, I rather see you go to college than fly to the moon, but where do they think we're ever goen to raise that kind of money? It costs money to go to college. Didn't you ever see those boys over there at the University of Virginia in Charlottesville? Them boys is rich boys. Their daddies have got money or they wouldn't be there in the first place."

"But with a scholarship you don't have to have money. Miss Parker and Mr. Goodson think they can get me one."

"I've read enough to know what a scholarship is. That don't take care of half the expenses. You've still got to eat. You've got to have clothes on your back. You've got to have books and pencils and ink and a fountain pen. We're poor people, son. Where we goen to get money for things like that?"

"Miss Parker said chances are I could find a job of work on the side. She and Mr. Goodson got it all planned out."

"Clay-Boy, you know I'd love you to go to college. If anybody in the world ever deserved an education you do, but it's wishen for the moon to even think about it."

"Mama, all I want to ask you and Daddy to do is listen to what Miss Parker and Mr. Goodson have got in mind."

"If they've got in mind to foot all the bills for getten you a college education then I'm all for it, but if they're just comen down here to put foolish ideas in your head then they can just say their piece and go home early."

"That's all I want you to do, Mama—listen to them."

"I'll listen," declared Olivia. She rose to take the sleeping baby to his bed. As she went up the stairs she called, "Clay-Boy, come here and take care of Pattie-Cake."

Clay-Boy went into the hall and there, seated halfway down the stairs, holding her head in her hands and looking forlorn, was his three-year-old sister.

"Get back in bed," Clay-Boy scolded. "You're supposed to be asleep."

"I can't sleep," she said mournfully.

"Why not?"

"I got to wee-wee," she explained patiently.

"Then go do it," he said. "You know where the bathroom is."

"Will you lift me up, Clay-Boy?"

"All right," he said impatiently. Pattie-Cake descended the stairs, procrastinating by pretending to find each rung of the banister so fascinating she could hardly bear to leave it. Clay-Boy followed her wearily to the bathroom, took off her pajama bottoms and set her on the toilet.

"Now, you go out and wait in the hall," she directed. "I want to be by myself."

"Oh Lord," mourned Clay-Boy loudly. "You'll be in here all night." He went out into the hall and was heading for the kitchen sink where he planned to wash his face and hands when there came a polite knock at the front door. He went to the front-porch door, turned the switch that connected with a naked bulb that hung in the center of the porch and saw Miss Parker and Mr. Goodson.

"You-all come in," Clay-Boy said, and held the door open for them. As he ushered the visitors into the living room, he explained that his mother was putting the baby to bed but would be down in a moment.

Miss Parker sat down and smiled reassuringly at Clay-Boy. She was an institution in the community. Some of the people regarded her with mirth, but those parents who had any concern about their children's education had high praise and respect for her. She was in truth a dedicated and gifted teacher and gave a dignity and purpose to learning that most of the children in New Dominion would never have known otherwise. The reason she was laughed at by some of the people was that she dyed her hair to keep the gray from showing and every time she dyed it it came out a different shade. That she was a spinster others found amusing simply because there were no other spinsters in the community. A girl grew up and found herself a husband. There was no other way.

Mr. Goodson, after his unfortunate introduction to the community, had succeeded in only a short time in winning the favor of his congregation. He had proved to be an agreeable, intelligent and pleasant man and the God he brought to his followers was a softer, more forgiving deity than the harsh and ever-watchful, ever-stern Saviour his predecessor had presented for their worship.

Now Miss Parker, Mr. Goodson and Clay-Boy sat in the living room and groped for something to say. Finally Miss Parker's eyes fell on the ferns that Olivia kept on stands underneath each window. They were rich, full plants that Olivia had dug up in the woods and brought indoors last fall to provide some greenery through the winter.

"Somebody has got a green thumb around here," observed Miss Parker. "Did you ever in your life see such luxurious ferns, Mr. Goodson?"

"I never did," said Mr. Goodson.

"Mama likes to grow things," volunteered Clay-Boy.

"I certainly must ask her the secret of her success," said Miss Parker.

"It's cow manure mostly," explained Clay-Boy. "She says it's the best kind of fertilizer." Clay-Boy bit his tongue. *Cow manure* was something you just didn't say in front of Miss Parker. She glanced away, but the first signs of a blush were beginning at her throat.

"Sunshine is the biggest thing with plants, though," continued Clay-Boy in desperation.

"Sunshine is the salvation of us all," said Miss Parker. "I am looking forward so much to sunshine once the spring finally decides to stay with us."

"Is your father going to be with us this evening, Clay-Boy?" asked Mr. Goodson.

"I hope so," said Clay-Boy. "Sometimes he has to work late."

At that point Olivia walked in the room. She had changed into her good dress, the green silk one she had made herself and wore only to church or for special occasions. She had used no lipstick or rouge, but she had combed her hair and powdered her face and looked so young and pretty it seemed impossible for her to have borne and raised her enormous brood of children.

"I'm glad to see you," Olivia said to the guests, shook hands with both of them and sat down. "I'm sorry Clay-Boy's daddy can't be here. He had to go down to Howardsville to see a man about some pigs he's buyen."

Clay-Boy cringed and wished that he and his mother had agreed on a story beforehand, but then he forgot his original embarrassment as the source of an even greater one strode into the room. Pattie-Cake, her pajama bottoms in her hand and her little rear bare, walked into the center and looked around uncertainly.

"I did a big wee-wee, Clay-Boy," she announced. "Now, can I go to bed?"

Clay-Boy could have gladly shaken the meat from her bones, but instead he picked her up firmly and marched into the hall. At the foot of the stairs he stopped long enough to put her pajama bottoms back on and then started up the stairs only to find his way blocked by Matt, Shirley, Becky, Luke, Mark and John.

"What are you doing out of your beds?" he whispered ferociously.

"Listenen," said Becky.

"Go to bed. Every one of you." His anger frightened them and each child scampered off to his room. He laid Pattie-Cake down in her bed and said, "If you get up another time tonight I'm going to spank your behind so shiny you can see yourself in it."

"I want you to kiss me good night, Clay-Boy," was Pattie-Cake's answer. He bent over the bed, gave her a quick kiss and then descended the stairs.

As he walked into the room he saw that the business of the evening was at hand. Miss Parker had just turned to his mother and said, "Did Clay-Boy tell you anything about our talk today, Mrs. Spencer?"

"A little bit," answered Olivia. "Mostly he just said that you and Mr. Goodson would be comen by tonight."

"I won't embarrass him by telling you in front of him what an exceptional boy Clay-Boy is," said Miss

Parker, "but his record at school has been something to be proud of."

"Well, Clay-Boy's always been just as smart as a tack," his mother answered. "These others I nearly have to take a broom to 'em before they'll do their homework, but Clay-Boy just sits down and does his. Always has."

"Do you and Mr. Spencer have any plans for him after graduation?" Miss Parker asked.

"Well," said Olivia, "his daddy has spoke to some people over at the DuPont Company in Waynesboro. His daddy worked over there for them during the Depression when the plant closed down here, and he always thought high of the DuPont Company. You see, we're both hopen he won't have to go to work in the mill. There must be somethen better he can do and still make a liven."

Miss Parker nodded her head vigorously. She herself was at constant war with the mill. All too often she had watched some promising child, some boy with a quick inquiring mind, and had waited for him to reach her class only to have him snatched from her hands to take some menial job at the mill. And it would break her heart to go past the place and see the boy in later years, pushing a wheelbarrow or bent over a stonecutting machine or else snickering with the other workers over some joke she was well aware concerned herself.

"What would you think of Clay-Boy's going to college?" asked Miss Parker.

"Lord, Miss Parker," replied Olivia. "We never

thought of anything like that. We always vowed we'd put every one of the children through high school, but even that's a strain. We've got nine of them to feed and clothe and I'll tell you the honest truth, we just have to stretch every penny as it is."

"But," said Mr. Goodson, "if a way were provided, would he be allowed to go?"

"Well, certainly he could go if he wanted to," replied Olivia, "but let me say one thing here and now; I don't want to see this boy get his hopes all up and then be disappointed."

"That is something we will have to risk," said Miss Parker. "And you must understand that, Clay-Boy." She looked at Clay-Boy and he nodded gravely.

"Just what did you have in mind, Miss Parker?" asked Olivia.

"It seemed to me such a crime that Clay-Boy's education should end with high school that I mentioned it to Mr. Goodson. He suggested that we apply for a scholarship and he has taken the liberty of finding out what scholarships are available at the University of Richmond. Mr. Goodson went there himself and I also happen to know that it is an excellent school."

"I found that a limited number of scholarships are still available," said Mr. Goodson. He hesitated a moment and then continued. "However, these scholarships are of a rather specialized nature."

Clay-Boy braced himself. He knew that the qualification that was to follow was a ticklish one.

"What Mr. Goodson is trying to say," said Miss

Parker, "is that the only scholarships left are ministerial."

"I don't know too much about scholarships," said Olivia. "What kind is that?"

"It means that if Clay-Boy were to receive one he would be obliged to become a Baptist minister," replied Miss Parker.

Until now Olivia had worn a look of bewilderment mingled with hope, but now the hope vanished completely.

"You mustn't refuse us until you've heard us out, Mrs. Spencer," said Miss Parker.

"I'd be wasten your time to let you go on," said Olivia. "I've heard enough now to know that it's something that just can't be."

"I fully understand that Clay-Boy has never felt any special call to be minister, and we would be playing a small deception on the University to pretend that he has, but it does offer a way for him to go to college, and even a ministerial education is better than none." Miss Parker cast an apologetic glance at Mr. Goodson, but he was nodding quietly in agreement.

"Oh, I realize all that," said Olivia, "but it just can't be."

"Maybe not," said Miss Parker, "but it's worth a try."

"No," said Olivia. "We can't even do that."

"I don't understand why not," said Miss Parker. She was determined to overcome any reasonable objection.

"The reason is," said Olivia, "his daddy would have a fit."

"If Mr. Spencer is willing to make the sacrifices you've already mentioned to put his children through high school, he must have a great respect for education," said Mr. Goodson.

"Oh, he's got respect for education all right," said Olivia, "but if there's anything in the world he can't stand it's the Baptists."

"I know that Clay is not what you might call a formally religious man, but I don't see why he should let that stand in the way of Clay-Boy's education."

"My husband might go along with it if it was anything but Baptist, but you just mention the word and he sees red."

"What exactly has Clay got against the Baptists?" asked Mr. Goodson.

"I wouldn't blacken my tongue by sayen some of the things he says against the Baptists," declared Olivia. "You don't know how it worries me. Sometimes when I think of all these little children comen along to hear the things that man says. It's awful."

Their attention was drawn suddenly to someone who appeared in the doorway. She was looking at Mr. Goodson and she announced to him in a grave voice, "I got to poop."

Clay-Boy rose and grabbed Pattie-Cake angrily by the hand and led her into the bathroom.

Sitting on the toilet and looking up solemnly at him with her big brown eyes she said, "You goen to be a preacher, Clay-Boy?"

"No," he growled, "and don't you ever let me hear

you say that again!"

"All right, Clay-Boy," she answered, but she continued to regard him with troubled eyes.

"I don't want you to go away, Clay-Boy," she said.

"Don't worry about that," he said harshly. "I'm never going to get away from here. I'll rot right here in New Dominion for the rest of my life."

"That's nice," said Pattie-Cake.

"Aren't you through yet?" demanded Clay-Boy impatiently.

"No," she said, and put her elbows on her knees, cupped her chin in her hands, and looked blissfully off into space. Clay-Boy went to the door, put his ear to the keyhole, and tried to listen to the conversation in the living room, but the voices were muffled and he could not hear what they were saying.

"I hear my Daddy," squealed Pattie-Cake all of a sudden. In the same second she jumped from the toilet and tried to run past Clay-Boy and out of the room.

"You wait a minute," he said and grabbed her. "You can't go out there without any pants."

As he was putting Pattie-Cake's pajama bottoms on her, Clay-Boy listened and realized that she was right. Somewhere down the road his father and a group of the men he worked with were on their way home. They were singing a song that Clay-Boy had heard them sing before. The opening lines were:

I've got a girl in Baltimore,
Streetcar runs right by her door, . . .

The closing lines of the song were extremely suggestive.

Clay-Boy spent the next few minutes praying that temporary deafness might visit his schoolteacher and the minister, but when he walked into the living room he could see that they had heard and understood every word of the bawdy song.

Everyone had been intently studying some spot in the linoleum that covered the floor. Olivia rose suddenly.

"Excuse me," she said and went through the hall and out onto the front porch.

"Clay," she called and then again, louder, "Claaaay!"

From down at the gate Clay separated himself from the group of men he had walked home with and called over his shoulder to them as they walked on up the road.

"That woman loves the tar out of me. Can't wait for me to get home."

A chorus of good nights and farewells followed his unsteady progress up the walk. At the foot of the steps he stopped and looked up at Olivia.

"If I can make it to the top of them steps," he said, "I'm goen to haul off and kiss you, old woman."

"You behave yourself," she admonished. "There's company in the house."

Suddenly he bounded up the steps and grabbed Olivia up in his arms with her feet off the floor and waltzed around and around the front porch with her. Paying no attention to her pleas to be put down he kissed her again and again.

"Clay, there's company inside. You stop it," she implored.

"I love you, woman," he declared and slapped her happily on the behind.

Clay was so intent on expressing his love and Olivia was so busy trying to release herself that neither of them heard Doctor Campbell walk up on the porch. He regarded them with amusement and was grinning broadly when Clay grew tired of his loving and lowered Olivia to the floor after giving her one final bone-breaking hug and a kiss that was intended for her cheek but landed somewhere near her ear.

"Good evening," said Dr. Campbell.

"What are you doen here, Doc?" asked Clay, as he released Olivia.

Doctor Campbell held out the piece of paper containing Clay-Boy's message. "According to this note Donnie has a broken neck."

"Oh God," wailed Clay and turned to Olivia. "Is that what you were tellen me?"

Composed now, Olivia explained, "Donnie fell out of his high chair a while ago and knocked himself out. He's all right now."

"Perhaps I'd better take a look at him just to be sure," offered Doctor Campbell.

"That's real good of you, Doctor," said Olivia, "but I'm sure he's all right. Why don't you come on in, though? Maybe you'd like a cup of hot coffee?"

"As a matter of fact I would," said Doctor Campbell.

Clay turned to enter the house but he found his way blocked by Olivia.

"What are you standen there for, woman?" he demanded.

"Before we go in, Clay, you better know that the Baptist preacher's in there."

"What's he tryen to do, get thrown out of the Baptist church again?" Clay said in a voice that could be heard for miles.

"Him and Clay-Boy's teacher come down here tonight to talk to us. It's somethen about Clay-Boy and I want you to listen to what they've got to say and not use any bad words."

"Doc Campbell," said Clay. "This woman just can't seem to get it through her head that I'm a natural-born cusser. If I couldn't cuss I couldn't talk."

"It's a bad habit, that's all it is," said Olivia with weary disapproval. It was an argument she knew she would never win, yet she felt it her Christian duty to register her position from time to time.

Olivia stood aside and opened the door. Clay led Doctor Campbell down the hall and into the living room. Doctor Campbell entered first and shook hands with Mr. Goodson and Miss Parker. Clay stood at the door for a moment. First he smiled at Miss Parker, then went over, took her hand and nodded silently. Next he went to Mr. Goodson, took his outstretched hand and smiled cordially.

"I'm happy to see you, Clay," said Mr. Goodson.

Clay smiled again, nodded agreeably and sat down.

Clay-Boy looked at his father anxiously. It was unusual that he had not spoken. Usually he entered a room and set everyone in it at ease with a single remark, but now he had not said a word and showed no intention of saying anything.

They all sat in silence. The only sounds in the house came from the kitchen where Olivia was preparing coffee.

The living room was so deathly silent that Clay-Boy became conscious of his breathing and tried holding his breath until his face turned red and he had to breathe again. When he finally began to breathe again he drew in his breath with such gulps that all faces turned on him and he became the center of attention. He turned his face imploringly to his father, but Clay merely sat nodding and smiling politely.

Miss Parker cleared her throat, turned to Clay and said, "It's been a great honor to have your son in my class."

Clay nodded but spoke not a word.

"I don't believe anyone in the history of the school has made such a brilliant record as Clay-Boy has," continued Miss Parker bravely.

She waited for some response from Clay. He nodded companionably, but a look of desperation had crept over his face. Clay-Boy had been studying his father closely ever since he came into the room. At first he thought his father was drunk and could not talk, but he discarded that idea. Clay was sitting quite straight and his eyes showed none of the brightness that whiskey sometimes put there. The trouble seemed to Clay-Boy to be that his father looked as if he were going to explode any minute.

"Daddy, are you all right?" Clay-Boy asked.

"Damn it all, I never been better, boy, but your Mama said for me to watch the way I talked and I ain't been able to open my mouth for fear I'd say somethen wrong.

"You see, ma'am," said Clay to Miss Parker, "ever since I was six years old I been usen cuss words and I reckon I'm too old a rooster to change. Oh, it bothers the old woman in there that I don't talk like somethen out of a pulpit, but I can't help it. I learned to cuss before I learned to walk. Now if that bothers anybody they can march their tail right out of here, but I'm in my own home and I'm goen to talk the only way I know how."

Miss Parker began to take hope. At least Clay was communicative and she preferred that to the idiotic headshaking he had been doing when he first came into the room.

"Now that's said and done," said Clay, "what the hell is goen on here?"

"We came to explore the possibilities that young Clay might go to college," said Mr. Goodson.

Clay's expansive mood left him. He looked at Clay-Boy sadly. "There ain't the chance of a snowball in hell," he said.

"Mr. Spencer," said Miss Parker, who was becoming so accustomed to the swearing that she barely flinched at each new word, "I think if you'll listen to Mr.

Goodson a moment you might see that there is a possibility."

"I'm listenen," said Clay.

"Miss Parker spoke to me some time ago about young Clay," said Mr. Goodson. "I wrote to some friends at the University of Richmond and found that they still have a few scholarships available."

"What kind of ship is that?"

"A scholarship is a fund set aside to help students who might otherwise not attend college at all. My guess would be that young Clay would stand a good chance of winning one."

"It's some kind of contest. Is that what it is?"

"No, you just have to fill out an application. I've taken the liberty of writing to the University and asked them to send young Clay an application. When it comes he'll fill it out, you and his mother sign it, and return it to the University. A record of his schoolwork will have to be sent to them at the same time and I'm sure Miss Parker will see to that."

"Yes indeed," nodded Miss Parker.

"Boy," said Clay, "if this thing comes through we'll get you down to Richmond somehow. If we can't get you a ride with somebody goen that way we'll find bus fare for you."

Olivia entered carrying a tray of cups and saucers already filled with coffee.

"Clay," she said, "it isn't as easy as all that. All a scholarship takes care of is the admission. He's still got to have a place to sleep and somethen to eat."

"What kind of cheap outfit are they runnen, they don't let the scholarship take care of everythen?"

"Clay, don't you have a brother down in Richmond?" asked Dr. Campbell.

"My brother Virgil's down there. He's worken down there. That's a fact," answered Clay.

"Maybe he'd take Clay-Boy in with him. That would take care of his room and board," suggested Dr. Campbell.

"That's asken a lot of a man, even a brother," said Clay, "To take some little old shirttail boy in and live with him. Virgil's down there chasen women and liven like a dude. Clay-Boy would just be in his way."

"No, I wouldn't, Daddy," said Clay-Boy emphatically. "I'd be studying."

"Boy," said Clay, "there's another thing. You ain't never been to no big city. You wouldn't know how to get on a streetcar. I know how it is with cities. Virgil took me down there to Richmond one week end and it nearly scared the pie out of me. Cars goen every whichaway and fire trucks janglen up and down the street all hours of the night and so many people you wouldn't believe it if you saw it. You'd get lost down there."

"He probably will get lost," said Miss Parker, "but not for long. I know that Clay-Boy is special to you, Mr. Spencer, because he's your son. But he's very special to me. I've been teaching school here in New Dominion for almost thirty years. I've taught my boys and girls to recite Shakespeare, and I've tried to open to them some of the beauty and wisdom they can find in books. I've taught them a little bit about how their government works and hope I've instilled in them some idea of the majesty and wonder of people governing themselves. I've tried to teach them in geography class that this is an enormous world full of opportunities for growth and learning and achievement. Once in a while a child comes along with a hungry look in his eye. He's not content just to memorize facts. He wants to know, he has an inquiring mind, and everything he learns only whets his appetite to learn more. Your son is such a boy, Mr. Spencer. I've taught him everything I know and he's still hungry. If the day comes that I go past the mill and see him stooped over a polishing machine, I think I will give up the teaching profession."

Miss Parker had made more of a speech than she had intended and she was near tears, but she tried to hide her distress behind her handkerchief.

"I wish I had a bottle," said Clay. "I'd offer you a drink. But the old woman pours out every bottle she finds so I don't bring it in the house no more."

"Thank you anyway," said Miss Parker.

"I'll tell you something," said Clay. "I never had no education myself, and maybe that's why I appreciate what a education means. I went to school maybe four or five days in my life, just long enough to learn a little writen and how to read a little bit and enough arithmetic so I can tell when the company's cheaten me on my pay. I admire a man with education and it's always been my heart's craven for my babies to get better than I had."

"Clay," said Dr. Campbell. "One of the trustees of the University of Richmond lives up in the part of Nelson County I do. I'd be glad to speak to her on Clay-Boy's behalf if you're willing."

"I don't see how I could hardly say no, Doc."

"I take it then," said Mr. Goodson, "that you have no objection to Clay-Boy's at least applying for the scholarship."

Clay considered for a while. After a long pause he looked at Clay-Boy and asked, "You want it, boy?"

"Yes sir," answered Clay.

"Suppose you go down there and fall on your butt?" said Clay.

"I won't . . . fail, Daddy," promised Clay-Boy.

"All right then, boy. I'll talk to Virgil about it and see if he'll take you in. Then you go down there and show them city folks somethen they never saw the like of before."

"I take it then that you will sign Young Clay's application?" asked Mr. Goodson.

"I by-God will," swore Clay.

"Very well," said Mr. Goodson, "I'll get the application to you right away."

"Much obliged, Preacher," said Clay, and then turned to Olivia. "Now that's done, Old Woman, how about putten some supper on the table. I'm hungry."

Later, when they were alone in the kitchen and Clay

was having a second cup of coffee, he said, "Livy, write a letter to Virgil and tell him all about this thing and see what he says."

"He's your brother," said Olivia. "I think you're the one that ought to write to him."

"Honey," said Clay. "It takes me half the night just to sign my name. Now, you get here to the table and write it and I'll tell you what to say."

Olivia agreed; when she had found one of the children's school tablets and sharpened a pencil with a butcher knife she sat down and waited for Clay to compose his thoughts. Finally when nothing seemed to come to Clay's mind she said, "I'm waiten."

"Durned if I can think of how to start out."

"Most letters start with Dear whoever it is you're writen to," suggested Olivia.

"All right, then. Put down, 'Dear Brother Virgil.'"

Olivia did as she was instructed. When she was finished writing, she looked up for further dictation.

"Dear Brother Virgil," said Clay, "Hope this finds you in the pink of health and getten plenty to eat."

Olivia wrote hastily as Clay warmed to what he was doing. "We are just fine and dandy here. The trout fishen is goen to start soon and I hope to hell you will be here for it."

"I can't say that," said Olivia.

"What?"

"Say 'hell.'"

"Why not?"

"Because it's going through the mails of the United

States Government. They'll arrest you for sayen a thing like that in the mail."

"How they goen to know if I write 'hell' and send it through the mail?"

"They're liable to open it," said Olivia. "That's how."

"Who gives 'em the right?" demanded Clay.

"Anything you send through the mail they got the right to open," said Olivia. "It's the law."

"Well," exclaimed Clay, "I got a good mind not to do business with 'em. They got no right tellen me what I can write to my own brother. Now you write it like I tell you and if they give me any trouble I'll deal with 'em. Take it down like I tell you. What have you got so far?"

Olivia read back what she had until she came to "The trout fishen is goen to start soon. . . .

"And I hope to hell," said Clay, "you will be here for it. Trout is goen to be plentiful this year from the looks of things and you come on up here and we will catch us a bushel." He paused for a moment to give Olivia time to catch up with him. "Are you writen it down just what I'm sayen?" he asked.

"Word for word," replied Olivia, who had substituted "heck" for "hell."

"Now you are probably wonderen what the devil I am doen writen to you," continued Clay.

Olivia put down the pencil and pushed the tablet over to Clay.

"I'm not goen to write that," she said.

"Well, say it someway else," he said and pushed the tablet back to her.

"You are probably wondering what the goodness I am writing to you about," wrote Olivia and waited.

"The reason is," Clay went on, "that Clay-Boy is just about to get a chance to go to a college down there and they are willen to pay for everything but a place for him to sleep and somethin' for him to eat. It seems to me if they wanted him bad enough they'd take care of that too, but I know about as much about college as Alabama Sweetzer knows about Sunday school."

"Clay!" said Olivia.

"Well, you know what I'm tryen to say. Put it down anyhow you want to."

Olivia composed the idea to her own liking, wrote it and waited for Clay to continue.

"What I want to talk to you about is maybe you'll take Clay-Boy in with you down there and see no harm comes to him while they're given him an education. He's a good boy and won't trouble you none and no matter how he turns out, I'll spend the rest of my life maken it up to you. Yours till the well runs dry. Clay Spencer."

CHAPTER 6

IN MAY CLAY-BOY graduated from high school. His graduation present, a great surprise, was his high school ring. Clay-Boy had not expected the ring because Clay had objected to throwing away good money on jewelry, but Olivia had finally convinced Clay that it was a symbol of accomplishment rather than a useless ornament.

Since no word had come from the scholarship committee at the University of Richmond Clay-Boy had no way of knowing whether the dream of his going to college would come true or not. In the meantime there were long days ahead. He discussed with his father the possibility of seeking a temporary job at the mill, but Clay would not permit it.

"I've said it all my life," vowed Clay. "Not one of my babies will ever work in that sump hole and my word still holds."

"But Daddy," objected Clay-Boy, "it would only be for a little while. Just until I hear what they decide down at Richmond."

"Boy," said Clay with unaccustomed harshness, "I have gone without clothes on my back so you could get a high school education. Your mama has scrimped and saved so you could buy paper tablets to do your homework on. Many's the night we've gone to bed not knowen where the money would come from to see us through the next day.

"But one thing was always certain. The school was there and as long as it was free, and we could keep shoes on your feet and clothes on your back, you'd go to it until you got education enough that you'd never end up ignorant and broken-backed and covered with mill dust like the rest of these poor fools around here.

But you, boy, you're different. You've got a high school education. Maybe that's all you'll ever get. Let's see what you can do with it."

As Clay-Boy discovered in the days that followed there was simply no demand in New Dominion for a boy with a high school education. In a larger community he might have found work as a drugstore delivery boy, or an usher in a movie theatre or a messenger, but in New Dominion there were no drugstores or movie houses or Western Union offices.

Although Clay-Boy was out of school he did not lack for things to do. In the morning he delivered butter, eggs, and buttermilk to his mother's customers— Olivia supplemented the family income by such sales. He helped his mother about the house, and he even developed the ability to operate the old manual butter churn with one hand, hold the baby with the other and somehow review one of his schoolbooks at the same time. He longed for more books to read, for there were only two books in the house. One was *The A B C's of Bee Keeping* which Clay had sent away for during the Depression when he thought he would try to make money selling honey. The other was the *Holy Bible*, and since these were the only two books and they were precious they were kept on a high shelf away from the destructive hands of children.

Twice a day Clay-Boy would make the trip down to the post office to see if any word had arrived from the University of Richmond.

One day on his way home from the post office he

stopped and began to examine an abandoned little one-room house that was tucked away at the curve of the road a few hundred yards from the mill. It had been built originally as a playhouse for the children of one of the former general managers of the company. As the mill expanded and encroached more and more on the grounds of the general manager's home, he had succeeded in persuading the company to build a larger and better home in a new location. The residence had been torn down, but the little playhouse had been of such small consequence that it had been left.

Now its windows were broken and the door had been removed and the floors were covered with cigarette butts and beer cans—the men of the village occasionally and unofficially used the little house for drinking bouts and poker parties—but still its floor was strong and the roof only leaked in a few places.

"Somebody could open a business of some kind there," thought Clay-Boy. He sat down on the edge of the road and tried to think of something there might be a demand for in New Dominion. He reasoned that because everybody in the village was so poor it would have to be something that would cost them the least amount of money possible but still provide them with such value that they would buy.

Several days went by before Clay-Boy had an idea, one that came from a chance remark made by his mother.

"I certainly do wish I had somethen to read," she said one night after the younger children were put to bed. "I don't know when I had a good book to read."

And that was when the idea of opening a rental library came into Clay-Boy's head. There was only one drawback. He had no books to rent, but still he thought the idea was a good one, and when he told it to Laura Parker she agreed enthusiastically.

"Let me talk to some people," she said, "and see if we can come up with some help."

"And just who do you expect will borrow the books?" asked Clyde Goodson when she took him to the abandoned little house and told him Clay-Boy's idea.

"Maybe the children," she said. "We've taught them to read, but aside from their school books there's nothing in their homes to read except an occasional Bible."

"But are you sure there are enough people who can afford to rent books?"

"No," said Laura, "the renting was Clay-Boy's idea. What I thought we could do was somehow get some books and provide them free and let Clay-Boy act as librarian with a small salary."

"Where's the money coming from?" inquired Mr. Goodson.

"That's why I asked you to come down and see the place. I want you to persuade your congregation to adopt this as a project and provide a weekly salary of ten dollars or so."

"You obviously don't know much about my congregation and their financial status. Ten dollars or so is about what they pay me."

"I expected as much," said Laura, "so I'll use Plan Two."

"What's that?"

"I'll go to the company."

"They'll laugh at you."

"You forget that as an old-maid schoolteacher who touches up her hair and adores Shakespeare I am the object of considerable ridicule already. Being laughed at is nothing new to me."

"I wish you luck," said Mr. Goodson. "You get the building and I'll see what I can do about finding you some books."

The highest authority representing the company in New Dominion was the general manager, Colonel Coleman. He had no secretary, made no appointments, so in order to see him Laura simply went to his office one morning at nine o'clock and sat until he arrived.

Laura had never been in the Colonel's office before; because of his title she had expected it to be a monastic, military, ordered room. It was not. One dirty window admitted enough light to reveal a desk, cluttered with papers and a gooseneck lamp. Along the window ledge were stacked small sample squares of soapstone. In the center of the room was a pot-bellied stove in which no fire burned. The remaining furnishings consisted of the chair with a broken cane bottom in which Laura sat and waited.

Colonel Coleman arrived at nine-thirty. He was a

tall, thin man with thin-blue alcoholic eyes and thinning blond hair. No one had ever seen him dressed in anything other than a riding habit and he carried with him always a short leather riding crop. While no one had ever seen him actually use the crop on a horse or a person, he often gave the impression that if angered he might.

He walked in the office, sat down at his desk and turned on the gooseneck lamp before he noticed Laura. When he did see her he said, without any show of surprise,

"Good morning."

"Good morning, Colonel Coleman," said Laura. "I'm Laura Parker."

"I know who you are, Miss Parker," he replied.

"I've come to see you about that little playhouse that's around the corner under the mulberry tree." Laura grew nervous under the Colonel's bland stare. "You know the place I mean?"

"Yes," he said disinterestedly. "I've been thinking of knocking it down. The men use it to drink and gamble in when they ought to be home sleeping. Why are you interested in the place?"

"I want to make it into a library," replied Laura.

"Miss Parker, if you hope to turn this rock pile into a cultural center you're wasting your time."

"That is not my intention."

"Then why?"

"Colonel Coleman, I have a student in my graduating class who I hope will enter college next fall."

128

"Good God," exclaimed the colonel. "Why?"

"Because he is an exceptional boy. I think it would be criminal for his education to stop with high school."

"What's the boy's name?"

"His father works in the gang room. He's Clay Spencer's boy."

"Clay is a friend of mine. We've often hunted together, and I know the boy too. Where's the money coming from?"

"We've applied for a scholarship at the University of Richmond. If they judge by scholarship, promise and the ability to learn and to grow, I'm sure he'll get it."

"Hope he does," answered the colonel. "But what's this got to do with your making a library out of that old playhouse?"

"The scholarship we're working for pays tuition. That's all. Clay-Boy will need every cent he can earn this summer and more. It seemed to me that the company has done little enough for the people it employs; why couldn't they set aside some small sum each week to pay a librarian?"

"Do you have any idea what a laugh that suggestion would get if I were to present it to the company?"

"Colonel Coleman, who is the company anyway? As long as I have taught here I have heard of The Company. Aren't there any people in the company?"

"No people," said the Colonel. "Just stockholders, mostly located in New York City."

"Will you at least try?"

"Why should I risk that embarrassment, Miss Parker?"

"Because as long as this company has been in existence, and I believe that goes back into the eighteen-eighties, it has paid the workers barely enough to live on. They have worked longer hours than any slave might have worked in the old days, at dangerous jobs or else jobs so tedious it's demeaning. The men are bent and old by the time they are forty. Their children are taken when they are still children and placed in jobs their fathers had when *they* were children. It makes animals out of them, not people! I can't see how you can look at it day after day without its breaking your heart."

"I am glad to say that I am not an emotional man, Miss Parker."

"But you are an intelligent man. Doesn't it stagger your imagination that out of this stone dust and red clay something has come alive in one of these children?"

"Not in the least. You forget, Miss Parker, that nobody asks these people to work here, to live here, or to stay here. They're free to go and find jobs somewhere else."

"But they don't know anywhere else, except this boy who's come along and wants to go and should go. I beg you to help him."

"You can have the house for your library. You'll have to clear the beer cans out and I'd advise you to put a lock on it so the men don't go in there at night."

"And the salary. Considering what it will go for I don't see that fifteen dollars a week is too extravagant. What do you think?"

"It's ridiculous for some kid who isn't out of high school yet. As long as you've rooked me into this thing I'll manage five dollars a week, and that's it."

"Ten, Colonel," said Miss Parker firmly.

"Miss Parker, I operate on a budget here. There's no allowance in it for a librarian. Five dollars a week perhaps I can bury somewhere under miscellaneous expenses. I can't get away with a penny more."

"Colonel Coleman, this is the first philanthropic gesture the company has made in nearly fifty years it has exploited these people." Laura rose and pounded her fist on the desk.

"Miss Parker," answered the Colonel coldly. "This is not a philanthropic organization, and I am not making this concession out of philanthropic motives. It just happens I think the boy's father is a fine man and if he's anything like his father he probably can make something of himself. You can have the house for your library and you can have five dollars a week to pay the kid to run it."

It was not all she had hoped for, but more than she really expected to get. Still she could not resist just one more try. Before she could open her mouth, Colonel Coleman saw her intention. He reached in his desk, pulled out a fifth of whiskey, filled a shot glass and held it out to her.

"Would you care for a drink, Miss Parker?" he asked.

"No, thank you," said Laura and began pulling on her white gloves.

The colonel threw his head back and tossed the bourbon down his throat with ease and relish. It might as well have been lemonade, thought Laura, who expected him to gasp and sputter.

Seeing her look of fascination, he held the shot glass out to her again.

"Are you sure you don't want one?" he said.

"Quite sure," she said. "Good-by, Colonel. Thank you very much."

That night Laura sat down and wrote to churches, libraries and friends telling them of her need for books. "Even popular novels would be welcomed," she wrote to one friend, "as long as they are not trashy, and the condition and quality of the bindings is of little importance."

After school hours and on Saturdays, she and Clay-Boy and sometimes Mr. Goodson would work on the little house, clearing it of debris, replacing the broken windows and scrubbing down the walls with lye. Clyde Goodson found some lumber stacked in the basement of the church, donated it for shelves and then contributed his sincere if not quite expert labor to building them.

The first shipment of books came a week or so before graduation day. And then they began to arrive at the post office almost every day. They came in boxes and barrels from New York and Richmond and Washington. One afternoon after school when the little room was ready, Miss Parker and Clay-Boy went down to start placing the books on the shelves.

With a crowbar Clay-Boy opened the first barrel. A shiver ran down his spine as he looked into the barrel and saw that it was jammed full with books. Titles danced before his eyes: *The A. B. C. of Poultry Raising*, he read. He laid it aside for *A Primer of The Occult*. The third volume he picked out of the dusty-smelling barrel was even more provocative: *Goat Keeping for the Amateur.*

Laura in the meantime had opened a more productive box. "Here's one you'll like," she said, and gave him *Martin Eden*. "This one you simply must read," she exclaimed, and laid *Cyrano de Bergerac* over the primer of poultry-raising. And over that she laid a copy of *Gulliver's Travels*, and then *Ethan Frome*, and *The Mill on the Floss*, and *Through the Looking-Glass*, and *Crime and Punishment*, until Clay-Boy was reeling with the prospect of seeing so many books at one time.

The task of placing the books in the shelves was slow. Over each book Clay-Boy hovered as if in a happy dream that might vanish in a second. Each title he repeated again and again to himself as he moved from container to shelf. All the time Miss Parker hummed to herself, pausing once in a while to announce rapturously, "How marvelous of them to send *Green Mansions*," or "Here's a volume of *Walden* that will fit right into your pocket. Don't put it on the shelf. Carry it with you."

The day after graduation the library was opened for business. The children had been notified at school and their parents had been told of the new asset to the community through notices on the company bulletin board and at the churches.

Clay, who was a little confused as to the function of a librarian, instructed Clay-Boy to "teach them heathens everythen you know" and to "let 'em know who's boss from the word go and you won't have a bit of trouble with 'em."

The hours were twelve to four. On the opening day, Clay-Boy, who had been sitting inside reading, opened the door at twelve o'clock promptly. His first customer was the last person in the village he had expected to see.

There was in the village a family named Sweetzer who named all of their children after Confederate states. Once Mrs. Sweetzer had been tempted to go outside the Confederacy for a name; that was when the twins were born. She had wanted to call them Vermont and Virginia because the two names sounded so pretty, but her husband insisted it would not be patriotic so the twins had become Virginia and Florida.

The Sweetzers did the best they could with their enormous brood, but one of the girls, Alabama, became the village derelict and would attach herself to whatever man would provide her with a place to sleep and enough small change for cigarettes and beer. At the moment that man happened to be the husband of Lucy Godlove, the night watchman at the mill.

Alabama Sweetzer was Clay-Boy's first customer at the new library.

"I heard all about it," said Alabama, "and I come right over here to see if you had somethen for Mr. Godlove to read. He's always carryen on about he don't have nothen to keep him awake at night so I just decided I'd come over here and put the whole thing in your hands."

"What kind of books do you think he'd like?" asked Clay-Boy.

"He's got an old Western magazine down there at the mill he's read front'ards and back'ards. You got anythen like that?" asked Alabama.

"We've got some Zane Grey books," said Clay-Boy, feeling efficient and proud that he was able to satisfy a request so quickly. He found several Zane Grey novels, selected two and taking the card out of the back cover signed the books out to Alabama.

"Appreciate it, Clay-Boy," said Alabama graciously. "Come again," said Clay-Boy, and she promised that she would.

Clay-Boy read for another hour before his next customer arrived. She was Geraldine Boyd, the tall, nervous daughter of the Episcopalian minister. Geraldine's mother had not felt that her daughter would receive a proper education at the New Dominion School and had educated the girl at home. Now she was eighteen years old and well educated but ill at ease whenever she left the Episcopal parsonage, which she seldom did in the daytime and never at night. She materialized in the doorway of the library and stood there waiting for Clay-Boy to finish his reading rather than interrupt him. He looked up with a start when he realized that he was not alone.

"Congratulations on your good fortune, Clay-Boy," said Geraldine primly. "I heard you will attend the University of Richmond."

"Well, it's not sure yet," said Clay-Boy. "We've sent the application down there but we haven't heard from it yet."

"Waiting must be very tedious."

"You said it."

"Of course I wouldn't know. I never had the opportunity to attend college."

"Why not?" asked Clay-Boy. "I mean your family could afford to send you, couldn't they?"

"Yes, but Mother and Daddy feel that once a person has a basic education learning is mostly a matter of reading and applying one's self. Still, college could provide so much more than learning. There's the companionship of good friends. One longs to know people one's own age."

"I guess I won't have time for much of that," said Clay-Boy. "I'm goen to have to find a part-time job and I guess after classes in the morning and work in the afternoon and then studying at night I'll be living like a hermit most of the time."

"In that case I think you are making a mistake by leaving home."

"That's a funny thing to say," said Clay-Boy.

"Not at all. If becoming a hermit is all this opportunity provides you then you shouldn't take it. Could you really be a hermit after all that activity at your house? Every time I go past where you live I walk a little slower so I can watch all those little children playing in the yard and hear your mother telling them not to get hurt, and your father puttering away up there in the back yard. It's all so noisy and happy and gay, I've always wanted to just come inside the gate and be a part of it."

"I wish you would sometime," said Clay-Boy. "It's like Daddy always says, 'Everybody's just as welcome as the flowers in May at our house.'"

"I expressed the desire once to Father and . . ." she broke off and blushed.

"What did he say?"

"I'm sorry, but I can't tell you."

"Why not?"

"It's not very complimentary to your father."

Clay-Boy grinned at the thought of what the Episcopalian minister must think of his own father.

"Why are you laughing?" asked Geraldine.

"I was just thinken that your Daddy probably objects to the things my Daddy is proudest of being."

"I'll tell you what he said if you promise not to tell your father."

Clay promised.

"Father wouldn't let me come to your house because he says your father uses bad language."

"He does," said Clay-Boy nodding his head and grinning.

"Do all of you children too?" asked Geraldine.

"No," said Clay-Boy. "Mama won't let us. Course a couple of the kids said *damn* for their first word, and Pattie-Cake said *hell* a couple of weeks ago, but Mama put a stop to it right away."

"How?" asked Geraldine.

"She washes their mouths out with soap," explained Clay-Boy. "It puts a stop to it right away."

"The interesting thing is that my own father uses those very same words himself and right in the pulpit. Life is so mysterious, isn't it? I really can't make any order out of it. My goodness, here I am talking your arm off and you are probably studying or something."

"I enjoy talking to you, Geraldine," said Clay-Boy sincerely.

"I'll tell you something," she said. "You are the only person near my own age I've ever been able to talk to. Around most people I'm silent as a clam, but somehow you seem interested, and I find myself talking a blue streak. Now I won't bother you any longer. Do you have any books by Jane Austen?"

"I don't remember putting any of them on the shelves, but we can look." Clay-Boy searched through the A authors and found nothing by Jane Austen. Suddenly he thought of a book he had just finished and went to the shelf and picked it out.

"Hey," he said, "Here's one you might like. I just finished it and it's wonderful."

"Oliver La Farge," she said, reading the dust jacket. "I've never even heard of him, but as long as you recommend it, I'll take it. It's really very dear of you to recommend it."

At that moment a voice spoke from the door, in a teenage imitation of Tallulah Bankhead, "What's going on here?"

Geraldine Boyd was so startled she dropped the book she was holding and Clay, recognizing the voice, came around in front of the desk.

"What's the password?" he said.

"Mountain dew," the voice said.

"What's the class song?" he demanded.

" 'You Are My Sunshine,' " the new girl answered.

"Eat your words," he said, and from the doorway the girl sang:

"You are my sunshine, my only sunshine,
You make me happy when skies are gray;
You'll never know, dear, how much I love you.
Please don't take my sunshine away."

At the end of the song the girl came running to Clay-Boy and they hugged each other affectionately. The routine was one they had worked out last summer when they had formed a club whose members could enter only after reciting the routine they had just been through.

The girl was Claris Coleman, daughter of the general manager of the New Dominion Stone Company. During the winter months Claris lived in Washington, D.C., with her mother—who was divorced from the

Colonel—but as soon as the weather turned warm she would appear in New Dominion.

Colonel Coleman did not understand his daughter, but for the time she visited him each summer he welcomed her and saw to it that the house was put in order for her. It always amazed him that she returned year after year, because on her visits they saw very little of each other. She was far too fascinated with the families of the men who worked in the mill, and she viewed them with the objectivity of a sociologist and with something else he often thought might be envy. It occurred to him that she found in these wild mountain people something he and her mother had never given her, a warm unquestioning acceptance, a sense of belonging to a close-knit group, bound together by love. Often she adopted an entire family, and their conversations, which took place mostly at breakfast and dinner, would consist of her well-informed and quite accurate observations of their folk ways, the stories they told and the way they lived.

On her visit last year she had formed an alliance with Clay Spencer's family. The Colonel knew Clay to be a decent and honorable man who did his best to raise his children well, so it was almost with relief that he learned that for the summer Claris had chosen the Spencer family to love, to observe, and to belong to. He had noticed, though it had not disturbed him greatly, that if any effect of her adopted family showed in the girl, it was a tendency to use profanity with skill and imagination.

"What did the spook want?" demanded Claris, breaking from Clay-Boy's embracing arms.

Clay-Boy had forgotten about Geraldine. He looked around, but she had gone. He looked back at Claris and found himself abashed by a maturity that had taken place since he had last seen her.

"You grew," he said.

"So did you, Spark-Plug," rejoined Claris. "What's this about you going to college?"

"They've put me in for a scholarship," he said. "Down at the University of Richmond. We don't know a thing yet."

"What are you going to take up there?" asked Claris.

"Just the regular course, I reckon," he said.

"God, you're ignorant," she observed. "There isn't any such thing as a regular course. You have to major in something."

"What are you majoring in?"

"I registered for a Phys Ed major, but then Mother found out and made me change it. It's a snap course but she said I'd end up muscle-bound, so now I'm taking Home Economics."

"What's that?"

"Oh, you slop around in an apron and bake cakes and learn how to hemstitch. There is one class I liked. Got straight A's. It's called Marriage and the Family—and boy-boy-boy, could I tell you a thing or two. Only I'm not going to."

"Oh, come on."

"Unh, unh."

"Why not?"

"You're so grown up all of a sudden."

"So are you."

"My measurements are thirty-two, twenty-two, thirty-two. That's quite an improvement over last year."

"It looks nice," he said.

No more customers came to the library that afternoon so Clay-Boy and Claris chatted raptly until the clock struck four. There was something new in their relationship this year. Last summer they had been buddies, as close as companionable brothers and sisters. Perhaps it had to do with the fact that Claris had spent a year in college. Clay-Boy had matured too, and whatever it was that was new between them, neither of them was able to speak about to the other.

Claris was more conscious of it than Clay-Boy, but he too recognized the difference and was conscious of it from time to time in their talk. Clay-Boy locked the library and they were silent until they walked out from under the dark green canopy formed by the old mulberry tree and were in the bright light of the roadway.

"You're a funny boy," said Claris. "What makes you such a funny boy?"

"I don't know," said Clay-Boy apologetically. Then he was furious with himself for letting her know he had ever thought of himself as funny.

"Even so," she said, "I like you."

"I like you," he said.

"You can carry my books for me," Claris said, and handed him the armful of books she had borrowed.

"What makes you such a funny boy?" she teased as they climbed the hill to where her father lived.

"Mama says I read too many books," he said.

"You don't read the right kind of books," she scolded and looked at the several adventure novels he carried to read at home. "I'll tell you the kind of books you should read. You should read Dickens, and have you read the Bible—as literature, I mean? And there's Thoreau, Emerson, Milton, Hawthorne. You should have a dictionary too. I'll give you a good dictionary so you'll know what the words mean. It's very important to have a good vocabulary. By the way, did you know that Mrs. Wirt Hazeltine is gravid?"

"No," he said, "I hadn't heard anything about it."

"Of course you haven't," she said. "You don't know what gravid means."

"I do too," he insisted.

"It means she's going to have another baby. I find that most interesting, don't you?"

Secretly Clay-Boy found it appalling because Mrs. Wirt Hazeltine already had more children than she could take care of, but hesitated to tell Claris he found it much less fascinating than she did.

"It would seem to me that you would observe such things," she teased.

"I guess I just don't pay enough attention," he said.

"I imagine one day you will try to make me gravid," she observed casually.

He looked at her in amazement and now he knew what it was that made them different this year from what they had been last summer.

"But of course I won't let you until we are married," she declared.

He stuttered something but it didn't make sense. He hated her because he could never find a reply for her bolder statements.

"You're crazy about me," she said. "Aren't you?"

"You're the one that's crazy," he said.

"Could I have my books, please?" she said and held out her arms. One by one he gave her the books to prolong their parting.

"Some day I'll give a party," said Claris with sudden gentleness. "I'll have lemon ice cream and lots of people. You'll come."

"Thank you," he said, and placed the last of the books in her arms.

"You're crazy," she said, and then she was gone into the house and Clay-Boy was alone and miserable, bewildered and in love.

CHAPTER 7

THE LIVING ROOM was silent. Once in a while a sigh would come from upstairs when one of the children murmured a soft sleepy word. The only sound that came with any regularity was the steady ticking of the clock in the kitchen which showed that the time was five minutes to eleven.

Clay-Boy was reading a book he had brought home from the library and Olivia was holding a two-day-old copy of the Charlottesville *Citizen* in front of her but she was nodding so with sleep that she hardly saw the words.

Clay-Boy looked up from his book and called quietly to his mother.

Olivia opened her eyes and was wide awake in an instant. "Why don't you go on to bed?" he said. "I'll wait up till Daddy gets here."

"I sure would like to," she said. "I'm so tired I can't see straight."

"Go on to bed," urged Clay-Boy.

"No," said Olivia, "If your daddy has gone off and spent his paycheck in sin and whiskey he's goen to have to answer to me for it when he walks in that door."

"Maybe he had to work late, Mama," said Clay-Boy.

"If he had to work late that's all the more reason for me to be up. I'll make him some supper so he won't go to bed hungry."

Clay-Boy returned to his book and Olivia resumed her pointless perusal of the daily *Citizen.* At a quarter to twelve they heard footsteps sound faintly down the road. Clay-Boy laid aside his book and Olivia dropped her newspaper as the-footsteps left the road, came up the front walk onto the porch. The door handle turned and Clay walked in.

Something had happened that had made him proud and cocky.

"Boy," Clay said, grinning at the two of them, "when you get married get yourself a woman like your mama. That woman loves me so much she'd sit up till the rooster crowed if I wasn't home."

"Where've you been, you old fool?" asked Olivia, trying to pretend that she was angry.

"I been off to Charlottesville loven them city gals," replied Clay. "Where'd you 'spect me to be on payday night?"

"I thought probably you were down there at The Pool Hall drinken and gamblen."

"Thinken it over, boy," he said to Clay-Boy, "don't get married at all if you can help it. Women have got a suspicious nature and they're pesky to live with. Get up there, woman, and round me up some supper. I'm hungrier than a bear in the springtime."

Clay-Boy followed his mother and father into the kitchen. Olivia was still trying to pretend that she was angry because it was midnight and Clay was just getting home, but she was pleased that he had not been drinking and this time when she demanded to know where he had spent the evening she was not so much angry as curious.

"Woman," he said, "you are looken at a man who owns a power saw."

Olivia was pouring the coffee she had kept hot for Clay. When she heard what he said she set the percolator down beside his place and looked at him in real anger.

"Clay," she cried, "have you gone and spent every

cent of the paycheck?"

Clay reached in his pocket and pulled out a roll of bills which he placed in her hands. Olivia started to count the money, but he said, "No need to count it. It's six dollars short."

"Where'd you ever find a power saw for six dollars?" she asked, worry over the six dollars already crowding out the relief that the entire amount had not been spent.

"Well now," explained Clay, "five dollars of that money was the down payment. The other dollar I paid to a feller to take me down to Old Man John Pickett's in his truck."

Mr. John Pickett was a rich man, the only person native to the country who could make that claim. Of course, Mr. John Pickett had done nothing to earn the money. It had simply come down to him from his family along with the remains of what had once been a great tobacco plantation on a high bluff overlooking Rockfish River.

"You see," said Clay, "I got word down at the mill that Old Man Pickett was sellen his power saw. Wanted thirty dollars for it."

"Don't tell me you got him down to five dollars!" said Olivia.

"No, I didn't," said Clay. "I know better than bargain with Old Man John Pickett, but I did make a deal with him. I'm buyen that power saw on the installment plan. Five dollars down and five dollars a month."

"Clay!" she said. "These children need shoes and

you go throwen your money away on a thing like that. I don't see what could be in your mind."

"It's springtime. Let 'em go barefoot for a while. It won't hurt 'em. And anyway, it wasn't money thrown away. Me and Clay-Boy are goen to work on the house first thing in the mornen."

"What are you goen to do? Go up there and dig some more on that hole in the ground?"

"No ma'am," said Clay. "I'm goen up there, and we are goen to start cutten down trees and sawen them trees into lumber. That's what took me so long tonight. The saw is already up on the mountain. I took it up there tonight."

"Clay," said Olivia, "why can't you just sit down and rest of a week end like other men do. Let the house go."

"Don't talk crazy, woman. Come here and sit down. Clay-Boy, get me a pencil and paper." Clay-Boy brought the pencil and a writing pad. Clay pushed his supper away and began to draw. "Look here, honey," he said. Olivia sat and watched as he sketched an outline on the paper.

"Now this here," he explained, "is where I'm goen to put you up a kitchen. It's goen to be big enough that when all my babies come home for reunions and all, they can bring *their babies* and there's still goen to be room for everybody to sit down and eat. I'll put you a big window right here in this wall because it looks out on the prettiest sight anybody ever saw. There's a clump of birch trees right under that window and I'm leaven them so you'll have somethen pretty to look at while you're washen your dishes."

It was a familiar story and listening to it again Olivia only half-heard what Clay was saying. His head was bent over the drawing and from this angle his face looked as young as it had been the night he first declared his love for her.

President Wilson had just declared war on Germany and that night in prayer meeting they had prayed for the Belgian babies and sung "Tenting Tonight" in memory of the boys from New Dominion who would be going over there.

After prayer meeting she had found Clay waiting for her in the shadows outside the church. Walking home he held her hand and asked her to wait for him while he was away. The next day Clay walked to Lovingston, the county seat, to offer himself to fight for his country. He did not know where Germany was or why they were at war with his country, but he was a crack shot and thought his country could use him. To his dismay he was turned down and he could never understand that the reason he was disqualified from fighting for his homeland was that he was only fourteen years old.

Having been turned down by the Army, Clay returned home to a good job. The company was particularly short of workers in the gang room, the place where the great diamond-tooth saws ground twenty-four hours a day to chew the stone into separate slabs. Here Clay found work as an apprentice.

In the years that followed, Clay Spencer became a

legend in the community. He could drink more whiskey, hold it down longer, and walk straighter afterward than any man in the community. He developed a flair for cursing and the swear-words he invented passed into the local language. He grew to a height of six feet two and always weighed two hundred pounds unless he'd been in a good fight and if the fight were worth the effort he would usually lose from four to five pounds and gain them back at breakfast.

He was always the first to arrive at a square dance and the last one to leave, and if the square-dance caller grew weary Clay himself would take over. While many of the mothers in the community expressed their disapproval of what they considered his wild ways, their daughters looked on him with favor.

One of the mothers who looked upon Clay with particular distaste was Ida Italiano. Ida was a strict Baptist and considered dancing, drinking and swearing among the most abhorrent sins, and since Clay excelled in all three she found him especially ineligible to court her daughter Olivia.

"I don't want that wild boy comen around here, Homer," she would say to her husband.

Homer, a carpenter at the mill as his father had been before him, would answer, "What you got against the boy, Ida?"

"He's a heathen, that's what he is. You got to tell him to stop comen around here."

"Livy don't seem to mind him comen."

"Livy's not old enough to have a mind."

Ida's statement had some truth in it; Olivia was only sixteen years old. A quiet pretty girl who sang in the choir at the Baptist church, Olivia was obedient to her mother in all respects but one. When Ida forbade her to see Clay Spencer, Olivia continued to see him. On Wednesday nights after prayer meeting, Clay would be waiting for her outside the church and he would walk with her home. Again on Friday night after choir practice she would find him waiting for her and they would walk home slowly—but not quite all the way home, for Ida had threatened dire things if Clay ever set foot in the yard.

The people of the village watched the romance and marveled that a boy with such wicked ways as Clay would choose such a religious girl.

"She's too tame for him," said the jealous girls, but the older and wiser women noted that Olivia might be just the right girl for Clay.

"Settle him down to have a girl like Livy," and it appeared that Olivia was already having a settling difference on Clay, for he began to drink less; he no longer appeared at the poker parties on the night he was paid and only occasionally would he show up at a square dance.

On a Wednesday night in June of 1922 Clay Spencer climbed the hill to where Olivia lived. The footpath was covered with a canopy of dogwood trees which emerged at the gate of the Italiano house. Clay stopped beside a lilac tree and was about to call out when Olivia came quietly from the shadows. When he took her in his arms, he whispered,

"Don't be scared."

"I'm not. I'm just a little nervous."

"How did you get away?" he asked.

"I told her I was goen to Prayer Meeten."

When he had stilled her trembling they went down the hill to the car Clay had borrowed for the night. They drove in silence to the Baptist parsonage where hand in hand they walked along the flagstone walk to the minister's house. Clay knocked once, a little nervously. From somewhere in the house they could hear footsteps and then the door opened and they saw Mr. Goolsby, the old Baptist minister. He held up a lamp to see who had knocked.

"Come in, children," he said.

Holding the lamp to light their way down a long dark hall he led them into a small, comfortable living room.

"I'm sorry we won't be able to have a long visit. I have to go in five minutes or I'll be late for the Prayer Service."

"We won't be needen more than that sir," said Clay. "We come here to get married."

"I thought probably you had," said Mr. Goolsby, "and I've been trying to decide what I should tell you."

"What do you mean," asked Clay.

"Children," said Mr. Goolsby, "marriage is a grave undertaking, not to be entered into lightly, not to be risked if there are factors that would seem to doom it from the beginning."

"Mr. Goolsby," said Clay, "if you've only got five

minutes hadn't you better save the sermon for another time?"

"I'm sorry, son," he said to Clay and then turned to Olivia. "Olivia, your mother is a good friend of mine. Knowing how she would feel about this marriage I cannot perform it."

Olivia began to cry and started out of the room.

"Come on, Clay," she said. "I told you he wouldn't."

"All right," said Clay. "We'll go." But turning to the preacher he said, "I just want you to know you are not the only damn preacher in the world."

They had nearly reached the front door when Mr. Goolsby called them back. "If that's the way you feel about it," he said, "I will marry you."

The ceremony took longer than five minutes because when Mr. Goolsby became nervous he stuttered, and he stuttered now as he realized the consequences that would come when it became known that he had joined together one of the fairest daughters of the Baptist church and the wildest devil in the county.

After they left the parsonage, Clay drove along the main road until they came to the foot of Spencer's Mountain. Here he turned off the gravel road onto a smaller roadway that led to the top of the mountain. He stopped the car at the edge of a pasture on top the mountain and led Olivia out into the field.

A brilliant moon shone down, so bright their shadows stood out sharp in the dark green grass at their feet. Below them they could see the village. The air around them was sweet with the scent of honeysuckle.

He took her hand and led her farther up in the pasture to where the land leveled off and a pleasant grove of trees stood. He looked at Olivia, watching for some reaction.

"It's pretty here," she said.

"This is where I will build you a house," he said. "A place to live in and bring up our family. A place all our own."

At night in the company-owned house, going off to sleep beside her he would say, "I will paint the house to your liken."

"White I would like," she would say, "with green shutters. I would like a flagstone walk goen down to the gate and a wisteria vine over the gate like an arch. I'll plant petunias down that walk on either side and we'll need a fence to keep the children inside so I won't worry when I can't keep my eyes on them every minute."

"White with green shutters is pretty," he would agree and drift into sleep.

"I've always been partial to green," she would say, and then realize that he had gone to sleep. Then she would join him and their dreams would be akin, of the house and the children and the scent of honeysuckle.

Looking at Clay now, Olivia realized suddenly how much he had aged. There was the beginning of a streak of gray at his forehead. The skin around his eyes and in his forehead showed deep wrinkles; sitting there over the drawing he looked stoop-shouldered, as if his back were permanently bent a little forward.

She did not have the heart to stop Clay's description of the work he would start the next day. It was only when Clay-Boy, half asleep with his chin resting on his hand, let his head fall forward with a jerk that Clay realized it was nearly one o'clock.

"God Almighty," said Clay. "It's goen to be daylight in an hour or two. If we're goen to get any work done tomorrow we'd better get some sleep."

Clay-Boy yawned "Good night," and stumbled off to bed. Olivia and Clay turned off the downstairs lights and then tip-toed quietly up the stairs and into their room.

Taking off his shoes as he sat down on the bed, Clay said, "I'm goen to finish off the basement first. It'll be a good place to store your canned goods."

"It's goen to take plenty of that to feed the hungry mouths around here," Olivia said. She lay down and Clay switched off the light by pulling the cord he had rigged to the bare electric globe in the center of the room.

"Night, sweetheart," he said.

"Night, Clay."

Men are strange creatures, thought Olivia as she yawned and rolled her head against the pillows; they really believe all the things they promise women. For seventeen years he had promised her the house and now he had renewed that promise. And women are just as foolish, she thought a moment later, for the vision of the house hovered in her mind. It was there so bright she could see the shining white clapboard in the sunshine and smell the honeysuckle sweetness carried on the wind. Then she went to sleep.

CHAPTER 8

AT DAWN THE FOLLOWING morning, Clay-Boy, still half asleep, followed his father across the meadow that rose to where Clay had started his house. The sun was just rising above the horizon and lingered there above a distant mountain. Fog rose from the damp meadow and the sun was a cool smoldering orange. Clay-Boy stumbled along behind his father but he came awake in a terrible rush of fear as a covey of young quail rose in startled flight around them. The covey dispersed in the air with fierce speed and then darted toward the ground and shelter and again the morning was still except for the tentative call of the hen as she assembled her chicks.

"Near about nineteen or twenty in that covey, I figure," said Clay. "How many did you make out?"

"About that, Daddy," said Clay-Boy.

"Them jaybirds is goen to make good eaten come fall of the year," said Clay. "Quail is plentiful this year. You come back here on week ends from that college course and we'll shoot us a mess of 'em."

"I wish I'd hear something from 'em down at the University of Richmond. I go down to the post office twice a day and not one letter has come from 'em yet."

"Well, I wouldn't bother my mind about it. They

156

probably take their time maken up their minds."

They walked on through the brightening morning until they came to the hole in the ground which was Clay's basement. Nearby was the new power saw. It consisted of a rotary blade attached to one end of an axle. At the other end was a band which connected to an old Model-T engine by a thick heavy leather strap. It had been little used and was in good condition.

"Don't you tell your mama, boy," said Clay, "but I paid ten dollars more for that saw than I told her. Old Man Pickett was asken fifty, but I got him down to forty. I told your mama thirty because you know how she is. You name a big amount like that and she'll worry her head off about how we're ever goen to pay for it. We'll pay it all right. It wouldn't surprise me if I didn't make money on this saw and get the house put up to boot."

"How you goen to make money on it, Daddy?" asked Clay-Boy.

"Well, there's plenty of dead wood on this land, chestnut mostly, that got killed in the blight. There ain't much else can be done with it, but it'll make good firewood. Once I get the house built I'm liable to go into the firewood business."

"I reckon there's money in it," said Clay-Boy.

"There is if you know how to make it," said Clay. "Now me, I ain't goen to waste my time sellen wood to these poor folks around here that can't afford lard to make bread. What I aim to do is get me a truck of my own, go over there to Charlottesville and peddle it there. That's where the big money is. Them city folks will pay money. Around here, all you'll get is a pat and a promise."

Just then the last wisp of fog vanished in the meadow and the bright light of the sun fell on the man and the boy and the hole.

"Better get started here," said Clay, and found a file with which he began sharpening the teeth of the saw.

When he was satisfied that the teeth of the saw were sharp enough, he started the Model-T engine. After a preliminary coughing it huffed away enthusiastically, splitting the quiet morning with its busy sound. Next Clay connected the leather pulley which led from the motor to the saw and the blade began a slow gradual building sound that ended in a steady metallic clawing scream.

"That buzz saw is ready!" shouted Clay to his son.

"She sure sounds it," agreed Clay-Boy.

Clay stopped the engine and the whine of the saw gradually subsided to silence. The boy looked at his father and saw that his eyes were glowing with pleasure.

"Let's cut lumber, boy," said Clay.

"Yes sir," said Clay-Boy.

They walked across the meadow and into the woods. Once in a while Clay would stop and examine a tree but reject it because it housed a nest of squirrels or because it was so old that it might have decayed sections. They came finally to a great oak which might have been a hundred and fifty years old. It was located near the edge of a clearing where it had received sunshine for most of its years and in its seemingly effortless growth toward perfection had grown a thick almost perfectly round trunk from which branches appeared at uniform intervals. Its leaves were a bright healthy green and when Clay saw it he recognized it as the wood he wanted for the underpinnings of his house.

Clay examined the tree carefully, observing weight and slant of branches above and determining which way he wanted the tree to fall.

"There's lumber enough in this old honey to build sixteen houses," he exclaimed to Clay-Boy.

"It's sure goen to make a whale of a crash," said Clay-Boy.

"I want her to fall out into the clearing," said Clay. "There's other trees in there she could knock over and I don't want to harm none of 'em if I can help it."

First Clay chopped out a triangular cut in the trunk in the direction he wanted the tree to fall in. He chopped with the axe in regular joyous strokes, chipping away at the wood—one stroke up and one stroke down—until he had cleared away a quarter of the diameter of the tree. Just as the tree began an almost imperceptible list he called out to the boy to stand aside.

They waited, but the gigantic thing held. Now the two of them with a double crosscut saw which Clay kept on the mountain approached the side away from the triangular wound and made a fresh cut in the untouched bark. Back and forth they tugged until the blade had sunk four inches into the trunk, making it nearly impossible for them to operate the saw. Clay inserted an iron wedge behind the saw and tapped it gently into the slit the saw had made. The tree groaned, and they began to saw again. The teeth of the saw ate steadily toward the center of the tree, tearing away in seconds rings which had taken a whole year to form until Clay pulled up on the saw and called to Clay-Boy to stop.

The tree was supported now only by the delicate threads of wood it had been in the first decades of its life. They had pierced now to its core, had sawed through wood and time until the tons of wood and leaves and branches and twigs that stood above them were held almost by a slender thread.

"She'll come down now," said Clay to the boy. "You get back."

"All right, Daddy," the boy said.

"You go all the way over yonder in the center of the field," his father said. "I won't drive the wedge in till you get there."

"Yes sir," the boy said, and ran. When he reached the center of the field he raised his hand and waved. He could not see his father any longer because he was lost in the shade of the tree, but in a moment he heard the pounding of a sledge hammer against the iron wedge. He watched with a mixture of melancholy and awe as the tree began to tremble at the top and then, like the folding of a gigantic fan, lean, then drop and explode with a great crashing sound back to the ground where it had started so long ago as a seed.

Clay-Boy ran back to the base of the tree. He found his father sitting on the raw stump. He was smoking a cigarette and looking at the tree thoughtfully.

"I felt it when she hit the ground," said Clay-Boy. "Way over there in the middle of the field I could feel it when she hit."

"A tree is a sorrowful thing to see layen down on the ground that way," observed Clay.

The tree had not yet settled against the earth. Even now a strong limb, caught in some awkward strained position, would snap; a branch would straighten itself out and fling its leaves out of the broken mass like a stricken arm trying to pretend that its trunk was not dead. Gradually a stillness came into the mass of broken limbs, no sound or movement came from it, and it was dead.

All morning Clay and the boy worked over the tree, cutting away each branch from the trunk. Clay examined each branch carefully. Some he designated as firewood, others he placed in a special pile, naming them by the use he would make of them.

"This one will make good two-by-fours," he would say. "Here's a prime four-by-four. Put that in a special pile over there."

By noon they had stripped nearly half of the tree of its branches. Soon they would be coming to the smaller limbs. Clay had already spotted limbs that he could use only for firewood and by the time they came to the tip of the tree he would be picking out the smaller limbs to be used for bean-poles in the garden.

At noon they heard voices and looked across the field to see Olivia and the children. The children ran on ahead, but Olivia was carrying the two youngest children and could not keep up with the others.

Shirley was the first to arrive. She ran to Clay, breathless and full of importance with the news she brought. "We got a letter," she said. "It came in the mail."

"Who's it from?" asked Clay-Boy.

"Mama didn't open it yet, but it says on the envelope it's from Richmond and she thinks it's from Uncle Virgil."

"They sent word from the post office that there was this letter down there," chimed in Becky, "and that somebody ought to come down and pick it up. Mama let Shirley and me go get it."

Olivia arrived, out of breath and tired from the long walk and from having carried two children. She placed Pattie-Cake on the tree stump and handed the baby to Clay-Boy.

"I think we've heard from Virgil," she said and pulled the letter out of her pocket.

"Why didn't you open it and find out what he said," asked Clay.

"It's addressed to you. I thought maybe you'd like to open it," replied Olivia.

Clay accepted the letter, opened it solemnly, and read the contents. Olivia and the children waited respectfully until he had finished.

"What in tarnation is a Jew?" asked Clay when he had finished the letter.

"It's some kind of religion. It's like a Arab or a Greek or somethen. There's some of them over in Charlottesville, I've heard. Why?" asked Olivia.

"Virgil says he's comen up here one week end soon and bringen one with him."

"One what?"

"One Jew. A girl Jew."

"What's he bringing her for?"

"Says he's thinken about marrying her."

"I'm glad Virgil's finally got a girl," said Olivia, "but what does he say about taken Clay-Boy in?"

"Says he'll talk to us about it when he gets here."

"I don't feel none too good about it if he's plannen on getten married."

"I ain't even sure I want Clay-Boy down there if he's goen to be liven in the same house with a Jew. They might be worse than the Baptists."

In the days to follow there was much discussion and conjecture about what a Jew might be, but the end result of it was that nobody had ever really seen or known one and there was not a soul in New Dominion who could tell what it was Virgil was bringing home.

Mrs. Estelle Watts, who happened to drop by selling mail-order products, said that Jews were people who wore little black bonnets and didn't believe in automobiles and there was no one to say that Mrs. Watts was wrong. Mrs. Frank Holloway stopped in the road one day to talk to Olivia and she said they were a religious group who went to Church on Saturday and were something like Shakers, and nobody disputed her. Mr. Willie Benblood told Clay at work that his son, Bibb, that went off to Washington, D.C., to live, had married a Jew and had even taken it up himself and that all he knew about them was that they didn't eat meat. Bibb never brought her back to New Dominion so what Clay heard was of no earthly use to anybody.

CHAPTER 9

CLARIS COLEMAN HAD become so much a member of the family that she did everything but sleep at the Spencer house. She would arrive usually as Clay was leaving for work and sit at the table till all the children had finished their breakfast. Sometimes Olivia enjoyed having her, but most of the time her observations made Olivia uncomfortable.

"Your baby must be nearly fifteen inches long now," she said one morning, observing Olivia's swollen stomach.

"My baby is none of your business, and if you don't want to wear out your welcome around here, don't mention it again," said Olivia.

"It's only that I'm so terribly enthralled with human reproduction at the moment. I've found a medical book at the house and it shows the development of the foetus from the moment the sperm and the egg unite until . . ."

"No more!" said Olivia.

"All right," answered Claris. "I was merely trying to make interesting conversation."

"You make interesting conversation about somethen else," suggested Olivia as she began gathering the breakfast dishes. Claris insisted on helping, and this only added to Olivia's distress. Usually they left the dishes to Becky and Shirley, who in a manner of speaking washed and dried them while Olivia made the beds. But with Claris there, Olivia was reluctant to leave the room for fear she might return to find Claris giving the girls a lecture on the reproductive process of tropical fish or the merits of Buddhism over Baptism. Now that Claris had become a part of the routine of the house Olivia altered her own routine so she could stay in the same room with her and thus halt or direct Claris' comments if they became what Olivia considered harmful or too clinical.

"Some day before I leave," said Claris, "I'm going to give you and Mr. Spencer a week's vacation."

"That's somethen I've never had," said Olivia. "That ought to be real interesten."

"Yes," dreamed Claris, "you and Mr. Spencer will just be free as birds for a whole week and I'll take over here and manage everything. I'll change the diapers and wash the dishes and make the beds and cook the meals and probably wear myself to bits, but it will he worth it if you and your husband can get off for a moment alone together."

"Just where would you recommend we go?" asked Olivia.

"I know you can't go very far because of your circumstances. What about Virginia Beach? Have you ever been there?"

"No," said Olivia, "I never have."

"Then that's where you should go. It's not terribly far and it shouldn't cost too much just for a week end, and there's dancing and swimming and sunbathing and it's very relaxing. Mother and I spent a week end there once and I'm sure you'll enjoy it immensely."

"I'm sure we would too, but I'd call it a vacation if I just got a chance to sit down out there on the porch for ten minutes," said Olivia, and started for the bed she shared with Clay.

"I'll help you make the beds," offered Claris.

"No thank you," said Olivia. "You sit out there on the front porch where Clay-Boy is and rest a while."

"Your mother and father are going to Virginia Beach for a second honeymoon," Claris informed Clay-Boy when she found him sitting on the front porch.

"You and I are going to be the mother and father while they're gone and sleep in their bed. What do you think of that?"

"You're crazy," he said.

"You really must learn to answer people sensibly," she said, "if you're going out into the world. I am not in the least crazy. What you really mean is that I am straightforward and that confuses you."

166

"Oh God," groaned Clay-Boy, "I pity the man that does get you one of these days."

"I do, too," said Claris. "I'm going to be hell on wheels to live with."

"Don't say that!" shushed Clay-Boy.

"Don't say what?"

"Don't say 'hell.' If Mama hears you she'll send you home."

"It seems to me your mother hears worse than that every waking hour of her existence."

"Oh, she does," replied Clay, "but she's not used to hearing it coming from a girl."

Claris cupped her chin in her hands and looked out on the morning. Often in the middle of one of their talks she would become silent and thoughtful. Clay-Boy had learned not to interrupt her thinking periods because they usually produced conversational fodder well worth waiting for, once she had come to a conclusion, if she would share it.

Finally she said, "If I could be anybody in the world do you know who I would be?"

"Who?"

"I would like to be your mother. She is the most fulfilled woman I have ever encountered."

"How do you figure that?" asked Clay-Boy.

"My dear boy, your mother has been delivered of nine children. I only hope that I shall be so lucky."

"You're crazy," he said.

"I'm crazy about you, but you're going to have to cut your hair differently when we're married. Oh, I shall

167

boss you about terribly. Tell me, what are you going to be when you get out of college? We ought to get that settled."

"I'd like to be an archeologist," he answered. He had read a book about an archeological expedition to Egypt, had memorized the methods its members had used and had been stimulated by the excitement of the accounts of their actually coming upon real relics. Thereafter he had combed the little library for books on archeology and had read everything he could put his hands on on the subject.

"Maybe I'll take that up too," Claris declared with enthusiasm. "We'll both become famous archeologists and we'll go to Egypt and dig up old bones and find lost Egyptian kings and get our pictures splashed all over every newspaper in the world. Then we'll write books together and give lectures and travel all over the world."

"Heck," said Clay-Boy, "you don't have to go to Egypt to dig up relics. I know a place not so far from here. I've been digging in it lots of times."

"Where is it?" she asked.

"It's an Indian mound," he said. "A place where they used to bury dead Indians."

"I want to see that," said Claris.

"It's too far away for you to go," he said. "And anyway it's a secret place that I'm the only one knows about."

"If you don't take me to see it, I'll go back to Washington and never speak to you again in my whole life."

"It's a long ways from here," he said.

"Where?"

"It's at the top of Spencer's Mountain."

"Next time you go will you take me?" she asked.

"Maybe," he said.

"I don't see why you can't say *yes* right off. Don't you want to take me?"

"I wouldn't mind, but I never took anybody up there before. It's a long ways and you're a girl. I don't know if you can climb that high."

"I can climb any mountain around here. Now you promise to take me or I'll scream and when your mother comes I'll tell her you tried to pinch my bottom."

"But I didn't," he said.

"Well, you'd like to, so it's practically the same thing. Now, are you going to promise or am I going to have to scream at the top of my lungs?"

"You're going to have to scream," he said.

Claris drew in a great breath of air, threw back her head and was about to shatter the morning with her scream when Clay-Boy knew she had defeated him again.

"Don't scream," he said.

"That's more like it," she said as soon as she could breathe again. "Now, when do we go?"

"One Saturday mornen when I can get away."

"Why do you fight me all the time?" she asked. "Why couldn't you just say yes right away?"

"I don't know," he said. "I guess I just never ran

169

into any girl like you before."

"Of course you didn't, silly," she said. "There aren't any other girls like me."

The sun was setting when Claris declared she had to go home. This was early for her to be leaving. Usually she stayed until every one of the children had been bathed and was ready for bed and by that time the night was so dark that either Clay or Clay-Boy had to walk her home. But tonight she was leaving early because her father had promised to drive her to Charlottesville for a movie and supper.

Clay-Boy walked with her home and when they reached her house she announced, as she had the first day in the library, that she was going to give a party.

"It's going to be the weirdest guest list you ever saw. I'm going to invite Miss Parker, Mr. Goodson, Geraldine Boyd, Alabama Sweetzer, Mrs. Lucy Godlove, your parents, and you, of course."

"Well, I'm not coming."

"Why not?"

"Because all those people would be uncomfortable with each other."

"Oh, I don't know about that. Mother gives very successful parties and she always makes a point of having people who are very different from each other. Wouldn't you just love to see what a lot of these oddballs would do if they got together?"

"I think it would be terrible," said Clay-Boy.

"Of course the Colonel will try to talk me out of it, but I can be very persuasive when I want to. Don't you think it sounds like an interesting gathering?"

"I can hardly wait," groaned Clay-Boy.

"Of course I can't let the Colonel know who I'm inviting or he'll bust a gut."

An item of unusual interest appeared the following Wednesday in Miss Eunice's column in the *Citizen*:

Miss Claris Coleman, daughter of Colonel Coleman, General Manager of the company, has announced a soiree to be held next Friday night at the home of her father. Music will be provided by The Saunders Family that plays for the Square Dance over at Buckingham County every Saturday night. Among the invited guests are Mrs. Lucy Godlove, Miss Laura Parker, Mr. Clyde Goodson, Miss Alabama Sweetzer, Miss Geraldine Boyd, and Clay-Boy Spencer.

The guests of honor will be Mr. and Mrs. Clay Spencer. Lemon ice cream, beer, cigarettes and after-dinner mints will be served, according to Miss Coleman who is down here from Washington, D.C., visiting her father.

"What in the name of God is this?" exploded the Colonel when he read the item at breakfast.

"I don't know, Daddy," said Claris. "What are you talking about?"

"It says here you're having a party Friday night. Is that true?"

Claris came around to her father's place and read the

item. Hoping that her mirth sounded convincing, she began to laugh.

"I don't find it so amusing," said the Colonel sternly.

"Don't you see? She fell for it hook, line and sinker. She was around snooping and trying to find out things one day so I made up the story on the spot. I've done it before. Don't you remember last year when I gave her that news item about a movie company coming to New Dominion on a talent search. She printed it."

"It serves her right," said the Colonel, beginning to smile a little. "But at the same time it seems to me you ought to have a few more friends around here than these hillbillies. I've a good many friends over in Charlottesville in my golf club. If you'd like to give a real party I could have them send some boys and girls over here your own age, more the kind of people you ought to be meeting."

"Sure, Pop," said Claris. "But may I have just one person from around here?"

"As long as it isn't one of the nuts on this list in the paper."

"Well, it is, as a matter of fact. Clay-Boy Spencer."

"Ask him. It's all right with me."

Word that the original party had been called off and a second one planned in its place lost no time in making the rounds of the village. That Clay-Boy had been invited to both and that he was the only local boy to be invited to the second party was mentioned in every kitchen gathering and over every back fence.

When he went to deliver Mrs. Moses Hughes' buttermilk she asked him into the kitchen and promptly began prying.

"I got it from Gilsee Joplin that you're steppen into high society next Friday night," she said.

"Well, I got invited. I couldn't hardly turn it down," he said.

"What does your mama say about you getten mixed up with high society?"

"Mama said I could go," he said. "It don't matter to her."

"I reckon your picture'll be in the Charlottesville *Citizen* and maybe the Richmond *News Leader*," Mrs. Hughes observed teasingly.

"I expect so," he said, trying to grin but succeeding only in pulling up the corners of his mouth.

"Well, it wouldn't surprise me if you didn't end up marryen into that crowd and ownen half the mill before you're through," she said.

She had hit a tender spot and his face betrayed him. He blushed.

"When you and that girl goen to announce your engagement?" Mrs. Hughes asked and prodded him in the ribs, her fat jolly face next to his.

"Mrs. Hughes, Mama told me to hurry home if you don't mind."

"All right, son, there's fifteen cents for the buttermilk there on the table. Don't you mind me teasen. I'm glad you goen to that party 'cause I know you ain't one to put on airs about it. You go and have yourself a good time."

"Thank you, ma'am," he said, took the fifteen cents from the table and fled.

On the afternoon of the party Clay-Boy came home from his job at the library and found his mother near tears.

"I wanted your good pants to be nice and clean so I washed 'em and I reckon they were just too threadbare at the knees. They couldn't take it."

He looked at the pants. They were knickers, the good pair he wore to church and any other time he had to dress up. He had no others except his two everyday pairs, which were in much worse condition.

"I reckon I'll just have to stay at home," he said. He tried to hide his disappointment, but he could not fool his mother.

"Of course you're not going to miss Claris' party," she said. "Now, there's a pair of britches your Uncle Virgil gave your daddy that are too small for him. They're in there in his closet. You go in there and try them on."

Clay-Boy had only to hold the trousers up to his waist to tell that his legs needed to be at least five inches longer if he were to get into his uncle's pants.

Olivia agreed that they just wouldn't fit. "If I had the time I could put new cuffs on them for you, but it would take longer than we've got. Well, I'll just have to do the next best thing. I'll darn those holes at the knees and nobody'll ever be able to tell the difference."

Olivia worked furiously, stopping only to make a

light supper for the family, and without taking any herself returned to her darning. At a quarter to seven she brought the darned trousers up to the boy's room where Clay-Boy was completely dressed except for his trousers.

"It isn't the best job of darnen I ever did," said Olivia, "but it's one of the best. Put 'em on and let's see how they look."

Clay-Boy pulled on the knickers and his mother looked him over. "You look just fine," she said. "And anyway, it isn't the clothes that count. It's the person that's in them."

After his mother left the room, Clay-Boy went to the mirror and examined himself. His hair was plastered down with water. His white shirt had been freshly laundered and ironed by Olivia that afternoon. His blue tie was knotted in a perfect bow. The knickers had been so perfectly mended that the darned places in each knee were barely visible. His shoes were shined to such a high polish that they almost gave off an incandescence of their own.

At seven-fifteen Olivia called from the foot of the stairs. "Clay-Boy, it's getten late."

"All right, Mama," he called back.

At the last minute he decided not to go. He didn't know exactly how he should be dressed but he decided that what he was wearing was completely wrong.

He spent the next fifteen minutes trying to imagine himself sick. At least if he became sick he would not have to give his real reason to his parents. He would also have an excuse to give Claris. Already he could see her disappointment which would express itself in lofty contempt and half-concealed wrath. But try as he might he could not make himself sick.

"Seven-thirty, son," his father called from the foot of the stairs. "If you're goen to that party you better get a move on."

"I'm not going," Clay-Boy said, and once the words were out of his mouth he felt even worse than he had before. "What's that?" his father called.

"I said I'm not going to the party." He tried to keep any feeling out of his voice but a thin edge of nervousness forced its way through. Clay detected it and climbed the stairs.

"How come you decided not to go?" Clay asked.

"Oh, I just decided it probably wouldn't be much fun," Clay-Boy said.

"I thought you liked that little girl," said Clay.

"I like her all right, but I got to thinking it over and I decided I'd just rather not go."

"That ain't the whole truth is it, son?"

"No, sir."

"Maybe you got yourself a little quivery and wrought-up about this party. Maybe that's it a little bit."

"Well, yes sir, a little bit."

"If you don't want to go that's one thing, but if you do want to go and you're scared that's somethen else. You see what I'm getten at?"

"Yes sir."

"If you let somethen scare you off the first time, the next time somethen come along that scares you, you might back off from that too. Now, if you honestly don't want to go to that party, you ain't got to, but if you're too scared to go then maybe you ought to think about it a little more."

Clay-Boy rose from the bed. He walked over to his desk, his shoes squeaking as he went, and without looking at his father he said, "I guess I'll go."

When he turned to face his father he saw that Clay was smiling.

"She wouldn't of asked you in the first place unless she wanted you, would she?" Clay asked.

"I reckon not," Clay-Boy said.

"Just remember this one thing," said Clay. "There ain't goen to be a soul there that's had the ancestry and the upbringing you have. If they say anything about the kind of blood they come from, you speak up and tell 'em you got stock in you that goes back to the beginning of this country. But don't you bring it up first because it ain't polite to brag about your background unless somebody else starts it."

"Yes sir," said Clay-Boy.

"And don't forget what you're goen for. You're goen to this party to have yourself a good time. When the time comes for eaten, eat like you're goen to bust a gut. Folks love a hearty eater. When the time comes to dance, get out there and sashay them gals till you wear out the fiddler. Squeeze 'em up a little bit. Gals say they don't, but they'll stick to you like honey in a bee tree if they find out you like a little squeezen now and again. And if there's any old folks there don't forget to say 'Yes sir,' and 'Yes ma'am,' to 'em."

"All right Daddy," promised Clay-Boy. "I'd better get going or I'll be late."

His whole family had gathered to see him off and as Clay-Boy walked down the front walk he could feel their eyes following him. He felt stiff and self-conscious. As he came to the corner of the sharp curve he looked back. His mother, father, brothers and sisters were lined up across the front porch, silently and gravely watching him. He waved farewell and was gone from them into high society.

He was late. As he came up out of the darkness he stood for a moment at the edge of the light thrown by the porch light and listened to the sounds of merriment within. Someone was playing the piano and shadows bobbed against each other and moved across the shades at the windows. Again Clay-Boy felt the unreasonable wave of fear. He felt clumsy and countrified. He wouldn't know what to say or how to behave. He took a deep breath and plunged into the circle of light.

At his ring the door was opened by an absolute stranger. A vision in white organdy ruffles whom he recognized only when she whispered in his ear, "What are you doing so late?"

Without bothering to wait for an explanation, Claris ushered him into a roomful of boys and girls. The girls were all dressed like Claris and all the boys, he dis-

178

covered to his horror, were dressed in blue serge coats and white flannel pants. He was the only boy in the room not wearing a coat, and not a single one was wearing knickers, to say nothing of knickers that were darned at each knee.

His entrance had interrupted a game they were playing and those in the room fell silent when he came in. Numbly he felt himself guided through a blur of names and faces until mercifully he found himself in a corner near the door he had come in. Afterward he had no recollection of a single name or of any intelligible response he had made to any introduction. He remembered only that after shaking each outstretched hand his right had gone down automatically to cover the darned place in the knee of his knickers.

"What's the matter with you?" Claris asked in a low voice when she brought him a glass of lemonade.

"I guess I'm not feeling very well," he said.

"You'll feel better once you drink that lemonade," she said. "There's a couple of shots of gin in it."

He sat gulping down the lemonade and stealing furtive glances around at his handsomely dressed, sophisticated companions. He admired the ease with which they talked to each other and their confidence. As each person had arrived Claris had given them party napkins designed to help everybody get to know everybody else. On the napkin was printed a thing which the bearer had to do. Clay-Boy realized suddenly that everyone was looking at him and that they expected something of him.

"It's your turn, Clay-Boy," called Claris from across the room.

"Oh," he said, and consulted his napkin. Tell a story, it said. Clay looked out at the faces in front of him. They seemed to have doubled. He tried to speak but his throat was full of dust.

"It says tell a story," he blurted finally.

"Clay-Boy Spencer is a master hand at telling stories," said Claris.

"Well, go on," somebody said after a moment.

"Which one?" Clay-Boy asked in a suffocated whisper.

"Tell the one about the natural-born homing pig," urged Claris.

"This is a story I got from my Daddy," Clay-Boy began, his voice hardly above a whisper. "It seems like one time Grandpap came down with the polio and left Grandma and all her children to take care of themselves. Grandma had this Uncle Benny Tucker over in Buckingham County . . ."

As he told the story he looked around; he saw that every eye was resting on him and that they were looking at him with interest. The attention of his audience encouraged him. His voice rose and he repeated the story exactly as he had heard it hundreds of times from his father. Once he faltered, trying to remember his father's version.

"And what happened then," someone asked, and he knew that they were waiting and wanted him to go on. He picked up the story where he had left off. He even embroidered it a bit, improving on it where he felt his father had left off, and when he came to the end of the story he was on his feet, acting out each bit, dramatizing each event as it had happened.

By the end of the story he had the fascinated attention of every person in the room.

"And as Daddy says," he finished, "he never knew if that shoat was in love with Uncle Benny Tucker or whether he was just a natural-born homing pig."

He sat down; as long as he lived he would never forget the laughter and applause that greeted the end of the story.

"Whatever happened to Jabez?" they wanted to know.

"Tell another story," somebody urged.

Clay-Boy had made his entrance into high society and they were his.

It was twelve-thirty when he arrived home that night. Clay and Olivia were sitting up in the living room waiting for him. "Did you have a good time," asked Olivia.

"I had a wonderful time," he said. He sat down on the sofa, pulled off his shoes, and yawned.

"What was it like, son," asked Clay.

"Just like any old party," Clay-Boy replied. "Them city people ain't no different from the rest of us."

CHAPTER 10

Mon.

Dear Brother Clay,

Will drive up and spend the day Sunday if it's all right with you. Tell Mama she's been pushing for me to bring a girl up there so I'm going to do it. Her name is Lisa and she's the one I told you about in last letter. Ought to be there eleven o'clock.

Yours truly,

Virgil Spencer

THE POST CARD HAD arrived on Wednesday. By nightfall everyone in New Dominion knew of Virgil's impending visit. The fact that he was bringing a girl home and that she was a Jewish girl heightened everybody's anticipation and was the subject of conversation at every supper table that night. Half the people in the village began making plans to be in the vicinity of Clay's house on Sunday morning on the chance that they might get a look at the Jew.

Claris Coleman, hearing the conjecture about what a Jew might be, had attempted to explain Judaism to Olivia, but since Claris' explanation centered entirely around the ill-founded contention that Jews were said to be against birth control and thus had large families as a rule, Olivia rejected the explanation as another aspect of Claris' obsession with sex and did not believe one word she was told.

Olivia was far more concerned with Lisa as a person than she was with her religion. It did not matter to her what the girl believed in, but the kind of girl she might be. Olivia's main concern was whether or not the two of them, Virgil and Lisa, would be willing to take Clay-Boy in while he was getting his college education.

"Virgil must mean to marry her," she remarked to Clay that Sunday morning at breakfast. "He wouldn't be bringen her up here for everybody to take a look at if he wasn't goen to marry her."

"Well, I hope that's what the boy's got on his mind," observed old Grandmother Elizabeth. "That boy needs a wife, somebody to do for him down there in Richmond. It's way past time for Virgil to have himself a little wife."

"That boy is haven himself a good time," chimed in Grandfather Zebulon. "He ain't figuren to settle down and I don't blame him. He's down there in Richmond frolicken them city gals and I don't blame him a speck."

"What do you know about city gals, old man?" asked Elizabeth dryly.

"I memorize the time I was down there in Richmond and looked 'em all over. Every one of them just dressed up in silk stockens and high-heel shoes looken like they stepped right out of the Sears Roebuck catalogue. That's the kind of woman I'd get me if I had it to do over again."

"Nobody short-changed you, old man," teased Eliza. "You never had cause to complain."

"What worries me about it," said Olivia soberly, "is maybe we haven't got any right to ask Virgil to take Clay-Boy in now. It's hard enough for two people to make a go of being married when it's just the two of them. Haven a third party around is asken a mighty lot."

"Virgil's goen to take Clay-Boy in. You mark my word," said Eliza. "And beside, Clay-Boy ain't goen to be that much trouble. He can sleep on a cot or a pallet on the floor for that matter. That boy ain't goen off down there for high liven. He's goen to get a college education."

"Anybody home?" a loud voice called from beyond the kitchen door.

"Come in, Papa," called Olivia.

Homer Italiano was a magnificent old man who at seventy, even though he enjoyed grumbling about imaginary aches and pains, was still as strong as he had been at thirty. Six and a half days a week he did his carpentry job at the mill, and five years before, when he had become eligible for retirement, he had rejected the small pension the company had offered him in favor of the promise of a steady job as long as he lived.

"I walked into that mill when I was a boy. Won't leave it till they carry me out feet first," he always said. He had a big head and his eyes, under a bushy umbrella of gray lashes, were warm and inquisitive.

"Mornen, everybody," he rumbled in his loud voice that could be heard half a mile away.

"Have some breakfast, Papa?" asked Olivia.

"Appreciate it, daughter, but Ida fixed me a little bite before we left the house."

"Where's Mama?" asked Olivia. "Isn't she with you?"

Although Homer Italiano was deeply devoted to Ida, he spent most of his time with or away from her complaining loudly of her latest foolish act. Homer regarded most women as foolish creatures prompted by mysterious and doubtful motives, all of them untrustworthy, and Ida the most suspect of all.

"Oh, that woman don't know what she's doen half the time," he said. "On the way up the hill she saw a patch of them black-eyed Susans, if that's what you call them, and nothen would do but she's got to haul herself over the fence and pick a mess of them to decorate the church. I told her she was goen to break a leg, old woman like her climben fences, but you know your mama, won't listen to a word of reason."

"You let Miss Ida be, Mr. Homer," said Eliza. "God never put a better woman on earth than Ida Italiano."

"I reckon you got no argument there, Miss Eliza," said Homer. "How you? You're looken right pert."

"I'm doen right good for an old woman," answered Eliza gaily.

"Story's goen around that Virgil's comen home today and there's talk he's bringen a girl of the Jewish faith with him," said Homer.

"We're holden judgment till we see her," said Eliza sensibly. "As long as she ain't no heathen I'm glad Virgil's got somebody he wants to marry."

"A lot of 'em been comen to me and asken how the family felt about a Jew in the family. I hadn't heard anybody express an opinion, but I said as long as she's Virgil's girl everybody's goen to make her feel right at home."

Clay, who had eaten four fried eggs, six biscuits, three thick slices of ham and three giant cups of black coffee, rose from the table and put on his blue denim working cap.

"Where do you think you're goen?" inquired Olivia.

"I thought I'd run up to the mountain and get as much done on the house as I could before Virgil gets here," said Clay.

"How's the house comen along, Clay?" asked Homer.

"She's comen, Mr. Homer," said Clay. "I got just about half the foundation put in. I figure by this time next year that house is goen to be ready."

"I'd be proud to see that, Clay," said Homer. "You've got yourself a good house right here. Not a thing wrong with it, but you never know when the company's goen to come along and tell you to move somewhere else."

Homer was feeling bitter toward the company because the house in which he and Ida had spent their married life was soon to be demolished. This was a frequent occurrence in New Dominion since quarries had to be opened along the vein taken underground by the soapstone. Actually, Homer's house was already hanging on the brink of a quarry and the company waited only to find a vacant house for Homer and Ida to move into before tearing their house down.

"That's one reason I'm builden my own place, Mr. Homer," said Clay. "As long as that house is mine no son-of-a-seahorse is ever goen to have the right to come along and move me and my babies to some place we don't want to go."

Wakened by the loud voice of their grandfather, the children began arriving for their breakfast. Clay departed for the mountain and the old folks moved to the front porch while Olivia fed fresh sticks of wood to the old cooking range and took up a position where for the next half-hour she fried two more pounds of ham and one egg after another until the entire brood was fed.

As soon as all the children had eaten she began getting the older ones ready for Sunday school. They were already clean from their Saturday-night bath so they had only to be dressed, have their hair combed, and proper shoes found for everybody. This was usually the hardest chore, because each pair of shoes was handed down from one child to another so that with repeated half-solings by Clay, every boy in the family might have worn the same pair of shoes at one time or another. Sometimes it was hard to know who had ownership rights at a particular moment.

Once the children were off to Sunday school, Olivia returned to the kitchen to clean up the breakfast dishes and start preparing her Sunday dinner. This was something of a challenge because after church every Sunday of the year relatives on both sides of the family would stop by the house. Everyone who stopped would be asked to stay to dinner, and it was not unusual for Olivia to set the table four or five times at midday on Sunday. Since she never knew exactly how many would actually stay for dinner it was a miracle that she was never short of food.

Olivia sighed with annoyance when a knock sounded at the kitchen door. There was much work to be done and she did not welcome the interruption.

"House was so quiet I didn't think anybody was home," said Eunice Crittenbarger.

"That's because all the kids are at Sunday school," said Olivia. "Come on in, Eunice."

"I thought about goen to Sunday school myself this morning," said Eunice, "and then I said to myself it would be just as Christian to go over there and give Livy Spencer a hand what with all that company she's got comen in." Eunice plunged her hands into the pan of sudsy dishes Olivia had been washing and set to work briskly.

"Any of 'em here yet?" she asked.

"We aren't expecten 'em before eleven," said Olivia, picking up a towel and beginning to dry the dishes Eunice was washing.

"You reckon Virgil is goen to marry that Jewish girl?" inquired Eunice.

"He said in the first letter he was thinken about it. That's all we know," replied Olivia.

"You think he'll still take Clay-Boy in if he does

marry her?" asked Eunice.

"How did you know about him taken in Clay-Boy?" asked Olivia.

"It's not a secret or anything, is it?" asked Eunice. "Everybody in New Dominion knows he's up to get a scholarship and that you and Clay are counten on Virgil to give him his room and board while he's getten his education."

"I vow," said Olivia. "You can't keep a thing to yourself around here any more."

"I wouldn't of brought it up if I'd known you were so sensitive about it, Livy."

"I'm not sensitive about it. It's just that we don't want Clay-Boy to get his hopes built up too high. It's a big thing for him to take on. He's counten on it something awful. I just hate to think how he'd take it if it didn't come through."

"Listen, Livy, you haven't got a thing to worry about with Clay-Boy Spencer. That boy is smart as a cricket. Don't you remember that Valedictorian Speech he gave when he graduated? A boy that can write a speech like that can be President of the United States if he takes his mind to it. Remember, I printed that whole speech in the Charlottesville Daily *Citizen.*"

Their conversation was interrupted by the arrival at the front gate of Clay's brother Anse and his wife and children. Following Anse came Luke and his family. Olivia returned to the kitchen just in time to see cars arriving at the back gate as members of the clan began coming in from that direction. Soon the house was buzzing with the sounds of conversation and laughter. On the front porch the Spencer brothers and their wives joined their parents and Homer Italiano. As soon as all the chairs were taken they began arranging themselves on the steps leading down from the porch, and when even more relatives arrived those who could not find seats spilled over into the yard.

Olivia was working alone in the kitchen. Eunice had deserted her as soon as the company began arriving and was now on the front porch gathering and exchanging gossip. The talk and the laughter had grown so loud that when it stopped quite suddenly Olivia walked through the house to the front door and looked out. She arrived just in time to see Virgil get out of his car, come around and hold the door open for someone to get out.

The girl who stepped out of the car was tall and dark and slight. She gave Virgil a nervous smile and then looked up at the crammed front porch and yard where the Spencer clan awaited their first look at her.

All the Spencers, the children included, fell silent as Virgil led the girl up the walk. At the foot of the front steps he looked around and exclaimed, "What the hell's wrong with everybody? Didn't you ever see a pretty girl before?"

"Bring her up here where I can get a look at her," called Eliza as the crowd parted to make way for Virgil and his girl.

"Mama," said Virgil, "this is Lisa. We got married yesterday."

"You're welcome here, child," said Eliza. She took the girl by the hand and pulled her down to kiss her on the cheek.

"And this is my daddy," said Virgil.

Old Zebulon was growing feeble. Some time ago the sons had taken his gun away from him and would allow him to hunt no longer. Lately they also refused to lend him their cars—which was even more irksome to Zebulon, for his two dearest friends, Miss Emma and Miss Etta Peabody, lived at such a distance that he could only get to see them if one of the boys would drive him there. When Virgil presented his bride, Zebulon rose with the aid of his cane and before Lisa knew what he was going to do, he embraced her warmly and kissed her full on the lips through his long handlebar mustache.

"You're about the prettiest little thing I ever laid eyes on," said Zebulon. "Sit down here beside me." He waved one of his sons aside and cleared a chair for Lisa.

"Thank you," the girl said weakly. She looked up at the sea of faces all looking back at her in friendly curiosity. She attempted to smile, but her lips trembled. She looked to Virgil for reassurance, but she saw that he had turned away and was talking to Olivia.

"Where's Clay?" he asked.

"Up yonder on the mountain worken on that house, same as he always is," said Olivia. "He said he would be back here before you came, but you know how he is once he gets to worken on the house."

191

"Let's run up and get him," said Virgil.

His brothers agreed and together they rose and left the porch. Virgil turned to Lisa and said, "You stay here and get acquainted. Livy, you tell her who everybody is," and then he was gone down the walk with his brothers. The eight of them piled into one of the cars, and then they were gone up the road toward the mountain.

Alone now with the women and children, Lisa seemed to be looking for a place to hide. All the faces were subjecting her to the closest scrutiny. Looking down at her open-toed shoes, she wished she had followed an earlier instinct not to paint her toenails; Virgil had told her that most of New Dominion was Baptist and not given to frivolity.

Watching the girl, Olivia remembered her own induction into the Spencer clan and recognized the cause of her nervousness.

"What do you think of all these Spencers?" Olivia asked in an effort to put the girl at ease.

"There sure are a lot of them," said Lisa.

"Well," said Olivia. "It'll take you years to get them all straight, but I'll just introduce you around anyway."

Olivia went the rounds of the porch, introducing Lisa to all the women, telling which woman was the wife of which particular Spencer man and pointing out their children in the crowd of cousins who were having a noisy reunion down in the yard.

Lisa responded to each introduction with a polite greeting. She was greatly distracted by the number of people who were passing on the road. Virgil had told her that the little village was practically deserted on Sunday, but whenever she looked down on the road she could see that it was heavily traveled by people on foot and in cars. Invariably the cars slowed to a crawl while curious faces peered up to the porch where she sat.

She discovered the reason for the unusual amount of traffic when a muddy old beat-up farm car slowed down to a stop and a woman leaned out to call up to the porch, "Virgil and that girl get here yet?"

"Shore did," Zebulon called back. "Here she is and just as pretty as a picture."

"Leave it to Virgil to pick a pretty one," the woman laughed. "You all come over to see us," she called, drew back in the car, and proceeded on down the road.

The Baptist church service was over now and more and more people were walking by on the road. Not one passed without stopping to peer up at the porch and each time Lisa seemed to shrink more and more into herself.

Sensing her discomfort, Olivia said, "Honey, why don't you come on inside and I'll show you around?"

"You can have her later, Livy," said Zebulon. "First I'm goen to take her around and show her New Dominion."

Lisa looked at Olivia as if to ask her permission, but the old man was already halfway down the steps and waiting for her to follow.

"Excuse me," Lisa said to the other women and fol-

193

lowed Zebulon down the walk.

"I reckon we'll use Virgil's car," said the old man as they walked out to where the cars were parked.

Lisa obediently got in the front seat and Zebulon climbed in the driver's seat and turned on the ignition.

"Old man, what do you think you're doen?" called Eliza from the porch.

Her answer was a roar from the engine and a jerky start as the car took off with all the speed it was capable of, turned the corner, and disappeared down the hill.

"Oh my God!" cried Eliza. "That old man hasn't driven a car in years, and he can't see the nose in front of his face!"

Lisa could not hear her but she had already come to the same conclusion by the time the car had reached the foot of the hill and Zebulon guided it in a wide screeching arc around the curve. Coming out of the turn he gunned the motor again just in time to arrive at another sharper curve at the corner of the mill. This one he took on two wheels. Neither did he slow down for the narrow little bridge over the creek or the rail-road crossing. This brought them to the center of the little group of buildings which made up the business district of New Dominion, but instead of stopping here as Lisa supposed he might, he zoomed through the village square in a swirl of dust and headed up the long hill that led to open country.

"I thought you were going to show me New Dominion, Mr. Spencer," said Lisa, half fearing to speak lest she distract him from his driving.

"That's all there is to it back there," said Zebulon. "Just a lot of shanties and mill dust. I decided to show you the only folks around here worth the gunpowder it'd take to blow 'em to hell."

"Who is that?" asked Lisa, already dreading that she would have to go on display again.

"You'll see," he promised.

They had come out of the hilly section of the country and there lay before them a long stretch of straight highway. Lisa began to breathe a little easier until she noticed a car coming toward them in the distance and even though the old man seemed to see it clearly he made no move to get the car out of the center and into the right lane of the road.

Somehow the other car managed to swerve around them just in time to prevent a head-on collision.

"That feller wasn't watchen where he was goen," growled Zebulon.

"Mr. Spencer," asked Lisa, "wouldn't you like me to drive the rest of the way?"

"Thanks all the same, daughter," replied Zebulon, "but I plumb enjoy it."

"Well, then would you please go a little slower so I can get a look at this pretty countryside?" pleaded Lisa.

Zebulon slowed down to about forty miles an hour, and while they still weren't going as slowly or as carefully as Lisa would have wished she began to breathe again and realized for the first time that her clenched hand against the door handle had begun to hurt from holding on, and she let go.

Almost immediately she grasped the door handle again, for without any warning and hardly slowing down at all Zebulon had wheeled off the highway onto a little wooded dirt road. He was forced to slow down now because the road was an old one, filled with mud puddles and sudden bumps and depressions.

"Hold on, daughter," he shouted. "It's just around the bend."

As they came out of the turn, Lisa saw ahead a driveway. It was bordered with ancient boxwood leading up to four graceful, ruined Grecian columns— all that remained of what had once been a charming old Confederate mansion. Zebulon brought the car to a screeching halt in front of the columns, pressed the horn furiously three times and got out of the car.

Followed by Lisa, Zebulon made his way through the decaying columns out into a cleared space where there stood a smaller replica of the original house. The front door was open and two elderly ladies in overalls were waiting just inside the screen door. Recognizing Zebulon, they hurried to meet him.

"Look here, Etta, who's come to see us!" said the older and stouter of the two women. "Isn't this a treat!"

"It's been a long time, Mr. Spencer," said the younger woman. "I was saying to Emma just the other day how we missed you and wondered when you'd make it down to see us again."

"It ain't every day I get hold of a car," explained

Zebulon, "else I'd be down here every day."

"I wish I'd known you were coming. Sister and I would have put on something nice instead of having you find us looking like two ragamuffins," said Etta.

"Ladies, I want to introduce my new daughter-in-law. This here is Virgil's girl and her name is Lisa."

"Virgil's girl, now!" exclaimed Emma. "Let me look at you."

Miss Emma looked at Lisa admiringly, turned to her sister and said, "Did you ever in your life see anything so pretty, Etta?"

Etta nodded pleasantly. "We're right fond of Virgil, honey," she said. "Virgil never goes up to New Dominion that he doesn't stop off to see us on his way back to Richmond."

"You-all come on in and make yourselves comfortable," said Miss Emma, leading the way into the house. "In honor of the company we'll sit in the living room. Etta, open some windows and let some air in there."

"Kitchen will do for us, Miss Emma," said Zebulon. "This gal ain't company. She's family."

"Whatever you say, Mr. Spencer. Please don't look at the house, Lisa-Honey, we're just two old-maid sisters here and don't have the help there used to be in the old days."

"It's a very pretty house," ventured Lisa.

"It's really what Grandpa used to call a *garçonierrie*," explained Miss Emma. "You see, he had so many sons he decided to build quarters for them away from the main house so he built this one exactly like it. The main house just fell in one day, so Sister and I moved on over here. We ought to keep it up more but we're so busy maken the recipe we hardly have time for anything else."

At the mention of the recipe Zebulon's eyes lighted up and as they arrived in the kitchen he looked around thirstily.

"Etta," said Miss Emma, "find Mr. Zebulon a container so he can sample that new recipe." She turned to address Zebulon. "I was sayen to Sister just a while ago I think it's the best run we've had in years."

Miss Emma rummaged through some cooking utensils in the sink until she found a tin dipper. She handed it to Zebulon, who went to a row of earthenware crocks, uncorked one and filled his tin dipper to the brim with the clear white liquid.

He took a sip and rolled it around in his mouth, savored it with his tongue, and then swallowed. "That's one hundred per cent," he announced and took a longer second drink.

"I always did say," remarked Miss Emma, "that nobody ever appreciated the recipe half as much as Mr. Zebulon Spencer. Etta, serve Virgil's girl some recipe."

Miss Etta washed a drinking tumbler and filled it from the same earthenware crock Zebulon had sampled and brought it to Lisa. Lisa raised the glass to her lips and took a small sip. A fire started in her mouth and worked its way down to the pit of her stomach.

The two sisters looked at her as if waiting for a verdict. "It's strong," said Lisa. "What is it?"

"It's Papa's recipe," explained Miss Emma. "Papa used to make it all the time and then when he passed on we used to get so many calls for it that Sister and I just kept on making it. Help yourself there, Mr. Zebulon, there's plenty."

Zebulon poured himself a second dipper of the liquor. "People come from miles around here to buy from Miss Emma and Miss Etta," said Zebulon.

"We had a gentleman stop off last week all the way from Raleigh, North Carolina," said Etta proudly. "He was a traveling man and somebody in Charlottesville told him about the recipe. He loved it so much he took a whole gallon of it back to Raleigh with him."

"It gives us something to do in our old age," said Miss Emma, "and it makes people happy so I can't see why we shouldn't keep right on providing. But gracious me, here I am rattling on about myself, and I haven't heard a word about you. Tell us about your romance with Virgil Spencer, how you met and fell in love."

She waved to the earthenware crocks. "While we're talking, Mr. Zebulon, since you know your way around, just make yourself at home."

Zebulon nodded his thanks and made his way to the row of crocks to refill his empty dipper.

When Virgil and his brothers returned to Clay's house they found their wives waiting for them on the

199

porch. Virgil noticed that his car was gone and when he came up to the porch he asked his mother, "Where's my car?"

"Your daddy took it and he took your wife with him. I'm near about worried to death he's wrecked that car and killed the both of them."

"We'd better go look for them," said Virgil to his brothers. They all returned to the car and piled in together.

"Where you reckon we ought to look for Papa?" asked Virgil.

"There ain't but one place Papa goes when he's on the loose, and that's down to Miss Emma and Miss Etta's," said Clay. "Wouldn't mind stoppen off to see them old ladies myself." he added.

Lisa had just come to the end of her recitation of her romance with Virgil when a horn sounded from somewhere in front of the house, and shortly thereafter a knock sounded at the door.

"My gracious," said Miss Emma. "Looks like we've got some more company. Go see who it is, Etta."

Miss Etta returned in a few minutes, followed by Virgil Spencer and his eight brothers.

"Well, if this isn't a treat!" exclaimed Miss Emma. "Etta, find chairs for everybody. Virgil, I want to congratulate you on finding the prettiest girl I've ever laid eyes on."

"Thank you, Miss Emma," said Virgil respectfully. He went to where Lisa was sitting and gave her hand a tight squeeze. Lisa, her glass half empty, was relaxed and rid of the nervousness that had nearly overcome her since her arrival in New Dominion and smiled back to tell him that she was all right.

"Clay, what's this your daddy's been telling me about you sending Clay-Boy off to get a college education?" asked Miss Emma.

"That's how it looks, Miss Emma," said Clay. "His teacher up at the school seems to think they can get him a scholarship or something. We're waiten to hear from it."

"Well, this certainly is a red-letter day for us, having all the Spencer boys and their daddy visit us on the same day. Etta, get everybody some of the recipe and let's celebrate this grand occasion."

Darkness was falling across the hills when Olivia went for what seemed the thousandth time to the front door to see if there were any signs of Clay, his brothers and Lisa. Her sisters-in-law were all in the kitchen and the cousins, tired from playing and hungry from the long wait for their Sunday dinner, were fighting and grumbling down in the yard.

"See anything of them, Livy?" asked Eliza, who had come up and stood behind her.

"Not a thing, Miss Eliza," said Olivia.

"They've got into whiskey somewhere," said Eliza darkly. "You watch what I tell you. Oh, I could just shake that old man for runnen off with that girl in the first place."

"I hate whiskey as much as the next one," said Olivia, "but I'd almost rather it be that than to have 'em off dead in a ditch somewhere in an accident."

It had been a frustrating day for Olivia. All day long she had wanted to speak to Virgil in private to find out if he might still consider taking Clay-Boy in with him and Lisa when it came time for Clay-Boy to go to the University of Richmond.

"I reckon we might as well go ahead and feed the children, Miss Eliza," she said. "If the Spencer boys are in their whiskey they won't be back till it's all gone, Lord knows." Raising her voice, she called, "Y'all come to supper," and an eager and hungry army of little Spencer cousins roared toward the house.

After the children and their mothers had eaten, Vinnie, Rome's wife, packed all the guests into Rome's car and began delivering them to their homes. Olivia sent all her children except Clay-Boy to bed and finally the house fell silent except for the sounds made by Clay-Boy and his mother as they washed the dishes. Eliza was upstairs hearing the younger children's prayers when Olivia heard a car stop down at the front gate.

A woman's footsteps echoed on the front walk and onto the porch; as Olivia came to the long hall that led to the front door she saw that the woman was Lisa. The girl was weary and exasperated.

"Olivia," she said. "They're all down in the car. They said they wanted to sit down there and sing a while."

"It's the whiskey," said Olivia. "They'll wear it off after a while."

From down at the front gate the strains of "The Old

Rugged Cross" drifted up to them across the darkening lawn:

". . . I will cherish the old rugged cross
And exchange it some day for a crown."

Olivia smiled at the girl.

"Now you're getten some idea what it's like to be married to a Spencer."

"You know," said Lisa, "I've been in New Dominion all day and still haven't met the one person I wanted most to meet."

"Who's that?"

"Clay-Boy," she replied. "Virgil says he's coming to live with us this fall."

The frustration and annoyance that had been building in Olivia all day long fell away. She took Lisa's hand to express her gratitude and then changed her mind and embraced her instead.

"Are you sure you can take two Spencers at the same time?" asked Olivia.

"It looks to me when you take one of them you take the whole family," said Lisa. "I won't be able to help him with his homework because I only had high school myself, but I'm a good cook and I'll see he gets plenty to eat."

"Bless you, honey," said Olivia. "Come on back here in the kitchen and get somethen to eat. I'll bet you're starved to death."

After Lisa had her supper, she sat at the table with

Olivia and Clay-Boy. All the time she had been eating Clay-Boy had been looking at her with a curious gaze.

"Is there anything you want to ask me, Clay-Boy," Lisa said finally.

"Yes," he said, "but I'm not sure it would be all right."

"Well, try me," she said.

"What is a Jew?" asked Clay-Boy.

"I'm a Jew," Lisa replied.

"I mean what makes you so different?"

"Do I look so different?"

"That's what I mean," the boy said. "You don't."

"It's a religion," said Lisa. "We believe in God and the Ten Commandments. We believe that man has a soul, that he should love good and hate evil and that his soul is eternal. We don't think we're the only religion there is. I remember hearing a rabbi say once, 'We Jews know there are many mountain tops and all of them reach for the stars.'"

"It's just what I thought it would be," said Olivia. "It's just about the same thing as being a Baptist."

Down at the car an unsteady voice started a new hymn.

"Throw out the lifeline!
Throw out the lifeline!
Someone is drifting awaaaaaaaaaaaay."

One by one the other voices blended in harmony.

"Throw out the lifeline,
Throw out the lifeline,
Someone is sinking today."

"You want me to go down and see if I can get 'em to turn in for the night, Mama?" asked Clay-Boy.

"Wouldn't do any good," said Olivia. "They'll just pull you in the car and keep you down there singen with 'em. You go on to bed if you're tired."

After Clay-Boy went to bed, Olivia and Lisa sat in the kitchen drinking coffee and talking.

It was midnight before the singing down in the car came to a quavering halt. After a while Olivia and Lisa took a flashlight and went down to investigate. With their arms around each other and tired happy grins on their faces, the Spencer men had gone to sleep.

"What are we going to do?" asked Lisa.

"I reckon we'd better get some sleep too," said Olivia, and they followed the circle of light from the flashlight across the dew-covered grass toward the house and rest.

CHAPTER 11

IT WAS GOOD FOR ALL concerned that Friendship Corner, as Clay-Boy's library had come to be called, was not run on a profit-making plan. During the weeks it had been open the library had attracted only a few regular customers. Geraldine Boyd came once a week.

If Clay-Boy were alone she would stay and make stilted bookish conversation. If Claris happened to be there Geraldine would make her selection quickly and escape as soon as possible from Claris' curious and merciless questions. Alabama Sweetzer quickly exhausted the supply of Western books which she supplied to Craig Godlove. At Clay-Boy's suggestion she had switched to murder mysteries, but Mr. Godlove consumed them so quickly that Clay-Boy was already wondering what to recommend when his supply of mysteries was exhausted.

Most of the time, left alone, Clay-Boy spent reading. He consumed more books during that summer than probably the entire population of New Dominion had read in a lifetime. At first he read indiscriminately. He would take down any volume from the shelf and paying no attention to the title or whether it was fiction or biography, a book on medicine or a single volume of an encyclopedia, he would read if from cover to cover. Every book he read only whetted his appetite to read more and he began forcing himself to read more slowly lest he finish all the books in the library before the summer was over.

Late one afternoon a shadow fell over the page he was reading and he looked up to see Claris.

"You and I are going places, son," she announced.

"I'm going home to supper," said Clay-Boy.

"Where would you like to go? Name it."

"Well, I'd like to go to Jerusalem and see the Dead Sea. I was just reading it's got so much salt in it you don't have to swim. You just float automatically."

"Would you settle for the Dixie Belle Traveling Tent Show? It's over at Faber."

"Sure I would, but how would we get there?"

"I'll drive us. The Colonel's gone to Tennessee on business and left the car. Said I could use it."

"I'd sure like to go," said Clay-Boy, "but I don't know if Mama and Daddy will let me."

"Son," said Claris, "you disgust me. Here you are, about to go out in the world and get yourself an education and you're still asking permission to turn around. When are you going to stop asking them if you can go and just go?"

"If I told them I was going to a carnival, I'd never get out of the house. Mama would say it was sinful and Daddy would want me to go with him to work on the house and there I'd be."

"Don't tell them you're going to the carnival. Tell them you're coming over to see me and I'm going to teach you to play the fiddle or something. God, you're dumb. I can't stand you."

"Then how come you're always hanging around?"

"I guess it's that soulful little choirboy face and the fact that you're the only hillbilly in a hundred miles I can talk to. Now, do you want to go or not?"

"If I can get away."

"I'll wait until eight o'clock. If you're not there by then I'm coming over and tell your family you've ruined me and you're going to have to do the right thing and take me to the preacher."

"Boy, you really talk big. I bet if I said *boo* to you you'd break a leg getting out of here."

"I really don't know what you mean," said Claris airily.

"I mean if I tried to do it to you," said Clay-Boy.

"Do what?" she asked.

"You know," said Clay-Boy and blushed.

"Pow!" exclaimed Claris and jumped up from her chair and strode around the room. "Pow! Pow! Pow!" she said, striking her fists against the book-lined shelves.

"What's the matter with you now?" cried Clay.

"Oh you hillbillies!" she cried. "All you can think of is sex, sex, sex!" She stood in front of him now, mocking and teasing him with her eyes. "I came down here, an innocent girl from the city, trying to be friends, trying to invite you to enjoy a pleasant evening with me at the Dixie Belle Traveling Tent Show, and I haven't been here more than ten minutes before you start making indecent proposals."

In spite of her words Claris was daring him with her body and suddenly, as much to his own surprise as hers, he reached out and took her into his arms. Her lips were still curved in a smile but no sound of laughter came from them. Through her half-closed eyes he saw that she had no fright and that she was merely waiting to see what he would do. He bent his lips to hers and held her in a long kiss.

With his body pressed close against her, Claris felt what the excitement was doing to him and whispered, "Not here. It isn't safe." But Clay-Boy hardly heard her. His hands began to explore the places they had longed to touch and the girl began to respond, guiding his hands and moving her body against his.

It was Claris who heard the sound. A high amused giggle sounded from the door. She began to struggle and Clay-Boy, mistaking her struggle for passion, struggled with her, whispered words to reassure her, until finally when she could rid herself of him no other way, Claris shouted, "Let go of me!"

She twisted out of his arms and retreated. When Clay-Boy started to follow her, Claris inclined her head toward the door. Clay-Boy looked and there stood his little sister Becky, looking at him indignantly.

"What do you want?" he demanded.

"Mama says she needs you. You come on home right away she says."

"You run back to the house and tell her I'm on the way."

"I'll wait and go with you, Clay-Boy."

"You do what I tell you. I've got to put the windows down and lock up here and everything."

"I won't," declared Becky.

"If you don't I'm going to spank your fanny," he shouted.

"If you lay hands on me, I'll tell Mama what I saw," threatened Becky.

"What you saw, Little Miss Smartie Pants, was Clay-Boy trying to get something out of my eye. I got a piece of mill dust in it walking around from the post office and Clay-Boy was just taking it out for me, weren't you, Clay-Boy?"

"That's right."

"He didn't have his hands nowhere near your eyes," objected Becky.

"You say that again, kid," said Claris, "and I'm going to clobber your jaw so hard you'll look backwards for the rest of your life."

Becky turned and ran out of Friendship Corner. Once she was safely out of the door and up the path to the road she shouted, "I'm goen to tell Mama on you-all!"

"Oh God," cried Clay-Boy, "I've got to shut her up before she tells the world. You lock up here."

As he ran for the door Claris called, "What about the carnival tonight?"

"I'll be there if I can get away," he promised.

"If you don't show up by eight o'clock, I'm coming over there after you," she threatened. "I'll tell your Mama what you tried to do to me down here, too!"

"I'll be there," he shouted in desperation and ran after his little sister who, safely halfway up the hill, was shouting her threat.

He saw Becky enter the house and doubled his speed, but it was too late. When he walked in the kitchen he found Olivia seated on a stool beside the kitchen range. She was cutting some vegetables into the soup she was making for supper and listening to Becky's story.

"And then," Becky was saying, "Claris said she was going to slap my face around to the other side if I said anything so I ran away from them."

"What's this child tryen to tell me, Clay-Boy?" asked Olivia.

"I don't know, Mama," said Clay-Boy. "What did she say?"

"She says that you and Claris were doen somethen bad."

"Well, we weren't."

"Becky, what have you got to say to that?"

"Mama, they were wrapped up together like two fishen worms," shrieked Becky.

"We were not!" shouted Clay-Boy.

A stricken look crossed his mother's face, and she drew in her breath sharply. Clay-Boy thought the pain was caused by the idea of what she thought he had done and that he had lied to her.

"Mama," he cried, "I didn't do a thing but kiss her. That's all we did. I swear before God."

"It's all right, Clay-Boy. I believe you." She had drawn herself upright on the stool but now she slumped into a more relaxed position. "I want you to run down to the mill and tell your daddy to come straight home from work."

"Why, Mama? Is anything wrong?"

"Nothing's wrong, but I think you and the children might be goen to spend the night with your grand-mother."

He realized then what had caused the pain he had seen in his mother's face. The only time he or any of the other children spent the night away from home they would return the following morning to find their mother in bed and a new baby beside her.

"I'll go get Daddy," he said and ran as fast as he could down the wall and out on the road toward the mill.

Olivia did not inform the smaller children that they would be spending the night with their grandparents until supper was almost over. Hearing this news, Shirley burst into tears.

"What's the matter, honey?" asked her mother.

"You're goen to hatch a baby," cried Shirley. "You always hatch a baby when we go to Grandma's and stay all night."

"That's right, honey," said Olivia, "but that's not a thing to cry about. A new baby is somethen to be happy about."

"Where is the baby now, Mama?" asked Luke.

"Doctor Campbell's got it and he's going to bring it over here in that little black bag he carries around," said Olivia. "Now Clay-Boy, I'm going to get the toothbrushes and pajamas together and you get everybody ready to go."

Clay had already left to alert Dr. Campbell that the new baby was expected and when Olivia went out of the room, as the oldest, Clay-Boy took charge.

He went from one upturned face to the other, smearing it quickly with the same wash cloth, giving it a fast drying dab with a towel. He tried not to show his nervousness for fear of upsetting the younger children. He knew what happened when children were born, could not believe it, did not see how such a mechanically impossible thing could happen; the idea of it clung in his mind, filling him with worry and pity for his mother.

Becky had been whispering something in Shirley's ear which caused Shirley to burst into crying.

"What's the matter with you?" Clay-Boy demanded. "Becky says the baby is in Mama's stomach and Doctor Campbell's goen to cut it out with a knife," sobbed Shirley.

"Becky's crazy," said Clay-Boy.

Becky stuck out her tongue at him and he slapped her face so that her cries blended with Shirley's sobs, which continued unabated.

"You stop that damn crying," snarled Clay-Boy to Becky.

Becky stopped long enough to say, "I'm goen to tell Mama you said a bad word," and began to whimper again. The baby in his high chair began to cry sympathetically. Pattie-Cake had crawled off the bench and onto the table, where she was merrily spearing a boiled potato with her index finger. John leaned against the table, thumb in mouth, regarding the chaos with mild indifference and Mark kept taking one biscuit after another from the bread plate and crumbling them in a neat little pile in front of him. Clay-Boy started for the baby to try to stop his crying, but saw that Pattie-Cake was about to overturn a bowl of gravy. He rescued the gravy, took Pattie-Cake off the table and placed her on the floor—where she began to yell as loud as her small lungs would allow.

Clay-Boy had an impulse to run out of the house and let he children go right on with their destruction. They seemed to him a wriggling nest of wicked little grasshoppers, each leaping from one destructive act to another. He was tired of his position in the family, of being the oldest, of having to manage the younger children and of having to set a good example always. Then he remembered the pain he had seen on his mother's face and he did what had to be done. Becky was still whimpering monotonously in her place at the table. He went over and slapped her cheeks sharply. She looked up astonished.

"Now you listen to me. If I hear another whimper out of you I'm going to tan your fanny. Now, pick up the baby, go to the door and stand there."

Stunned, she obeyed. Next he seized Matt, placed him behind Becky and threatened him with death if he dared move. One by one he lined the children up just inside the door, and that is how Olivia found them when she returned with a suitcase.

"Clay-Boy said a bad word, Mama," tattled Becky.

"Did you, Clay-Boy?" Olivia asked.

"Yes ma'am," replied Clay-Boy firmly.

"I'll tell you somethen, boy," Olivia said. "Sometimes I feel like sayen them myself, and then I remember God sees everything we do. You remember that and maybe it'll help you not to say bad things."

"I'll try, Mama," said Clay-Boy.

"You all run on over to Mama's now," said Olivia. "Be good babies and mind Clay-Boy."

She kissed each of them as they filed out of the door. "Have a nice baby, Mama," said Becky, and Olivia promised she would.

"I hope it's a baby rabbit," said Luke.

"One day I'm goen to catch me a baby," said Shirley, "and tame it for a pet."

With Clay-Boy in the lead carrying the baby and Becky, holding Pattie-Cake by the hand, bringing up the rear, the children walked down to the gate and out onto the road. Olivia watched them to the turning of the road and when they were gone from her sight she turned into the house.

When she had washed the dishes and straightened up the living room she went to the bedroom and took from a drawer the clothes she had made for the new child, a band to cover its severed cord, a little flannel under-shirt, some folded diapers and a long nightshirt. When these were laid out where they always had been for past births she went to the bathroom and bathed herself.

After she had bathed she dressed in a nightgown and went to the bedroom. The bed had a cast-iron head and footboard. It was painted white and was covered with a crocheted bedspread which had been a wedding pre-sent from Eliza. This was the bed on which Olivia had given birth to all of the children and two of the rungs in the headboard were permanently bent forward where her hands had clung during her labor. Once she had thought of asking Clay to straighten them out because they spoiled the symmetry of the headboard, but she decided not to speak to him. How could a woman explain to a man a pain so great that to endure it she would bend a sturdy metal thing and still endure it again? Such things were not for a man's mind, so the bent rungs remained as they were, evidence of pain that she forgot once it was endured.

Olivia removed the bedclothes and took a rubber sheet from the bottom of the dresser and placed it on the bed. She covered the rubber sheet with an old cotton sheet, one old enough that it could be thrown away without being missed too much. The crocheted spread she folded and placed in a dresser drawer.

Now there was nothing more to be done. The pains were gradually increasing in frequency and in intensity and they seemed less severe if she were standing so she walked back and forth in the room. She was glad she was alone, and when the pains were sharpest could relieve herself by moaning aloud.

"I declare if here don't come Cox's Army," said Ida as Clay-Boy and the children flocked in the kitchen where she and Homer were finishing their supper.

"Well, now if this ain't a treat," said Homer, sweeping a few of the younger ones up in his arms and hugging them until they could hardly breathe.

"Y'all had anything to eat?" asked Ida.

"Yes ma'am," said Clay-Boy, "Mama fed everybody and they're all washed and ready for bed."

"I'm hungry," said John. "Me too," chorused several other voices and soon they were all seated around the table, munching Ida's thin crisp biscuits dripping with butter and peach preserves. Afterward, when she had washed their sticky fingers, Ida took them into the parlor, a room that was almost never used. Ida had furnished it with money she made taking orders for a mail-order house, and the stiff-back chairs and settee upholstered in a black composition material were a source of great pride to her. Homer had built her a little bookcase which sat beneath the window; on the bookcase there stood all year the cards she received at Christmas. From the wall a tinted dimensional likeness of a brown-bearded Jesus looked down with eyes that would follow you no matter where in the room you stood. The children, awed by the grandness and solemnity of the room, sat reverently and quietly while Ida played hymns on the wind-up Victrola.

All the children were enjoying themselves except Clay-Boy. As he watched the light of day fading outside the window he grew more anxious. Worry over his mother was increased by the fact that Claris had threatened to come to the house if he did not meet her by eight o'clock. If she did go to the house there was no telling what she might do. In his mind Clay-Boy could see her being sent away only to sneak back to stand underneath the bedroom window for anything she might see or overhear. He did not know how he would do it, but he knew he had to keep Claris from going to his home.

As yet he had devised no way of getting out of his grandparents' house for the night, but as each child began to nod he would take him upstairs, dress him in his pajamas and put him to bed.

After many trips upstairs, he returned to the parlor where the Victrola pledged softly that it would cling to the Old Rugged Cross and exchange it someday for a crown. His grandmother sat in a dreamy trance, her eyes fixed on the face of Jesus. His grandfather sat holding Donnie, the baby. Donnie was fast asleep, breathing the soft untroubled sleep of a tired child.

Ida looked up as Clay-Boy entered the room.

"Look's like the party's over," she said.

"I'll take Donnie on up," offered Clay-Boy.

"I'll take care of him. You look sleepy. Go on to bed."

"Yes ma'am," Clay-Boy said and left the room.

"Past your bedtime if you're goen to work tomorrow, Homer," Ida reminded her husband.

Homer was looking down at the sleeping baby in his arms.

"It sure feel good to hold 'em when they're this size," he said. "I never for the life of me see how they get so big so quick."

"One minute they're steppen on your feet. The next thing you know they're steppen on your heart," said Ida. "Don't sit there holden him all night. He'll rest better in bed."

Ida rose and went out onto the porch. Across the little valley where the mill and the town square lay she could see the lights where Olivia and Clay lived. She felt she ought to go and see if she could be of any use. Yet she did not really want to go. Witnessing birth, hearing it, being near it brought back the pain and blood with which she had borne her own six. Even now the thought of bringing a child into the world left her trembling and reeling with vertigo.

Ida walked upstairs, grasping the handrail as she took each step, and then tiptoed across the creaking old wooden floor to the farthest room. At each door she listened to the breathing of the children and when she was satisfied that they were all asleep she went downstairs once more and into the parlor where Homer was half asleep and hunched over the sleeping baby he held in his arms.

"You better put that baby in the bed before you fall over asleep." called Ida.

Homer's head rose with a start. He gave a half-snore and looked at his wife angrily. "What do you mean scaring me that way?"

"Put that baby to bed," she said. "I'm goen over to Livy's and see if I can be any help."

"You're just goen to be in the way over there," said Homer. "Why don't you stay home where you belong?" What he really meant was that the two of them had slept next to each other on the same bed for so long that, no matter how tired or how much he needed sleep, he could not sleep without her beside him.

"I'll be back time to fix your breakfast," she said. She took the gray cardigan sweater from the nail behind the door and slipped it over her shoulders.

"I'd like to borrow your flashlight if you don't mind," she said.

"And how you expect me to see if one of them babies wakes up in the night? I ain't got no cat's eyes like some people I could name."

"All right," she said. "I reckon I can feel my way down the path." She went out through the screen door, closed it softly behind her; feeling her way along in the semidarkness she made her way down the stairs and onto the path that led down the hill. She had hardly stepped onto the path when a beam of light pierced the darkness, found her and then went down to show her the path.

In the darkness she smiled. "O'nery old devil," she thought to herself. "Wonder what he'd do if he didn't have me?"

Now safely on the roadway, she made her way toward the oasis of light that surrounded the mill. There was still a stretch of darkness after she had passed the mill but Ida had walked the road so many times to deliver her mail orders that she knew it by heart and had no fear.

Olivia's house was strangely quiet as Ida came up the walk. At the door she called and Olivia answered from the bedroom. She found Olivia lying on the bed looking lonely and frightened.

"I sure am glad to see you, Mama," said Olivia. "With all the children out of the house and this one gone quiet and still all of a sudden, you know how they'll do just before they start out, I was getting the jitters."

"Where's Clay?" asked Ida.

"He went after Doctor Campbell and found out he's down at Howardsville delivering Ruby Carter. Clay's borrowed a truck to go after him and he ought to be back any time. Sooner the better would suit me."

"You want me to get you anything, Livy?"

"No ma'am," Olivia replied. "Just sit and talk."

"What you hopen it's goen to be?" asked Ida.

"A boy," said Olivia firmly.

"Why another boy? What you got against little girls?"

"Oh, I ain't got a thing against girls," said Olivia. "God knows I love mine better than I do myself. It's just that I feel so sorry for little girls. I reckon maybe it's because I'm pregnant, but the other night I was washen Pattie-Cake and I looked down at her little body and I started thinken about one day she'd be grown up and a woman and some man would take her and she'd be haven babies of her own. I don't know what it was, but just all of a sudden I felt so sorry for her I started cryen. I didn't want her to see me cryen so I went out of the room until it was over. Wasn't that silly?"

"I don't know," said Ida. "It's harder on a woman than a man. A man's got so many things to fill his mind. He's got his job and his hunten and his fishen and bringen home the firewood to keep the place warm. But he don't know what it's like to have a baby, or sit up all night with a sick one, or to be home with them all day long with them runnen wild and then expect you to be just layen there in the bed waiten for him at the end of the day. Men are strange people, I'll tell you. I listen to their talk sometimes and I think *crazy, the whole lot of 'em.*"

"Clay talks, but he's a man that gets things done too. You take now what's goen to happen once I'm on my feet again. He'll be up there worken on that house night and day. He always does that whenever we get a new baby."

"It's a waste of time, if you ask me. Clay Spencer is never goen to get that house up. How many years has he been worken on it now?"

"I don't care how long it's been," said Olivia. "He has poured too much heart and time and money in that place not to finish it. That house is his life and his dream, and I know people laugh at him and say he's foolish in what he's tryen to do, but if you'll take notice it's them of small vision that hold him up for ridicule."

"I never poked fun at Clay," replied Ida. "It just seems to me there's not a thing wrong with the house he's got here."

"This is a good house," said Olivia, "but Clay's proud and the idea of liven and dyen in a house you can't call your own on land that belongs to somebody else just galls him."

She drew in a deep breath and closed her eyes as a spasm of pain rose like a tide in her body.

"That was a good strong one," she said as the pain ebbed away. "This baby is liable to get here before Doctor Campbell."

Reluctantly Ida went to the kitchen and began gathering the things she might need just in case Olivia should deliver before Clay and the doctor returned. She was afraid and she prayed to Jesus for strength, both for Olivia and for herself.

Clay-Boy lay in bed in his grandparents' house beside his brother Matt. He still wore his clothes and had taken off his shoes, letting each of them drop with exaggerated noise to notify everybody that he had gone to bed.

He did not know what time it was but guessed that it was close to eight o'clock. He listened while Ida left the house and then crept out onto the second-floor balcony just in time to see his grandfather turn off the beam of light which had seen Ida safely down to the roadway. Clay-Boy waited anxiously for his grandfather's next move, and when Homer turned back into the house, Clay-Boy, shoes in hand, crept down the stairway, down the hill and onto the road where he put on his shoes and ran toward Claris' house.

He could see the headlights of a car winding down the driveway from Colonel Coleman's house and sprinted to reach it before it arrived at the main road. The car and the boy reached the junction at the same time and an imperious voice called from the car, "Get in."

"I'm not going," said Clay-Boy.

"Don't be silly," said Claris. "Get in the car."

Clay-Boy propped his arms on the car door and

leaned in the window so he was face-to-face with Claris. The car radio was going quite loudly and a vocalist was proclaiming huskily that she didn't want to set the world on fire, but just wanted to start a flame in somebody's heart.

"You know how you talk sometime?" Clay asked. "You talk like you own the world. Well, you don't own me and don't you ever pull up to me in a car like that and tell me to get in. You are not the boss of me."

"If you didn't talk so corn-poney," said Claris, "you'd sound exactly like Humphrey Bogart."

"If you don't like the way I talk you can find somebody else to hang around all the time," said Clay-Boy.

"You are the most conceited thing I ever laid eyes on," Claris cried and slapped him hard on the cheek. Stunned, Clay-Boy withdrew just as Claris released the brake and went speeding off down the road.

He stood for a moment rubbing his cheek and cursing the girl softly. Hundreds of things he wished he had said came to his mind and if there were any satisfaction for him in what had happened it was only that for once he had not given in to her bossiness.

He swore that he would never see her again, but even before he reached his grandparents' house he had begun to miss her and he knew that the days ahead would be long and empty without her.

When he came to his grandparents' home everyone was asleep, and as quietly as he could he crept to bed.

For a long time he tossed and turned but sleep would not come.

His mind divided itself into two parts; each half kept arguing with the other. One half insisted he might just as well have gone with Claris to the carnival while the other half insisted he had done the right thing, that she was a bossy girl and needed a lesson. Nothing had really resolved itself in his mind when he began to doze and thought he was dreaming that he heard his grandfather's voice.

"Clay-Boy, come down here, son."

He woke, went to the head of the stairs and looked down. Standing at the foot of the stairs, clad in his long flannel underwear, was his grandfather. Standing beside him, her face streaked with tears, was Claris.

"This little girl wants to have words with you," said Homer.

"I came to tell you I'm sorry," said Claris when Clay-Boy reached the foot of the stairs.

"It's all right," said Clay-Boy, conscious of his grandfather's irritation at being roused from his bed. "How did you know I was here?"

"I only went a little way and turned back to find you. When I couldn't I went to your house."

"Oh no," said Clay-Boy.

"Don't worry," she said. "I didn't misbehave."

"Was anything happening?" asked Clay-Boy.

"It already happened before I got there," replied Claris. "Twins!"

"Twins!" thundered Homer.

"That's right," said Claris. "Mr. Spencer came to the door and told me. And guess what they're going to name them."

"Daddy always said he was going to name it Caboose if it was a boy."

"The little boy is going to be Franklin Delano and the little girl is going to be Eleanor."

"It's a shame it wasn't triplets or they could have named the other one after Henry Wallace," said Homer with a loud yawn. "And now if it's all right with everybody, I'd like to get some sleep."

"Good night, Mr. Italiano. I'm sorry I woke you," said Claris.

"Good night, little lady," said Homer.

"See you tomorrow, Clay-Boy?" asked Claris.

"See you tomorrow," he said happily and watched as she made her way down the hill to the car, and waited until the car was out of sight.

CHAPTER 12

CLAY-BOY WAS SITTING at his desk in the library when he heard quick footsteps across the front porch. He was surprised when he looked up to see his mother's sister, Frances, the postmistress of New Dominion.

"Look here," she said, and laid in front of him a letter.

"Is that it?" he asked. His palms became moist with excitement and his heart was beating double time.

"Open it up, boy," said Frances. "Let's hear the good news."

Clay-Boy could only stare at the letter, reading and rereading the return address: University of Richmond, Virginia.

"Wouldn't you know it?" said Frances. "Usually there's half a dozen people passing by if I want to send word to somebody. Today there wasn't a soul so when I couldn't get word to you to come to the post office, I just closed it and brought it to you special delivery."

"I'm almost scared to open it," said Clay-Boy.

"Why?"

"Suppose they've turned my scholarship down?"

"Well, honey, that wouldn't be the end of the world—now, would it?"

"It would for me," said Clay-Boy. "Even though they've accepted me I couldn't go without the scholarship."

"Listen, Clay-Boy," said Frances. "If you were meant to be a great man in this world you'll be one no matter whether you get to college or not. They haven't got all the education in the world locked up down there at the University of Richmond. You can read, can't you?"

He nodded.

"Well," she said, "if they've turned you down you write back to them and ask for the names of the books they teach. I'll bet between the gang of us we could get hold of those books. It might be a little bit slower than goen down there and taken the courses, but it's one

227

way. You open that letter and take it like a man, no matter what they say."

He smiled and tore open the envelope. His hands trembled as he removed the letter and unfolded it. "The scholarship committee announces the following appointments for the Fall and Winter Semesters," he read. There followed a list of names, but the name of Clay Spencer, Jr., was not among them.

Without a word he handed the letter to Frances. She scanned the list and when her eyes met the boy's he could see that she shared the misery of his rejection.

"It was kind of like asken for the sun and the moon and the stars, once you think about it. Wasn't it, honey?" she said.

He turned away so she could not see the hot tears that were welling in his eyes. The world had become for him a party he would never attend. Somewhere boys with not half the heart and mind and craving to learn and to do something with that learning would be accepted by colleges and they would accept it as their due. For Clay-Boy a window had been briefly opened into a world he had only dared to dream of and all he could see at that moment was that the window had been slammed shut in his face and would never open again.

"If I had my way, honey," said his Aunt Frances, "you'd be President of the United States." She walked around and kissed him on the cheek, and then at the door she turned and said, "I know you won't believe it now, but tomorrow it won't hurt so much and it'll hurt even less the day after tomorrow." And then she left him and returned to the post office.

Clay-Boy welcomed the solitude. He wondered why he had failed and he thought of the people who would share his disappointment and his sense of failure.

Miss Parker had written a quotation in his autograph book in the spring when he had graduated from high school and it returned to haunt him:

"Heights of great men reached and kept
Were not attained by sudden flight,
For they, while their companions slept,
Were toiling upward in the night."

The words had sustained him. Now they were meaningless. The world which had been so bright with its promise of the endless heights to which he could rise seemed now drab and more hopeless than it had ever seemed before. During the time he had waited for the scholarship and counted on it he had lived in a world of imagination. He had visions of himself walking across a grassy college campus to some ivy-covered hall where he would sit with other hungry young men at the feet of inspired teachers and drink in wisdom which would enable him to help realize the dreams of his younger brothers and sisters, his own dreams, and those of his mother, and to build for his father an even grander house than Clay himself had imagined.

Now the world he had imagined was only a bitter memory. He had returned to a ridiculous little village in the foothills of the Blue Ridge Mountains, a monotonous isolated grouping of dust-covered houses hemmed in by hills. There were no roads out of town, no escape; he was imprisoned forever.

He walked up and down the little room swearing every curse word he had ever heard his father use, and when he had exhausted his vocabulary he wept.

At breakfast the following Saturday morning Clay announced that he was going to Richmond for the day.

"You lost your mind or somethen?" asked Olivia.

"I never had no mind to lose, woman," said Clay.

"Then what are you goen all the way down to Richmond for?" she asked.

"I'm goen down there to talk to whoever turned down Clay-Boy for that scholarship to go to college."

"They won't let you inside the fence," said Olivia. "They're educated people down there."

"Listen to me, woman," said Clay. "I've talked to educated people in my time, and I'll tell you the truth, some of them make a heap more sense to talk to than these ignorant rattlesnakes around here. Now you get Clay-Boy in his Sunday clothes. I'm aimen to leave here just as soon as he's ready."

"Not with him," said Olivia. "He's not goen."

"How come?" asked Clay.

"I won't have him suffer disappointment all over again. That boy got his hopes up so high he was treaden on the stars and he's been sick at heart ever since he found out they turned him down. He's getten over it a little bit now and I'm not goen to have you build his hopes up just so he can have his heart broken all over again."

"I never thought of it that way," said Clay. "Maybe you're right."

"I know I'm right," said Olivia, "and it wasn't all his fault. We all got puffed up with pride and sin. We bragged on him and got to feelen we were better than anybody else around here just because we had a smart boy in the family. It got to the point where it wouldn't surprise me if it wasn't the Lord himself that stepped in and saw to it that Clay-Boy didn't get that scholarship."

"Now why the tar would He do that?" demanded Clay.

"To teach us that it's sinful to crave worldly goods. If the Lord put you on the earth poor, poor you were meant to be. If you were born ignorant He meant you to die ignorant."

"Now where in hell did you get that information?" cried Clay in disgust.

"It's in the Bible," said Olivia, "and you stop swearing in front of me."

"You show me where it says that in the Bible," said Clay.

"I don't know where it says it exactly," said Olivia, "but I've heard preachers say the same thing many a time and quote the Bible to back them up."

"Woman, you've been listening to too many preachers. Don't you know anybody in the world can find somethen written down somewhere to back up everythen they say? Maybe I never been baptized and maybe I've never set foot in a church since I was knee-high to a grasshopper, but I've got a good acquaintance with Old Master Jesus and the One I say my prayers to ain't One that would set His foot down on one of my babies betteren himself in the world."

In the end Clay agreed that it would be better not to encourage Clay-Boy's hopes again and he left for Richmond alone. He took the old road that at Scottsville met the James River and follows its curving course down through Columbia, the State Farm, Goochland, Manikin, and finally he came to the out-skirts of the city of Richmond.

When he saw the city limits sign he stopped at a filling station and asked his way to the University. He found himself on Three Chopt Road, riding along past estates so beautiful and past driveways so imposing that he began to think that each one might be the col-lege, for he had no idea what a college might look like. Finally he found a road that led through a series of pleasant hills. Scattered through the rolling hills and surrounded by areas of clipped green lawn were many buildings covered with ivy and because once in a while Clay saw a boy or group of boys carrying books along the paths he reasoned that he had found the University of Richmond.

Finally Clay spotted a lone boy walking along the road. He pulled up beside him and let the motor idle.

"Howdy," called Clay.

The boy nodded and said, "Good morning."

"I reckon this is the college?"

"Yes sir," said the boy.

"I'm looken for the boss or the foreman or whoever runs it."

"Runs what?" asked the boy, slightly apprehensive.

"The college," answered Clay.

"Well, the president and the dean and the people like that all have offices at the Administration Building. It's the one right up the hill there." The boy pointed.

"Much obliged," said Clay and, waving genially, started up the hill in his truck.

In the Administration Building, Clay opened the first door he came to and approached a woman with beautiful white hair who sat at a desk typing briskly.

"Good morning," she said, without looking up or slowing the least bit at her typing.

"I want to see the head man," said Clay.

The woman stopped her typing and turned to look at him. She smiled and said, "I'm Miss Montrose, the registrar. Tell me your business and perhaps I can help you."

"I didn't come eighty-four miles and spend all that money on gas to talk to no woman," said Clay.

"I'm sorry," said Miss Montrose. "You won't tell me who you want to see or what you want to see him about. I don't see how I can help you."

Clay reached in his pocket and pulled out the letter. "This is what I come about," he said. "I want to see why my boy's name isn't on that list."

Miss Montrose scanned the letter. "What is your boy's name," she asked.

"Clay-Boy Spencer," replied Clay. "Junior," he added.

"Please have a seat," she said. She went into a door behind her and in her absence Clay walked around the small reception room. He looked from one distinguished scholarly old face in the portraits to the other and while they looked smart enough to Clay he could not get rid of the feeling that none of them had ever done a decent day's work in his life.

"Mr. Spencer, would you come this way, please?"

Clay turned and asked, "Where you taken me?"

"In to see Dean Beck," said Miss Montrose. "He just happened to be in this morning. He wants to talk to you."

Clay followed her into a book-lined room where he half-expected to meet a face similar to those whose pictures lined the walls of the waiting room. He was pleasantly surprised. The man who rose to meet him was a pudgy, round-faced man who extended his hand in a friendly way; after a quick appraising glance at Clay, his face broke into an unexpectedly merry smile.

"Delighted to meet you, Neighbor Spencer," said the round little man, who called everybody "neighbor," from the janitor to the president of the college. "I'm Dean of Men here, and I understand from Miss Montrose you want to discuss your son. Have a seat."

Clay sat in a big, old leather chair worn thin by the uncomfortable seats of countless college students.

Clay himself had grown somewhat uncomfortable because he did not know quite what to make of Dean Beck.

"Now sir," Dean Beck said, "what can I do for you?"

"Well sir, since you put it that way," said Clay, "what you can do for me is to give my boy another chance at that scholarship."

"Neighbor Spencer, I'm sure you appreciate the fact that only a limited number of scholarships are available here. Each applicant is considered most thoroughly, and the awards must be granted to the young men we feel are best qualified, who have not only the strength of character and the drive and the will and whatever mysterious thing it is that makes for an inquiring mind, but also the preparation, the tools he needs for implementing these things once he begins a course of study."

"Yes sir," said Clay, who understood in a general way what the man was saying.

"I happen to sit on the Scholarship Committee and I remember your son's application especially. His scholastic record was impressive. His outside interests were commendable and he seemed on the whole to be a perfect candidate for a scholarship. I assure you he would have been awarded the scholarship except for one insurmountable deficiency. He had no Latin."

"I don't rightly know what that is," said Clay.

Dean Beck was shocked, but at the same time he was disarmed by Clay's frank admission of ignorance.

"Latin," he explained, "is one of the ancient languages; the knowledge of Latin is almost totally necessary for any real study of other language. In other words, your son would not have had the necessary background to have made the most of an opportunity to study here."

"How long does it take to learn this Latin?" asked Clay.

"Most of our freshmen have at least one high school semester, or the equivalent in some language."

"Like what?" asked Clay.

"French, German, or Spanish."

"Nobody talks that up in New Dominion," said Clay. "I reckon we'll just have to make it Latin."

"I don't follow you," said Dean Beck.

"What I'm aimen to do is find somebody to teach him up on that Latin. After that, if you could see your way clear to give him a second chance I would be mighty obliged to you."

"Friend Spencer," said Dean Beck, "may I say that if he doesn't get the scholarship, would you try not to be too disappointed? And may I remind you that some of the greatest men in our country never graduated from college."

"You can tell me that, sir," said Clay, "but I don't think that it would mean much to tell it to my boy. He's got his heart set on comen here. Only it's more than that. It's somethen I don't understand. Lord God Almighty, I never went to school more than five or six days myself and I've near about broke my back just to keep all of my kids in school. But I never let one of them quit and never will till they graduate from high school. Their mama feels the same way."

"I am sure that if your son wants badly enough to be a minister he won't let this setback stand in his way."

"I didn't quite understand you, sir," said Clay.

"I said I'm sure that if your son's passion to preach the gospel is strong enough he'll find some way to prepare himself," said Dean Beck.

"That boy don't want to be no preacher," said Clay. "He just wants a college education."

The dean consulted the application in front of him. "But he's applied here for a ministerial scholarship," he insisted.

That Clay-Boy could have done so terrible a thing seemed inconceivable to Clay. He could only conclude that a monstrous error had been made, that someone had failed to read the small print or that the wrong kind of application had been sent to Clay-Boy in the first place.

"Friend Beck," said Clay, "somebody has got things screwed up somethen royal. I'd rather see that boy of mine a jailbird than a Baptist preacher."

"What have you got against Baptist preachers?" asked the dean.

"Well, it ain't a thing against the preacher. That one we got up at New Dominion seems to be one hundred per cent. It's the Baptists that galls me. I don't know what kind you got down here, but where I live we got the Hard Shells. They don't allow smoken, drinken, card-playen, dancen, cussen, kissen, huggen or loven in any shape, form or size. They're against lipstick, face powder, rouge, and frizzled hair. I know what I'm talken about, Mr. Beck. I'm married to a Baptist and she might bring my children up Christian, but I'll be damned if I'll have a Baptist preacher in the family."

"I'm certain that if your son knows your feelings on the matter, then this application was in error," said Dean Beck.

"He ought to know," Clay said. "And I'll make double-sure he knows when I get home. Now, let me get somethen straight. You teach anythen else down here beside the preachen business?"

"Yes," said Dean Beck, "we have courses of instruction in business administration, the social sciences, the arts, and medicine and law."

"Well, Clay-Boy ought to find somethen he'd like out of one of them," said Clay. "Now, let me ask you another thing. If that boy of mine learned himself a little Latin between now and the time this college opens up again, would you take him in?"

Dean Beck considered for a moment. Fathers had tried to bully, to coax, to bribe or to beg him to accept their sons. None of them had been so direct or so determined as the man who now confronted him.

"Suppose I were to say *no* to you, Neighbor Spencer?" asked Dean Beck. "What would you do?"

"This ain't the only goldurned college in the country," said Clay. "I'd find another one."

"I don't think that will be necessary," said Dean Beck. "Bring young Clay back when he's completed one high school semester of Latin. If the boy's anything like his father I believe he'll be an asset to all of us."

"Thank you, sir," said Clay sincerely.

"However, it is too late for a scholarship this year. Perhaps that will come later, but the first semester, if he proves himself acceptable that is, he will have to pay the regular college fees. You'll find them all listed in this catalogue."

"Thank you, Dean," said Clay accepting the catalogue. The two men rose and shook hands. "If you're ever up in Nelson County," said Clay, "I hope you'll drop by and pay us a visit."

"I will indeed," Dean Beck promised.

After Clay had gone Miss Montrose went to the dean's office, opened the door and said, "Bravo!"

Dean Beck was leaning back in his big leather chair. He was smiling a satisfied smile while he bit on his pipe.

"What else was I to do, Miss Montrose?" he laughed. "He's right. This ain't the only goldurned college in the country."

CHAPTER 13

DARKNESS WAS FALLING when Clay arrived back in New Dominion. He was hungry and he knew that supper would be ready, but before going home he decided to report the day's happenings to Miss Parker. Miss Parker boarded with a family over in the section of New Dominion called Riverside Drive. Clay found her sitting alone in the porch swing reading in the fading light of day from *The Complete Works of William Shakespeare.*

"Miss Parker," said Clay, "I've been down to the University of Richmond. I found out why they turned Clay-Boy down."

"I would be most curious to know," said Miss Parker.

"Seems to go to college you got to know the subject of Latin, and Clay-Boy never took it up," said Clay.

"I knew it had to be something of that kind," said Miss Parker. "He was so qualified in every other way. If I'd only known I could have found some way for Clay-Boy to have studied Latin."

"I talked to a real nice feller down there, name of Beck . . ."

"The Dean!" Miss Parker exclaimed.

"That's what he said he was," continued Clay. "And I found out somethen else, Miss Parker. That boy had signed the wrong kind of paper or somethen, because they got the fool idea from somewhere that Clay-Boy wanted to be a Baptist preacher."

"They got that fool idea from me, Mr. Spencer," said Miss Parker. "If the blame rests anywhere it must be on me because I was the one who talked Mr. Goodson, your wife and Clay-Boy into the idea in the first place."

"Miss Parker," said Clay, "I always took for you a lady."

"Then you were mistaken, Mr. Spencer," said Miss

Parker. "I'm only an old-maid school teacher who self-ishly wanted to see just one of her children make something of himself."

"Maybe you still will, Miss Parker," said Clay. "I got the preachen business all straightened out. He'll take some other kind of trade at the College."

"You don't mean there's still a chance?" exclaimed Miss Parker.

"If Clay-Boy can get one high school semester of Latin here there's still a chance," answered Clay.

"Then we will get it for him by all means," said Miss Parker. She had been depressed ever since Clay-Boy's scholarship had been turned down. Now that there was a new opportunity for the boy, a new light came into her eyes and a quiver of excitement sounded in her voice.

"There's not a soul in New Dominion who knows Latin," she said. "That's why we've never taught it. Perhaps in Charlottesville we could find someone to tutor him."

"That wouldn't be much help, Miss Parker," objected Clay. "I've got no way to get him over there."

"That's the least of our worries," said Miss Parker. "I'll see that he gets there. The first thing we'll have to do is find him a teacher."

When Clay reached home he walked into the kitchen and looked sternly at Olivia for a moment.

"What's the matter with you, you crazy thing?" she demanded.

"Thought you'd put one over on me, didn't you?" he said.

"I don't know what you're talken about."

Hearing his father's voice, Clay-Boy walked from the living room into the kitchen.

"Howdy, preacher," said Clay in a sugary voice.

Clay-Boy stared at his father sheepishly but could not speak.

"What is the subject you are goen to talk on down there at the Baptist church in the mornen?" asked Clay. "Maybe you ought to talk about the sin of conniven against your daddy, and maybe your mama and Preacher Goodson and Miss Parker can all sit up on the front row so they can hear real good."

Clay-Boy could not tell if his father's anger were real or if it were pretended, but he began to suspect that Clay was not as disturbed as he seemed to be and that his father might even be enjoying the role he was playing.

"Daddy," he said, "it didn't mean I had to become a preacher. It just meant I could have become one if I wanted to after I graduated."

"Boy," said Clay, "as near as I can make out, it would have been the same as apprenticen as a plumber and then taken up the electrical trade. Now I've been down yonder in Richmond all day long and I've got this thing straightened out. They're goen to give you another chance and this time you can take your pick of anythen they're offeren."

"How come they're given him another chance, Clay?" asked Olivia.

"Well, there's somethen he's got to do first," answered Clay. "He's got to learn some kind of foreign language named Latin."

"There's a Latin grammar down at the library," said Clay-Boy. "Maybe I could teach it to myself."

"Well, you go ahead and try it," said Clay, "but I've already talked it over with Miss Parker and she seems to think she can find somebody over in Charlottesville that can teach it to you."

As it turned out, a teacher was found much closer to home than Charlottesville. When Mr. Goodson heard from Miss Parker the reason the scholarship was not awarded to Clay-Boy, he came immediately to the Spencer home.

Clay had been up on the mountain working on his house, but he arrived home soon after darkness had fallen. He found Olivia feeding the children at the kitchen table.

"Clay," she said, "go on in the liven room. Mr. Goodson's in there and he wants to see you."

"I've been wanten to see that ripstaver myself," said Clay. "Just to warn him never again to try to make a preacher out of my boy."

"Clay," admonished Olivia, "don't you say a word about that unless he brings it up. Now go on in there. He's been waiten a long time."

Clay-Boy had been left in the living room to entertain Mr. Goodson. The two of them had been talking earnestly, and when Clay entered the minister rose and offered his hand.

"Keep your seat, friend," urged Clay, but Mr. Goodson remained standing.

"I know you're anxious to get on with your supper, Clay," said Mr. Goodson, "so I'll tell you why I'm here. I understand from Miss Parker that if Clay-Boy can get one high school semester of Latin before fall there's still a chance they'll accept him at the University."

"That's about the size of it," said Clay. "Yes sir."

"Well it happens that I took Latin when I was a student at the University of Richmond. I believe I can teach it to Clay-Boy."

"I'll be a ring-tail squealer!" exclaimed Clay joyfully.

"Of course, I'm not a recognized teacher," said Mr. Goodson hastily.

"That don't make a damn to me," said Clay. "You could give him a guarantee or a warrant or somethen sayen he can talk Latin as good as anybody else, couldn't you?"

"Yes, I could do that."

"Honey, did you hear that?" asked Clay of Olivia, who had come to the door.

"I certainly did, and I want you to know we appreciate it, Mr. Goodson," said Olivia.

"That brings up somethen we ought to talk about right now," said Clay. "How much are you goen to charge to tell this boy about Latin?"

"I wouldn't think of taking anything," said Mr.

Goodson. "It would be a great pleasure for me."

"No, sir," said Clay. "I wouldn't think of letten you do it for nothen."

"You don't have to pay me anything," insisted Mr. Goodson. "But if you really want to do something for me you can take me fishing with you again."

"Preacher," said Clay solemnly, "we've been fishen together for the first and last time. I like you too much to lose you."

"All right then, Clay," grinned Mr. Goodson, but then with an innocent smile he added, "however, if you still insist on doing something for me to pay for Clay-Boy's lessons, there is nothing that would mean more for me than to see you in church."

The full impact of what the preacher had said did not strike Clay right at first. But then as the meaning of what had been said began to sink into his brain, Clay whitened, but then his face turned red with frustration as he groped for words and not even profanity would come to his lips.

Mr. Goodson, still smiling his innocent smile, held out his hand and said, "See you Sunday?"

"I'll be there," said Clay grimly and took the preacher's outstretched hand.

"And I'll see you at the parsonage tomorrow morning at nine o'clock, Clay-Boy."

"Yes sir."

"I have all the textbooks we'll need, so you don't need to bring a thing. Good night, all."

Olivia walked to the front door with the minister.

When she returned to the kitchen she found that Clay had joined the children at the table and was busily buttering biscuits. He looked up at her and grinned wickedly.

"I'd like to shoot you with a gun," Olivia said.

"What's the matter with you, old woman?" he said.

"Promising that preacher you'd come to church," said Olivia. "You know good and well the roof would fall in if you ever set foot in it."

"You wait till Sunday morning," said Clay. "I made a bargain with that feller and I aim to keep it."

The following morning at nine o'clock Clay-Boy reported to Mr. Goodson at the parsonage. No mention was made of the price that was being exacted for the lessons. Together Mr. Goodson and Clay-Boy set out on the make-up program and by lunch time they had covered the first five lessons of Latin grammar.

In the afternoon at the library he reviewed what they had covered that morning and when night came, after supper, when all the dishes had been cleared away from the dining table, he sat down to study again.

"I want it quiet around here so that boy can learn his Latin," Clay said to the younger children. "If I hear a peep from anybody from now till bedtime they're goen to get a tannen."

All evening the children, the grandparents, Clay and Olivia went about their work or their preparation for bed as quietly as they could while Clay-Boy in the kitchen prepared his homework.

Somehow during the week word leaked out that Clay

Spencer was going to join the church. Since he had been known from his boyhood to be a heathen who smoked, played cards, drank whiskey and did all those things abhorrent to the Baptists of New Dominion, many doubted the truth of the rumor.

Clay's brother Anse came to him at the mill and said, "There's a lot of funnen and joken goen around about you joinen the church and I thought you ought to know about it."

"It's the Lord's truth, Anse," said Clay. "I've got religion."

"I never thought I'd see the day," said Anse wonderingly.

"I reckon I've been heathen enough for two men in my lifetime." said Clay. "Looks like it's about time for me to get on the right side of the Lord."

"You're doen it for Livy. Is that it?" asked Anse.

"Nope," said Clay. "I'm doen it for myself."

"Well," said Anse, "I think it's only fair to tell you that there's a whole crowd getten together to come to the church on Sunday just to see if it's true or not."

There was an extraordinarily large congregation at the service at the Baptist church the following Sunday morning. Often a woman had trouble dragging her man to church with her, but this morning as many men as women had attended. Standing aside from the group of regular churchgoers was another group, made up of known sinners and rousers.

There was Obed Miller, the village drunk, sober now and chuckling softly to himself for no apparent reason.

Slim Temple, the champion pool-shooter of the village, who was almost never seen outside The Pool Hall and who was closer to a church this morning than he had ever been before, stood uncomfortably at the edge of the crowd. Even Odell Harper, the village dandy, had turned up. What made Odell a dandy was that he traveled with a fast crowd of gamblers in Charlottesville and wore a suit all week end and even some working nights. All of them were good friends of Clay's.

Five minutes before the service was due to begin a little procession made its way out of Clay Spencer's yard and down the hill to the Baptist church. At the head of the group were Olivia and Clay. Following them, two by two, hand in hand, came their brood of red-headed children.

Only once did Clay show any sign that he recognized the stir their appearance caused. He was starting up the steps to the Baptist church when one of his cronies called out, "Great God Almighty, Clay Spencer's really goen in."

Clay turned, and over the head of the worshipers who were coming in behind him, called, "You're damned right I'm goen in there and it wouldn't do you bunch of heathens no harm to come on in neither!"

Olivia was blushing to the roots of her hair when Clay took her by the arm and led his family to a pew near the front of the church. As they entered every fan stopped dead and every whisper ceased. Clay had never been with his family to church before, but he was conscious that his entrance had attracted the eye of every worshiper. Olivia and the children sat stiff and straight, their eyes cast straight before them. But Clay sat still only for a moment before turning to examine his neighbors. Some of the men he had difficulty recognizing because he was so accustomed to seeing them covered with dust from the mill, and the women he had never seen before in their Sunday finery. Finally Clay's eyes met those of his mother-in-law, who sat looking with thanksgiving because the soul she thought was lost might now be saved after all. Clay returned her look with a reassuring smile and she said softly, but in a voice that could be heard by everyone in the silent room, "Welcome to the House of the Lord, Clay Spencer."

"I'm proud to be here, Miss Ida," he said and the fans began to fan again and the hushed voices began to whisper again and at least the initial crisis was over.

Preacher Goodson came out of his little study behind the rostrum. When he reached the pulpit he announced that the opening hymn would be Number 37.

Ordinarily the burden of the singing fell on the choir, which was led by Lucy Godlove and was composed of the best singers of the church. The others of the congregation merely held their hymnals in front of them and followed the words with their lips or hummed along with the choir.

Olivia found Hymn Number 37 and when she held the hymnal up Clay noted with pleasure that it was one of his favorite hymns, "When the Roll Is Called Up Yonder"—a spirited hymn and a joyous one to sing.

After the pianist's introduction the choir began to sing heartily, but from the congregation itself only one voice raised itself above a whisper. It was Clay Spencer and he was singing with a vigor that matched the entire choir.

When the trumpet of the Lord shall sound,
And time shall be no more,
And the morning breaks, eternal, bright and fair;
When the saved of earth shall gather
Over on the other shore;
And the roll is called up yonder, I'll be there.

Clay sang the opening stanza practically solo because even the choir had stopped to listen to his singing, but when the second stanza began Lucy Godlove gave a signal and the choir joined in the refrain. Then some members of the congregation began to sing, and by the end of the hymn it was as if a contest had developed between the choir and the congregation to see which could outsing the other.

For the remainder of the service Clay sat and listened attentively to Mr. Goodson's sermon. When people began streaming out of church after the closing hymn, Clay found his way blocked by Lucy Godlove.

"Clay Spencer," she cried, "a voice like yours was made to sing the Lord's praises. Next Sunday we'd be honored if you'd sit with the choir."

Olivia had been wondering whether Clay might continue going to church or if he had come only this once to satisfy the bargain he had made with Mr. Goodson, so she waited for Clay's answer with more than ordinary interest.

"You can count on me, Miss Lucy," replied Clay.

"Amen," said Lucy.

"Likewise," said Clay, and nodding amiably to people on all sides, he led his wife and brood out of the churchyard and up the road to his house.

For Clay-Boy time melted into one continuous Latin lesson. He worked with Mr. Goodson in the morning and alone in the afternoons and evenings. If he happened to look up from his book and catch sight of his sister he thought *puella*. If he saw a farmer on his way to the library he said to himself *agricola,* and if Patti-Cake, as she sometimes did, would throw her arms around him and say "I love you," he automatically repeated in his mind, *amo, amas, amat, amamus, amatis, amant.*

One night when it was near bedtime and when all the other children were asleep, Clay-Boy, tired of sitting, stood and walked around the kitchen, holding the textbook in his hands, and tried to keep awake. Once he came to the door to the living room where his parents and grandparents were talking quietly.

"How you doen, son?" Clay called.

"Pretty good, Daddy," he said, blinking out at them and becoming aware of his family for the first time since he had sat down to study three hours before.

"I can even read a little of it," he said proudly.

"I've never even seen what Latin looks like," said Olivia. "Let me take a look at that book."

She opened the book and examined the strange-looking words. "I don't see how you can make head nor tails of it," she said wonderingly. *"Larentia carnem cupit,"* she said. "What does that mean?"

Clay-Boy took the book. "It's an exercise you're supposed to translate into English. *Larentia carnem cupit.* That means Larentia wants meat. *Itaque Faustulus cum cane ad silvam discedit.* Which means, 'Therefore Faustulus,' I guess that's the husband, 'with his dog goes out into the woods.'"

"What happens next?" asked Clay, his attention attracted by the sound of a good hunting story.

Clay-Boy continued his translation slowly and with difficulty. "The man takes a bow and arrow. He sends his dog out there in the forest. Vegator—I guess that's the dog's name —runs through the forest. Faustulus waits down by the river. Finally the dog comes down through the woods chasing a deer. He runs quickly through the woods. The deer falls . . . flees to the river. Faustulus wounds the deer with an arrow and then kills it with a spear. With care he carries the deer home."

"I'll be damned," exclaimed Clay. "They must of been some kind of Indians or somethen shooten with a bow and arrow."

"No, they were Romans," explained Clay-Boy. "They lived over there where it's Italy now, where Mussolini lives."

"I'd like to shoot that old bohunk with a bow and arrow," commented Clay.

Old Zebulon stirred. Everybody had thought he was asleep but he had been listening to the story.

"It was a white deer," muttered the old man. "I told everybody when it happened it marked that boy."

A shiver went down Clay-Boy's spine. He had forgotten his grandfather's prophecy, made that day in the fall when he had killed the white deer.

"That boy will break new ground." the old man said. Clay-Boy had lived with superstition all his life and he did not find it at all difficult to believe that the killing of the deer had been an omen. But an omen of what? He did not have the time to speculate. He was too occupied learning Latin.

Claris came to the library every day. When he first began the Latin lessons he had been rude to her, had insisted that her visits took up his time, but she had adapted herself to the ordeal he was going through. She became less frivolous and cut out her teasing altogether, and when she offered to help him by hearing his vocabulary or translations he had accepted her help and she became as devoted to his cause as he was.

By the middle of August Clay-Boy and Mr. Goodson came to the end of the textbook. They spent a week in review and on Monday Clay-Boy spent three hours in examination. When Clay-Boy came home he carried a note which read:

This is to certify that Clay Spencer, Jr., has completed the equivalent of one high school semester of Latin. I believe him to be as proficient in the language as most college freshmen.

Clyde Goodson

When Clay-Boy gave the note to his father, Clay nodded with satisfaction and said, "Fine. We'll take it down to Dean Beck first thing in the mornen."

The campus of the University of Richmond was oddly deserted when Clay-Boy and his father arrived there at eleven o'clock the next morning. Clay remembered the building where he had found Dean Beck on his previous visit and was lucky enough to find it again. After parking the pickup truck he led Clay-Boy up to the Administration Building but found when he tried to open the door that it was locked.

"They must be closed here for the week end or somethen," said Clay.

He pounded on the door, but the sound of his knocking faded away and the pervading quiet settled over the morning again.

"Damn it," swore Clay, "I reckon we're just goen to have to come back another day. Might as well look around while we're here though."

Clay-Boy was wordless. The campus was the most beautiful place he had ever seen. He had tried to imagine how it might look, but had succeeded only in summoning up vague images of classrooms and blackboards and bearded professors. Now that he was here and walking along the pathways that crossed each other, each opening on a vista more beautiful than the last, he had the feeling that at any minute he might wake and find himself in his bed at home and the whole thing a dream. They came into a quadrangle where the Science buildings faced each other and Clay-Boy's mind surged with the realization that behind those windows, somewhere in those buildings lay the College Education, a magic passport to some unimaginable new and wondrous world.

Clay looked at his son and he could see the thrill and delight that were in the boy's eyes.

"It's a right pretty place, ain't it, son?" he said.

"I don't know what I'll do if they don't take me, Daddy," the boy said.

"They'll take you," said Clay. "You've done your part. From now on it's up to these folks down here."

They had started walking back to the parking lot behind the Administration Building when they saw coming toward them a man who was dressed in paint-spattered coveralls and carrying a ladder.

"Morning," the painter called. "Help you folks?"

"We come down here to see Dean Beck," said Clay. "But it looks like they're taken the day off."

"They're closed for vacation," said the painter. "Nobody around here but a few workmen."

"When they goen to open up again?" asked Clay.

"First week of school. Sometime in September usually."

"Damnation!" exclaimed Clay. "We've got to see that feller before then."

"I'd try up at his home, if I was you," said the painter. He gave them instructions for finding the dean's house and Clay-Boy and his father set out up the walkway, across the streetcar tracks into the wooded area where the members of the faculty lived.

When they came to the house the painter had described Clay's knock on the door was answered by Mrs. Beck, a handsome woman whose kind smile put both the boy and the man at ease immediately.

"I'm looken for Dean Beck," said Clay.

"Won't you come in?" she said.

Clay and the boy entered the house and were ushered into a warm and beautifully furnished living room. All the while Mrs. Beck chatted away about the beautiful morning and how pleasant the summer had been, and though neither Clay-Boy nor his father had uttered a word they felt that they had taken part in a brilliant conversation. Saying that she would go find the dean, Mrs. Beck disappeared somewhere into another part of the house.

Clay and Clay-Boy sat solemnly side by side on a comfortable sofa which had been covered for the summer in a light flowered slip cover. Clay lit a cigarette and after hesitating for a moment over a little glass dish, decided that it might be the ashtray and dropped his match there. Hearing footsteps approaching, both Clay and his son stood as the dean entered the room and came bouncing toward them.

"Neighbor Spencer, I'm delighted to see you again," he said.

"I'm sorry to butt in on your vacation," said Clay.

"Not at all," said the Dean. "It's the only time I have the time to really visit with anybody."

"This is my boy," said Clay.

The dean turned and looked at Clay-Boy in a quick but appraising glance.

"I'm glad to meet you," he said.

"How-do, sir," said Clay-Boy, returning the dean's firm handclasp.

"Sir," said Clay, "the last time I was here you said if Clay-Boy got a semester of Latin you'd let him in the college."

"I did indeed. I spoke to the other members of the Admissions Committee after you were here and they agree that young Clay should have every opportunity."

"Show him the note, son," said Clay.

Clay-Boy extended the note Mr. Goodson had given him. Dean Beck read it, folded it and placed it in a pocket in his jacket.

"Give my regards to Goodson when you see him," the dean said. "Registration and orientation begin the second week of September. I'll see you then, young man."

"Don't you even want to hear the boy speak any Latin, Dean?" asked Clay.

"Goodson's word is good enough for me. By the

way, is he a good preacher? He showed great promise when he was a student."

"I'll tell you how good a preacher he is, Dean," said Clay. "I been a heathen all my life, hadn't been to church since I was a boy, and right now I'm sitten in the Amen Corner every Sunday mornen."

"And it was Goodson who persuaded you to come to church?"

"I wouldn't say he persuaded me," grinned Clay. "Starten to church was the price he charged me to give Clay-Boy them Latin lessons."

"Forsan et haec ohm meminisse iuvabit," said the dean with a wink at Clay-Boy.

Clay looked puzzled.

"He said something good might come of that bad luck," explained Clay-Boy.

"Somethen already has," said Clay with a smile. "The rest of the choir has to sing so loud to keep up with me that we near about drown out the Methodists."

Clay and Clay-Boy sang all the way home. Mixed in with the Baptist hymns Clay would sometimes do a solo from his vast store of bawdy songs while Clay-Boy would grin in sheepish merriment.

It was only when they were in sight of home that Clay-Boy asked the question that had to be answered.

"Daddy," he said, "where are we going to get the money?"

"I'm goen to get that money, boy," he said. "I'm goen to borrow it off Old Man John Pickett."

"It's right smart money, Daddy," said Clay-Boy. "Are you sure he'll lend you that much?"

"I'm putten up the kind of security that Old Man John Pickett can't turn down," said Clay.

"What security you offering him, Daddy?"

"You'll see when the time comes, boy," said Clay. "Right now, looks like we're home."

He drove the truck up into the back yard. As soon as the truck stopped, the back door of the house flew open as Olivia, the grandparents and all the children came running toward them to learn the good news that was written all over the faces of Clay-Boy and his father.

CHAPTER 14

"THIS IS GOEN TO BE the catfish of the waters," Clay warned Clay-Boy as he looked up at the old oak tree he had decided to cut down.

The tree was diseased and would be pushed over by the wind in time to come. Clay had chosen to get rid of it now; if it fell in a storm it was close enough to the house Clay was building that it would undo all he had done.

Clay walked around the tree studying it carefully. He decided to cut it with an axe rather than slice through the trunk with the cross-saw he and Clay-Boy usually used.

"Too dangerous with all that rot in there, boy," he

said. "You back off a ways where it's safe and I'll tend to her."

Clay-Boy ran to the site of the new house and climbed over the foundation Clay had built and sat down. The foundation of the house was beginning to take shape now. Already the skeleton outline was visible for the kitchen, the pantry, the living room and the two downstairs bedrooms. If work went slowly now it was only because of time and the fact that Clay would accept no inferior piece of wood. If a two-by-four or a four-by-four went out of proportion in the sawing, Clay would reject it and start all over again. The sawing was all the more laborious because the power saw was designed for sawing firewood, not finished lumber. Yet Clay worked with joy every week end from sunup until darkness forced him to quit.

Sometimes Clay-Boy would watch his father sweating and cursing joyfully over the house, and the boy would wonder how it was that his father could envision the finished house so clearly. The boy could only see what had been accomplished; each new addition was a revelation to him. It also added to the pride he felt in his father when Clay would make some addition that brought the house closer to reality. He knew from his visits to the kitchens of the villagers when he delivered buttermilk and butter that some of the people felt his father was dreaming a foolish dream and that the house never would really be built. For a while Clay-Boy had shared these doubts, even though he defended what his father was doing, but now, during this summer, Clay-Boy saw that the house was no longer a dream but almost daily was assuming the shape of a good strong house.

He knew that his father expected to finish the house during the summer of the next year, and Clay-Boy planned to spend the entire summer vacation helping his father with the finishing touches, the painting of the inside walls, sanding the floors and plowing the yard so that grass might be planted. It was not a thing his father had asked him to do. The boy had promised it and the promise pleased Clay.

While Clay-Boy dozed in the sun and his father wrestled with the tree, farther down the hill from them Zebulon Spencer was cleaning up the family grave-yard. It was a job he did several times during the summer, and while there was really very little work to do there he used it as an excuse to go and sit in the place and think.

The graveyard was located in a grove of pines. A still whispering wind seemed forever moving through the green canopy overhead, and underfoot blue periwinkle covered the row after row of Spencer dead. The old family burial ground had been used for so many years that many graves were merely unmarked mounds. Others had sunk in, but Zebulon never failed to leave the place sobered and thoughtful after communion with his ancestors.

Zebulon threw out some pine branches that had fallen from the trees overhead and noted with pleasure that the white rhododendron they had planted on his mother's grave was growing well. Farther down the row he came to the grave of his brother, Ned. Chiseled in the soapstone marker were the words: *Ned Spencer. Fell at Bull Run. August 30th, 1862.*

Old ghosts came alive in the quiet morning and Zebulon remembered the days of his own growing up. He had been too young to go off and fight with Ned, but he had gone with his father in the wagon down to the train station at Esmont where the train stopped in those days and where they had left Ned's coffin off. His earliest memories were of Ned's being returned to them dead and then of the other boys coming back with tales of what had befallen them at Chickamauga, Antietam, Manassas and Chattanooga.

The old man dreamed for a long time, and when he woke he thought for a moment that he was back in the time when he and Eliza still lived on the mountain and that all he had to do was to walk up the hill and he would find the house they lived in and all the boys would be small again. But then as his mind became more fully awake and he heard the rhythmic sound of an axe eating its way into a tree, he remembered that Clay was cutting a tree this morning, that the old house was gone, had settled down into a pile of decayed wood.

He had not seen the house Clay was building in several months, so the old man left the graveyard and made his way up the hill.

He thought with pride of the house Clay was building. There were not many boys like Clay. Most of the men in New Dominion were happy to sit around all week end swilling down beer or Miss Emma and Etta's recipe, but not Clay. The boy was a cut above the other men in the village, and his father had always been proud of him. Another year and they'd all be living in the new house and they would all be back on the mountain again. There had been times when he had feared that Clay might follow the other boys' example and sell his part of the mountain, but now that the house was well under way, the old man was sure that Clay would never let the land go, had indeed promised his father that he would never let it go, and the knowledge that at least part of the mountain would always remain in the family had been a comforting thought to Zebulon.

Clay-Boy, half-asleep on the foundation, thought at first his father was calling to him.

"Papa, go back!" were the words he heard, but then as he sat up and looked to where the voice had come from every muscle in his body went rigid with the horror of what he saw. His grandfather stood transfixed, unable to move as he looked up at the tree which slowly and gently had begun to fall toward him. In that same instant Clay-Boy saw his father throw his axe aside and run toward his father, shouting as he ran, but even before Clay reached old Zebulon a splintering groan came from the tree trunk as it separated from its stump and then the crashing mass of green enveloped the old man and Clay.

As Clay-Boy ran toward the fallen tree he cried

aloud to God making incoherent promises and impossible bargains that he would keep if only somehow he could find his father and grandfather alive under the mass of green ahead of him.

Reaching the outer edges of the fallen tree, Clay-Boy, wild with fear and dread, tried to claw his way into where he thought his father and grandfather lay, but the crushed and broken branches were too thick, and even his animal-like efforts could carry him no further.

He heard someone screaming "Daddy! Daddy! Daddy!" and when he recognized his own voice and the hysteria in it he realized he must gain control of himself before he could be of any help to his father and his grandfather if they were not already beyond help.

Slowly, trying to regain reason, he backed out of the entangling leaves and limbs and ran to the base of the tree and inched himself along the trunk through a tunnel of green. The hysteria returned as he called again and again, "Help me, God. Help me, God. Help me. God."

Suddenly, when he had come midway the length of the tree he saw underneath him his father's shirt.

"Daddy," he called, but no answer came. If only the shirt might move or show some sign of life. He waited, fearing to know if life were there or not, for if his father were dead—if all that vitality and strut and swagger and joy could have gone so quickly out of life—then the world might as well be dead. Nothing would have meaning without him. Immediately beneath Clay-Boy was a medium-sized branch of the tree. The boy reached down and slowly pulled the branch toward him and as he did so he revealed gradually the chest and then the throat and finally the face of his father. Clay's eyes were open, whether in life or in death, Clay-Boy could not tell.

His hand was shaking violently, but when he reached down and touched his father's chest and felt life there, he began to cry and pull at his father's body in insane belief that he might extricate him from the tree. Finally he realized that he could not do it alone and the boy clawed his way out of the twisted and broken branches and ran down the mountain toward the village for help.

He had run so hard and fast that he could hardly speak when he came to the house closest to the mountain. It happened to be the Baptist parsonage and as soon as he had sobbed out to Mr. Goodson what had happened, Mr. Goodson sent him off to find more men and the doctor and went roaring off toward the mountain in his car.

Continuing on into the village, Clay-Boy stopped at one house after another until a stream of men and cars was set in motion toward the mountain. Finally he reached the doctor's house.

Doctor Campbell was writing "Am delivering the Bland baby" on the slate that hung outside his door, but when Clay-Boy told him what had happened, he said, "Estelle Bland has had enough babies to know what to do. Jump in the car, son."

By the time Doctor Campbell and Clay-Boy reached

the mountain the men had removed Clay from the wreckage of the tree. He was stretched out on the ground and he was alive.

"I'm all right except for this leg, Doc," he said. "Go in there and see if you can do anything for Papa."

Clay-Boy looked down at his father's leg and saw with a wave of nausea that below the knee the leg was bent in a way that no leg should he.

Doctor Campbell knelt and looked at the leg, but Clay said. "Dammit, Doc. Take care of Papa."

Doctor Campbell went to the trunk of the tree and made his way along it to where a group of men were sawing and chopping at limbs and branches in order to get to Zebulon. "Ain't this hell, son?" said Clay.

"Is Grandpa dead, Daddy?" asked Clay-Boy.

"I hope to God he ain't," said Clay. "I wasn't halfway through that tree; it didn't appear anywhere near ready to fall. I heard her give a little and then I looked out there, and God Almighty, there was Papa. I hollered at him, but either he didn't hear me or he was just froze to the spot."

After a while the doctor came out of the tree and knelt down beside Clay.

"He's alive, Clay," said Doctor Campbell, "but it won't be for long. He's broke nearly every bone in his body." He took a pair of scissors out of his bag and began cutting away at the trousers around Clay's broken leg.

"Son," he said to Clay-Boy, "there's a bottle of whiskey over in the glove compartment in my car. Get it for your daddy. He's going to need it."

Incredibly, old Zebulon was still alive when the last branches of the tree were cleared away, and he clung to life while his body was somehow placed on a stretcher and started down the torturous twisting wood trail that led to the foot of the mountain.

Clay-Boy had run on ahead to prepare his mother and grandmother. He found his mother in the kitchen and he forced himself to stop trembling before he entered the door. Nevertheless, Olivia knew.

"Son," she cried, "what's happened?"

"Daddy's all right, Mama," Clay-Boy said, "he's all right."

"Then what's the matter?" she cried. "You're white as a sheet."

"They had a little accident . . . up on the mountain," Clay-Boy said, attempting to keep calm.

"Who?"

"Daddy and Grandpa," answered Clay-Boy.

"Oh God," screamed Olivia. "What happened?"

"Mama," said Clay-Boy, "you've got to sit down and listen to me. They're all right. They're bringen them home now, but they're all right. It was the tree Daddy was cutten. It fell on Grandpa and Daddy came runnen, and it fell on him too, but he's just got a broken leg. Grandpa's a little worse, but the doctor's with him and he's doen everythen he can."

Once more Olivia screamed, "Oh God," and ran out into the yard, gathered up the children and herded them all into the kitchen where she left them in Clay-Boy's care. Sensing that some terrible thing had happened they sat in unaccustomed quiet and whispered in fear and apprehension.

And then the sound of unfamiliar voices, hushed and sympathetic, came into the house as the neighbors brought Clay and his father home. They placed Clay, with his leg in a temporary splint, on the sofa in the living room. The old man they carried into his room and without removing him from the stretcher laid him out on his bed.

Doctor Campbell allowed Eliza to stay in the room with him while he worked most of the afternoon on Zebulon. Once he came out and in a quiet conversation with Clay and Olivia suggested that Virgil be sent for. The other sons who lived in the community had already arrived and were sitting quietly on the front porch.

When he had done all he could do for the old man, Doctor Campbell left him alone with Eliza and gave his attention to Clay.

Sitting beside Zebulon's bed, Eliza suddenly heard him whisper her name. She took his hands in hers and bent to hear what he was trying to say.

"I'm goen over, old woman," he whispered.

"Rest now," she said.

"I want my will made out," he said.

"No need for that. You rest," she said.

"Get somethen to write on," he insisted, and Eliza left the room and returned a moment later with a pencil and one of the children's school tablets.

"Write it like I tell you," he said, and as Zebulon dictated Eliza wrote down his last will and testament. When it was over he sank back into a coma and was carried farther and farther away from her.

Through his last moments the old woman knelt beside his bed, holding his hand in hers. In the beginning, when she knew that he would die, she had faced the inexorable fact and yet hoped that prayer might return him to her for a few more days at least; she had prayed over and over again:

"Lord Jesus, give him time. Let him stay a little while longer. Lord God, be merciful on his soul." On and on her plea had sounded until it had become a mumble and the mumble had become a whisper and finally when she knew that not even God could keep the feeble flicker of life going she had composed herself and held his hand.

When life ebbed away, when the blood no longer made its spasmodic voyage through the hand she held, she looked at his face. The fierce old beautiful visage relaxed, and something not quite a smile, but akin to it, took its place, a waxed artificial slack expression that was neither pain nor joy but was simply death.

Something she could not name rose from forgotten wells and the old woman remembered her husband in the vigor of his youth. He had been a man to be proud of and the tears that fell from her old eyes were the tears of a young girl. Her grief spent itself when at last she took her warm hand from the cold dead one and prepared herself to tell those who waited beyond the door.

She opened the door and they knew.

"The old man's gone," she said with dignity and suddenly the arms of her sons were around her and they clung to one another and wept.

All that night the house was ablaze with light. The children were sent to their Grandmother Italiano's and Eliza sat in a chair in the upstairs room used by the girls. The women in the family took turns sitting with her while she sat, not speaking, her eyes set far away on some past, remembered thing. The other women busied themselves in the kitchen while in the living room the men were drinking whiskey and telling stories about the old man.

"I remember the only time he ever whipped me," recalled Anse. "I sassed him, and I don't remember what I said or what it was about but he near-about killed me. Used his strap and I'm here to tell you I never sassed Papa again to this day."

"Wasn't much of a hand for getten mad, but if you crossed him the wrong way, Papa was a good man with his fists," said Rome.

"Best hunter in his time till his eyes went bad on him," said Clay.

In the afternoon of the following day Clay was driven to the graveyard early and placed in a chair because of his broken leg. He waited there as neighbors and friends of the old man gathered to pay him their final tribute.

Then through the crowd, on their shoulders, his sons bore the body of the old man and lowered the coffin into the grave. They listened quietly while Mr. Goodson spoke the ritual, and when he had finished, Clay, who was the sweetest singer of all the sons, with a voice that was tight and choked began what had been the old man's favorite hymn.

On a hill far away stood an old rugged cross,
The emblem of suffering and shame;
And I love that old cross where the dearest and best
For a world of lost sinners was slain.

But as he sang his voice sweetened to the words and other voices joined his and they sang it so beautifully that no matter how far away, no matter where the old man might be listening, he could not have failed to hear the words:

So I'll cherish the old rugged cross
Till my trophies at last I lay down;
I will cling to the old rugged cross,
And exchange it someday for a crown.

When it was evening the whole clan gathered again in the living room at Clay's house. Eliza was composed now, and sat with her sons and their wives and told them stories of Zebulon in his young manhood and of their life together in the early days. Finally when it was late and the time had come for rest, she said, "Before everybody goes, we're goen to read his will."

"Papa never made out no will, Mama," said Clay.

"Yes he did, son," said Eliza. "I got it in yonder in my bureau. Everybody wait here for a second and I'll go fetch it."

When the old woman returned from her room she carried the sheet of paper from the children's school tablet. All noise in the room ceased as she sat down in her chair, put on her glasses and began to read:

"The old woman is writen this for me because I never learned to write myself. When you boys read this I'll be gone from this world and I hope you won't think hard of me for taken your hospitality all these many years and never letten you know I had money of my own. I was saven it hopen that when I died it wouldn't put no burden on nobody to bury me, but now the time is comen when I've got to face the Old Master and I want this money to go for somethen good. It's my heart's craven all my earthly riches go to my grandson, Clay-Boy Spencer, and for him to use it down at that college to make something of himself, for the good of him and the rest of the family too if they can get any benefit out of it. God bless each and every one of you. Stick to your guns; pay all debts; don't run with evil; and . . . and . . ."

Eliza began to cry and the paper fell out of her hands onto the floor.

Anse picked it up and read the closing words: "And take care of my old woman who has been a joy and a blessing to me all the time we endured together. Good-by from Zebulon Spencer."

Later that evening Eliza turned over to Clay-Boy the gold watch and the worn old black wallet which had belonged to his grandfather. In it were thirty-seven one-dollar bills.

At first Clay-Boy objected. "You keep it, Grandma," he said.

"No, boy," she replied. "It's your granddaddy's way of showen his faith and trust and it wouldn't be right for you not to take it."

Clay-Boy placed the money in his mother's hands for safekeeping. In the days that came he would think about the money and it became a kind of assurance to him. It was only a small fraction of the amount he would need, but it was a beginning.

CHAPTER 15

SLOWLY THOSE WHO lived in the house began to adjust to the loss of the old grandfather. Eliza could not endure to sleep in the room they had shared for so long together and went to visit some of the other sons, spending a week or two with each one before going on to stay for a while with a different set of in-laws and grandchildren.

Clay's leg was mending, but even so he sat on the front porch and cursed and grumbled at the passing of precious time he might have spent working on the house. When the summer's heat grew intense the skin beneath the cast began to itch, and every time Doctor

Campbell came to inspect the leg Clay would threaten to cut the cast off himself unless the doctor did it. Doctor Campbell was able to persuade Clay to keep the cast on only when he warned that premature removal of the cast might permanently injure Clay's leg.

One week Clay became obsessed with the notion that his house on the mountain was being stolen board by board, that thieves were carrying off his tools and his power saw and the treasures he had collected there. One morning, to put his father's mind at rest, Clay-Boy offered to go up on the mountain to check on the house.

Clay-Boy went through the kitchen to tell his mother where he was going.

"You want to go too?" he asked Claris, who was helping his mother bathe the twins.

"Sure," said Claris. "Just wait till I throw some powder on old Franklin Delano."

"I'll take him," said Olivia, retrieving Franklin Delano from Claris, who handled him as if he were a sack of potatoes.

After Clay-Boy and Claris disappeared down the road Olivia went about her work absent-mindedly. She was sorry she had allowed them to make the expedition. There were snakes on the mountain and all sorts of wild animals. But after a while Olivia admitted to herself that it was not danger from wild things that worried her, but the possibilities open to two young people alone on the mountain with no one to chaperone them.

"The best way to go," said Clay-Boy when they came to the foot of the mountain, "is up the creek bed. We won't run into so many snakes that way."

Claris shuddered. "You didn't tell me there'd be snakes."

"There won't be, except for water snakes, and most of them don't bite. Come on. Let's go."

Clay-Boy led the way. He stepped from one stone to another above the clear shade-dappled water that tumbled peacefully down the mountainside. Through one cool mossy glade after another, over the icy spring-fed water, Claris followed in his steps, agile as a boy. Once Clay-Boy saw a cottonmouth moccasin coiled around the base of a frond of ferns. He knew he should kill it because it was poisonous, but he was impatient to reach the top of the mountain and kept on past the snake, which did not stir.

"That's trailing arbutus there," he said, and pointed to a patch of the plant, "and over yonder under that pine tree is some creeping cedar."

"The arbutus is lovely, but I don't like anything that creeps," said Claris. "Where did you find out so much about plants?"

"My Grandma Spencer. She used to take us walken along the road and every time we'd see a plant she'd tell us the name of it. When I was a junior in high school I picked sixty-two different kinds of plant leaves and knew the names of all of them."

"Botany is not one of my passions," she said. "I'm

more interested in sociology. Give me a hand."

Clay-Boy turned back and helped her step up a slippery stretch of rock. It occurred to him that she was behaving more like a girl today than she usually did, and the thought made him feel vaguely superior and protective so that he started pointing out places where she should step with care or else he would wait and escort her over a place where she might have fallen or slipped.

Once when they found a broad rock that split the little stream they sat for a while and rested.

"This is the forest primeval," recited Claris, "the murmuring pines and the hemlocks."

"It sure is," said Clay-Boy. "Plenty wild."

"It's just as if there were just the two of us left in the world. Everybody else gone off somewhere," said Claris.

"Just us and the wildcats," said Clay-Boy.

"Are there any of those up here?" asked Claris with a shudder.

"Maybe," he said. "But they're nothing to be afraid of. Willie Beasley killed one one time and I saw it. Wasn't much bigger than a good-sized tom cat."

"What would you do if a wildcat jumped down here on this rock right this minute?"

"I'd say 'Go way, cat. I'm resting.'"

"No, I mean honestly."

"There isn't any point in talking about it because it isn't going to happen."

"All the same, I'm scared." They were lying on their

backs looking up at the patch of blue sky visible through the branches. Claris moved a fraction closer to Clay-Boy and feeling her near him he brought his arm over and around her protectively. Just as quickly she moved away indignantly.

"Now, don't go trying anything like that with me!" she exclaimed.

"Like *what?*"

"Like what you were trying to do just then."

"What was I trying to do?"

"You were trying to touch me and you know it."

Clay-Boy rose with equal indignation, but she did not give him time to speak.

"Just don't get any ideas," she warned. She got up from the rock and stepped out into the little brook again. Clay-Boy followed after her, sullen and angry that she had mistaken his protective gesture for anything more than what it was intended to be.

"Hey," he called suddenly. Claris stopped and looked back at him. "I'll go first," he said, "you follow me." Obediently she waited while he walked abreast of her, and then as he was about to go past her, Claris reached out and touched his arm and he stopped.

"I'm sorry I screamed at you," she said.

"I didn't try what you thought I did," he said.

"I'm a little jumpy today," she said.

"It's all right," said Clay-Boy. With Clay-Boy in the lead they continued on up the mountain. Once he stopped and pointed off through the trees.

"If you'll look right through that clearing in the trees

where the wood trail turns you'll see a stump," he said.

"What's so wonderful about a stump?" asked Claris.

"It's where I killed the deer," said Clay-Boy.

"Let's go over there," said Claris. "I'd like to see it."

Clay-Boy had not visited the spot since he had killed the deer there. Now as he stepped into the edge of the clearing he felt as if he were in some haunted place. The trees were in leaf now, and trillium and lady's slippers grew where he had plunged the deer's antlers into the snow. Remembering, a shiver went down his back and when he looked at Claris he found her gazing at him curiously.

"What?" he said.

"What are you thinking about?" she asked.

"Oh," he said. "That story my grandfather used to tell."

"Do you believe it?" she asked.

"Do you?"

"Something's happened to you since last year."

"What?"

"You're not a boy any more."

"It took you a long time to notice that," he said.

"No, it didn't," she said. "I just like to tease you."

"Come on," he said. "Let's look at Daddy's house."

They did not return to the creek bed but followed the old wood trail that led to the summit of the mountain. The skeleton of the house Clay was building remained as he had left it. Claris walked about on the floor joists and examined the exterior studs which would soon be ready for rafters while Clay-Boy checked on all his father's tools and equipment and found them intact, just as Clay had left them.

When he was satisfied that all was in order, Clay-Boy called to Claris and they started back down the mountain.

"You want to see an Indian mound?" asked Clay-Boy.

When Claris agreed that she would, he led her off the path into a field where the Indian mound was located. There was in the field the quiet of remote places where people seldom come. This field was broad and filled with high grass and bordered with pine trees. There was little sound and not much movement either, only the gently swaying grass as the wind passing through and the occasional swift flight of some bird disturbed the wild and private silence of the place.

Following a path that Clay-Boy knew, they came to a place where the tall grass had been flattened down. Clay-Boy said, "Some deer spent the night here. That's where they bedded down, there where the grass is all bent and broken."

Claris ran into the small bowl of flat grass and threw herself down into it.

"It's still warm from their bodies," she said.

"No, it's not," he said. "They've been gone since sunup. It's warm from the sun."

"It's nice," Claris said. "Come try it."

Clay-Boy came to where she was and sat down beside her. Her eyes were closed and she lay completely still. The aroma of the crushed grass and the earth and the sun-drenched air rose up around them, and for a long time they lay with their eyes closed and the warm noon sun caressing them.

"Just think," said Claris. "Only a few hours ago some wild beautiful thing lay here."

"I hope they didn't have fleas," said Clay-Boy.

"Oh, if you're going to talk like that, don't talk," said Claris crossly.

"All I said was . . ."

"Don't repeat it," interrupted Claris. "I thought you had a soul. I thought you were my wild witch boy of the mountains and all you can think about at a very important moment like this is fleas."

"It wasn't all I was thinking," said Clay-Boy.

"Oh, I know what else you were thinking," she said. "It's never out of your mind, is it?"

"What?"

"You're always thinking about it. I can tell. I can read minds and I've known all along you brought me up here just to try something."

Clay-Boy was wordless. Suddenly he realized that *it* could very well happen. He had dreamed of it, imagined it, anticipated it, yearned for it, and now it seemed that the mysterious and impossible thing could actually happen. He flushed with the pleasure of having, without really planning it, arranged the occasion so artfully. He knew he must make his next move with the utmost care. Too sudden a word might frighten or startle her and ruin his chances forever. While he searched about in his mind for just the right word to use, Claris spoke again.

"If you could be anything in the world you wanted to be, what would you be?"

"I'd like to be rich so I could go to college," Clay-Boy answered. "What would you be?"

"I'd be a nudist," Claris replied lazily.

"I guess that would be kind of fun," agreed Clay-Boy.

"I'd go off somewhere to the end of the world, some place without fences or people where nobody could see me and just let the sun and the wind seep right down into the marrow of my bones. I think that's what God intended us to be anyway. I'd be one right now if you weren't here."

"I could leave you alone for a while if you want," replied Clay-Boy.

"Do," said Claris. She sat up in the grass and stared at him. "What are you waiting for?"

Clay-Boy moved out of the grass where the deer had slept and into the path.

"You could use a little sun yourself," she called as he moved away.

Clay went a few yards and when he came to a turnoff he stepped off the path and into a sunny clearing beside a scrub pine. First he peered up toward where Claris was but the foliage was too thick and he could not see her. Next he proceeded to unbutton his shirt, fighting all along with his strait-laced Baptist conscience. It was only when he made a half-hearted promise to himself that he would only get out of his clothes and right back into them again that he allowed himself to remove his shirt and trousers and toss them over the pine tree. Standing there in his underwear and his shoes and socks he felt uncomfortable and conscious of the picture he would present if someone should happen by.

Discarding his undershirt and shorts he felt even more uncomfortable, and it was only when he shed his shoes and socks that he began to enjoy the sensation of being absolutely naked in the noonday sun.

Cautiously he stepped out of the clearing onto the path again and there above him, her back to him, was Claris. She was loosening the coils of hair at the back of her head, running her hands through them to shake them loose. Clay-Boy could hardly breathe.

When she turned he expected her to run screaming back into the grass. Instead, she continued to run her hands through her hair and asked in a half-teasing, half-serious voice, "What do you think of me?"

"I think you are beautiful," Clay-Boy heard himself say.

"You're not. You're all bony and knobby-kneed and your neck is red and the rest of you is white as flour." She gave him another critical look and with a sudden surge of modesty his hands went down to cover himself.

Suddenly Claris ran at him and pushed him so violently that he fell backward into the grass. When he got up she was running through the grass away from him. He watched her for a moment and then ran after her.

She did not look back, seeming not to know or to care if he were behind her.

When at last he caught up with her, he reached out and touched her shoulder. She gave a sharp cry and spun around to face him. She met him in the full force of his running and it carried them with their arms around each other to the grass.

The shadows of the late afternoon sun were lengthening across the field when they returned to where they had left their clothes. Clay-Boy dressed quickly in the spot where he had left his. They were hot from the sun and it was only when he was dressed that he remembered how sensitive his skin was to the sun, but it was too late now and his skin began to chafe and grow even hotter under the sun-warmed clothes. Nevertheless he felt pleased and possessive and full of love as he came up the path to where he had left Claris.

For the first time since he had known her she was shy with him, and she offered no resistance when he put his arms about her and held her to him.

"Tell me again that you love me," she said.

"Why?" he asked.

"I just like to hear it," she said.

"I love you," he said. Hand in hand they walked down the mountain. Claris chattered like a jaybird all the way home and Clay-Boy listened, silent, amused, indulgent, inflated with love and ownership of that most precious possession—his girl.

It was only when they came back into the village that

they let go of each other's hands; at the gate to her father's house Clay-Boy wanted to kiss her again, but he did not for fear her father might be watching out of the window.

"I hope I'm not pregnant," said Claris, looking up at him impishly.

"What made you say that?" he asked, his voice betraying the horror he suddenly felt.

"Good night, lover," she said and went running into the house.

When he came to his own home Clay-Boy found his father sitting on the front porch and he reported that the house on the mountain was in good order and then Clay-Boy went directly to his room. What had happened, he felt, must clearly show in his face and he was not yet ready to confront his mother.

He delayed going to supper that night until his mother had called him three times, and when he came to the table he had no appetite.

"What's the matter with you?" his mother asked. "Nothing, Mama," he said.

"Somethen's the matter with you," said Olivia. "You're all flushed and looks like you're comen down with somethen to me. Let me feel your forehead and see if you've got a fever."

Olivia felt his forehead and he flinched, feeling that what troubled him was so obvious that she might guess what it was merely by touching his head.

"Just feel a little sunburnt," she said and placed a heaping plate of food in front of him. "I been keeping your supper warm for you. Now eat."

Clay-Boy made himself eat the food, hoping that would avert their suspicions. As soon as he could, he excused himself from the table and went into the bathroom.

His father might have guessed part of the truth for after Clay-Boy left the room, Clay said to Olivia, "I think that boy's in love."

Olivia grunted despairingly. "That little girl will be gone in a week or two and I'll be glad to see it. You know what she said to me? Sitting there at the table she asked me if my uterus was back in place yet from having the babies. Where she ever learned such things in the first place is beyond me."

"What did you tell her?"

"I told her it was none of her business. She's always talken like that, and the things she must have put in Clay-Boy's head God only knows."

In the bathroom Clay-Boy was applying Noxzema to the more painful portions of his sunburned skin when the door opened abruptly and Shirley started into the room.

"Get out of here!" he shouted.

"I just want to use the bathroom," said Shirley indignantly. "You aren't using it. Why can't I?"

"Oh God," moaned Clay-Boy, "can't I ever have any privacy around here?"

"All right then," said Shirley, "but the next time I'm using it, don't you holler at me to hurry up."

She slammed the door and marched in the kitchen

where she announced, "Clay-Boy's the craziest thing."

"Well, honey," said Olivia, "you ought not to walk in the bathroom when somebody else is usen it. Just wait your turn."

"He's putten Noxzema on his fanny," said Shirley.

"What in God's name is he doing that for?" asked Olivia. "Clay, you go in there and see what he's doen. He won't let me in the bathroom with him any more. Says he's too big. You go in there and see what that boy is doen."

When Clay walked into the bathroom he could see that even though Clay-Boy had smeared the white salve over his buttocks *they* were still a bright and angry red.

"Let me give you a hand there, son," he said, and taking the jar of Noxzema he covered the places on Clay-Boy's back which the boy had not been able to reach.

"You want to talk about anythen, son," Clay asked after a while.

"What do you mean, Daddy?" Clay-Boy asked innocently.

"Son," said Clay, "if a man's been away all day long with a girl and comes home with his backsides all sunburned, that don't mean but one thing, in my way of seein' it."

Clay-Boy turned and faced his father. He could not tell if his father was angry or pleased.

"I'd appreciate it, Daddy," he said, "if you wouldn't let on to Mama."

"I don't see no point in it," said Clay. "There ain't a damn thing anybody can do about it now. Except next time, if I was you, I'd try to find a shady place."

Claris appeared quite dramatically a few evenings later while the Spencers were at supper. Most of the summer she had worn blue jeans and a shirt, but tonight she had on a suit and was wearing high heels.

"Hi there, little girl," said Clay, "sit down and have some supper."

"Thank you, but I really can't stay. Daddy's waiting for me down at the front gate. He's in a terrible hurry, but I just couldn't go without saying good-by to my favorite family."

"You're leaven early this year," said Olivia, only half-concealing her relief.

"Yes," said Claris mysteriously. "Something's come up."

"I always use you for my almanac to tell me when summer starts and when it's over. Looks like with you goen back to Washington, D.C., now, we're in for an early frost."

Claris gave everybody a hug and a kiss except Clay-Boy. When she came around the table to where he was sitting she said, "You can walk with me down to the car if you want to." He rose and followed her out of the door. In the front yard he pulled her over behind a forsythia bush where they could not be seen.

"What's this all about?" he asked.

"Something wonderful is going to happen," she said.

"What?"

"I don't want to spoil the surprise now," she said. "I've got to wait until I'm sure. I'll write to you."

"I hate to see you go."

"Do you love me?" she said.

"I really do," said Clay-Boy and took her in his arms.

"It's going to be so fine," she said.

"What?" he asked.

"When we're together always," she said, then broke out of his arms and ran to the waiting car.

Within three days after Claris left Clay-Boy received word from his Aunt Frances, the postmistress, that a letter was waiting for him and that it could be picked up at the post office.

He opened the letter with pleasure and read it with mounting horror.

Dear,

You may wonder why I do not address you as "Dear Clay-Boy" or "Dear Lover" or "Dear One," but all those names merely limit our relationship so that when I call you "Dear" it is to imply that you are dear to me and also that you are Dear Lover, Dear Clay-Boy and Dear One.

My return home was quite dramatic. I found Mother quite inebriated entertaining oceans of guests and they welcomed me into the circle and gave me sips of champagne which I adore. Of this I tired quickly and transported myself to the kitchen where I threatened Hazel I would tell everyone about her past if she didn't give me a full glass which she did poste haste, I can assure you. Afterwards feeling quite gay, I rejoined the party and entertained them for hours with anecdotes about life and love in them thar hills. I was divine.

The above paragraph is an abominable lie. What really happened was that Mother met me (God, how can I lie so?) at the station and was quite severe with me for not having written all summer and scolded me endlessly for my fingernails not being Borax clean. She says I look "womanly" and I was dying to tell her about us and of course I will have to if anything develops. At the moment my belly is still dismally flat but then it's still too early to know.

I love you desperately and think of your funny freckles and your beautiful red hair and the funny way you blush when I am outspoken. Please write me of your love. Please never think of it as an affair, although I suppose it was that too, but please, please, please, never call it that.

Give my enduring love to all those adorable little brothers and sisters.

Please don't worry.

Yours till the kitchen sinks,
Claris E. Coleman

P. S. I met a cute boy on the train but I did not flirt. Be true to me.

Clay-Boy tore the letter to shreds and threw the

pieces away. Later he returned to where he had thrown the pieces, collected as many as he could find and burned them.

He became a sleepwalker and both day and night went about like a person in a daze. Some nights he would toss and turn in his bed, his whole body flushed with dread of the day her father would come galloping up to the door on his horse. In some of his dreams the Colonel rode right into the kitchen and without even dismounting slashed the air with his riding crop and demanded vengeance.

Clay-Boy would imagine the disbelief and then the sorrow that would cross his mother's face when she realized that it had indeed happened. He had ruined the daughter of the manager of the company. He had no idea what the Colonel would demand of him, but it was certain that his father would lose his job at the mill and with no way to make a living in New Dominion they would have to move to some other place.

CHAPTER 16

THERE CAME A DAY when Clay could no longer stand the cast on his leg, so on a Saturday morning he took his fishing rod and reel and hobbled down to Rockfish River. After carefully casting his baited hook out into a productive-looking pool he sat down on the edge of a rock and gently lowered his cast-encased leg into the water.

Late that afternoon Olivia sat on the front porch to get a breath of fresh air before going into the kitchen to prepare the evening meal. She could see Clay coming up the road, but it was not until he came through the wisteria arch over the front gate that she saw him clearly. He was holding a long string of catfish and as he came toward her Olivia saw for the first time that the leg he had broken was bare from the knee down.

"Clay," she cried, "what happened to your cast?"

"I threw it in the river," he said happily.

"You come up here and sit down," she demanded. "I'm goen to send for the doctor."

"Don't do that, woman," he said. "I don't need *any* doctor to tell me when my flesh is well."

"It wasn't your flesh," said Olivia. "It was your bone."

"Flesh or bone, whatever it was, it's all well now," he said and continued on around to the back of the house, where he proceeded to skin the catfish for supper.

It was little Shirley who made the comment which was to forecast what the day might bring when at breakfast the following morning she observed, "Daddy don't look like Daddy."

Because Clay was going to Mr. John Pickett's place that Sunday to borrow the money to send Clay-Boy to college he had dressed in his white shirt, white duck trousers and white oxfords Virgil had given him many summers ago.

Clay didn't dress in light colors often. Weekdays he

wore blue or gray denim shirts and trousers to match. To church he usually wore his dark blue suit, but no one had ever seen him all in white before.

"You look nice, Clay," said Olivia. "You ought to dress in that outfit more often."

"Don't I look like a peacock though!" he replied and came up behind Olivia, who was frying eggs, and kissed her on the back of her neck.

"Stop that, you old fool. I'm tryen to get these children some breakfast."

"You better be careful how you talk to me, woman. With these glad rags on it wouldn't surprise me if I wasn't kidnapped by some good-looken woman before the day is over."

"She's welcome to you, you silly old rooster."

"Lord, that woman loves me!" said Clay to the children and winked broadly at them. "How are my babies this mornen anyway?" he made the round of the table, kissing and hugging everyone.

After breakfast Clay took the tin milk pail and went to the barn where Chance, the cow, had been lowing for her breakfast. As usual Chance had taken her position in front of the trough where she was always fed and where Clay usually milked her, and that is where he found her. Following his usual procedure he mixed her feed and went past her head and dumped the mixture in her trough.

Ordinarily Chance was a peaceful cow. She had never kicked and was by nature so gentle that Clay had seen no reason to have her dehorned, so that from her head sprouted two gracefully curved and quite sharp horns.

This morning she was fractious and though Clay noticed her erratic behavior he failed to realize that Chance just did not recognize him in his white clothing. When Clay poured the feed into her trough, hungry as she was she lifted her head, refused the food and bolted past him out of the barn and into the pasture. A few yards away she turned and looked back at the barn, peering distrustfully at Clay in his white shirt and trousers and lifting her head up and down in a troubled way.

"Come back here, you hellion!" shouted Clay as he came out of the barn in pursuit of her. As he advanced toward her Chance backed away. At first she had only appeared to be frightened, but now her eyes grew angry. She was hungry and needed to be milked and had no time for the advancing white-clad stranger.

But Clay was a stubborn man and the faster she backed away from him the faster he advanced upon her. Finally she stopped and something in her eyes told Clay that he would be wise to advance no farther. He realized too that she had lured him too far out into the pasture for him to run to safety if she should advance on him.

Chance evidently realized her advantage, for she charged. Coming at Clay with a fury he had not known she possessed, her head down, the horns aimed squarely for him, he realized that his only chance was to try to outrun her.

Because of the leg he had broken he could not run as fast as he thought he could, but still he was only a few yards from the barn when Chance caught up with him. When she did she caught him full in the seat and, tossing her head up, sent Clay flying through the air. The entire seat was ripped out of his pants and two long red streaks showed on his backside where her horns had made their mark.

Oblivious to Clay's curses and with threads of his white trousers still clinging to her horns, Chance trotted calmly into her stall and began to eat her breakfast.

"Lord God, Clay," cried Olivia when Clay came to the house and set the bucketful of warm foaming milk on the table. "What happened?"

"Oh," said Clay casually, "one of them good-looken women *did* try to kidnap me. I fought her off, but still she bit me powerful bad."

After his wounds were dressed and he had changed into another pair of trousers, Clay escorted his family to church as usual. As soon as the service was over he loaded his family into the pickup truck he had borrowed for the day and set out for Mr. John Pickett's farm. Olivia and the twins rode in the front seat with Clay while it was Clay-Boy's job to ride in the body of the truck and see that the younger children sat down so that they would not fall out.

Mr. John Pickett lived on a high bluff overlooking Rockfish River twenty miles from New Dominion. According to legend, his home had been designed by Thomas Jefferson; in the early days Mr. John's family had been people of means and influence. Now there was only Mr. John who lived alone in a house full of Federal antiques and pictures of his relatives. That he was rich was widely known. He even boasted of his money when he was drinking, but when he was sober he pretended to be the poorest man in the county.

He was sitting on the front porch dozing in the summer sun when he saw the pickup truck stop at the front gate and a man and a woman and an army of small children start up the walk.

"How you doen, Mr. John," the man called heartily.

"Clay Spencer, ain't it?" the old man said, peering down at the approaching group. "Who's that you got with you?"

"Brought the whole family," said Clay.

"Y'all come on up here and find a place to sit," said Mr. Pickett. "How you, Mrs. Spencer?" he said and shook hands with Olivia. "Sit down there, Clay. I didn't expect to lay eyes on you till hunten season. Birds is plentiful this year."

"I'm glad to hear it, Mr. John," replied Clay. "Mr. John, I come down here on a matter of business."

"Sit down, Clay," urged Mr. John. "Talk."

"Mr. John," said Clay, "I come down here to borrow a piece of money off you. I wanted you to know that right off the bat. There ain't a thing I can offer you for collateral but what I stand for. That ain't much in dollars and cents, but I figure what I've got here in this woman and these babies is worth more than a million dollars. You know me and my family before me and I don't have to tell you we've been decent people because Mama and Old Papa brought us up that way. You know Livy there and never a soul wore shoe leather better than her mama and daddy. Well, we've got ourselves a passel of babies there and I want you to take a good look at 'em."

Mr. John peered willingly at the group of smiling children who were seated quietly on the steps.

"That biggest boy there is my oldest," continued Clay. "He's named after me, and I don't mean to brag, but he's just as smart as a pistol. That boy graduated from the high school up at New Dominion last May and he made the highest score anybody ever set up there yet.

"Next one there is Matt. He ain't but eleven years old, but that boy can do anythen with his hands. He's got mechanical ability I've never seen in a grown man. That boy is goen to turn out to be a master mechanic one of these days or I'll eat my words.

"That little girl sitten next to him is Becky. She's independent as mud and ain't scared of the devil. She says she wants to grow up and be a nurse and I'll be damned if I don't believe she'll do it.

"That one sitten next to her is Shirley. Named her after Shirley Temple, and if I could raise the money I'd send her to Hollywood, California, and get her in the movies. She's a little prissy, but she'll get over it in time to come.

"You got a piano in the house, Mr. John?" asked Clay.

"I did have once, but some chickens got in there and roosted on it one time when I was off somewhere and it don't play no more," said Mr. John.

"Reason I asked," said Clay, "is I wish you could hear that Luke there play a piece of music for you. That boy is a master hand at piano-playen. Nobody ever showed him how. It was just born in him to make music and one day he seen a piano, went up to it and started playen. I think that is a right remarkable thing, but it's the truth as long as I live.

"Sitten next to him there is Mark. Now that boy is goen into business one of these days. It wouldn't surprise me if he didn't open his own store or fillen station or somethen. He's got it in him to make money, and there ain't a lazy bone in his body.

"That little feller down on the bottom step is John. We don't know what he's goen to be yet, but he's got a knack for drawen things. You ask him to draw somethen and he'll make you a picture of it plain as day.

"That little girl there is Pattie-Cake and it's too early yet for her to do anything but kissen and huggen and she's pretty good at both.

"The baby is Donnie and there's two more down in the truck. I'll bring 'em up here for you to take a look at if you want to see 'em."

"You got yourself a mighty fine family, Clay," agreed the old man.

"Thank you, Mr. John," said Clay. "If they're turned out to be a bunch of throwbacks, maybe I wouldn't care so much, but every one of these babies is thoroughbreds. That's why I got heart and craven to see 'em amount to somethen in this world and that's why I'm aimen to send that oldest one there off to college. I figure if he can get a start in life he can help Matt, and Matt can help Becky, and it can work right on down the line. I'll tell you another thing, Mr. John. It ain't just for my family I'm tryen to see this thing work. I figure it'll be a benefit to the whole country because if just one little boy or girl can go on to make somethen of theirselves then that'll clear a path for the other deserven ones to follow."

"I sympathize with you, Clay," said Mr. John.

"Well, sir, I hope you sympathize enough to put up a little cash money."

"Clay, I don't lend money to everybody."

"I know that, Mr. John."

"And I ain't got as much money as I let on sometimes when I've had one or two drinks."

"I ain't asken to borrow a lot, Mr. John."

"How much you figuren you're goen to have to lay out to get that first one educated?"

"Well, sir," said Clay, taking a notebook out of his pocket. "Here's how she adds up. My brother, Virgil, down there in Richmond is given him his food and his board. The boy is goen to find himself a job of work at night so he can take care of his streetcar money and books and supplies like that. That leaves the sum of two hundred and thirty-five dollars that's got to be paid in cash money to the college on the day he starts. I don't know what a one of these things is, but there's a sixty-dollar payment for what they call a College fee, five dollars for a Contingent Fee, twenty dollars for a Student Activities fee, and ten dollars for a Laboratory fee. There's something else called a Tuition that comes to a hundred and fifty dollars a year, but they'll take seventy-five dollars now and we've got till February to raise the other seventy-five. What I'm asken you to lend me, Mr. John, is the sum of two hundred and thirty-five dollars."

Mr. John took off his hat and scratched the rim of gray hair that bordered his bald skull.

"Dependen on whether I can scratch it together, Clay, how you aimen to pay me back?"

"Me and the old woman have put considerable thought to that. We've worked it out so we can save ten dollars a month. I'll bring it down to you the first of every month, same as I did when I bought that power saw off you. If I die or anything you'll still get your money because the company carries a five-hundred dollar life insurance policy on every man that works there and Livy here will see that it's paid in full out of the insurance."

Olivia nodded her agreement and took heart from the expression on Mr. John's face, for he seemed about to agree to the loan.

From time to time Clay had been conscious that someone or something had moved behind the curtain that hung over the window facing the long porch. When he had finished his plea to Mr. John Pickett a voice spoke from behind the curtain.

"Mr. John," it said. "You come in here. I want to have words with you."

Mr. John looked sheepishly at Clay and Olivia. When he did not speak for a moment the voice came again. It was young and it was female and it pouted.

"You hear what I'm tellen you, Mr. John?"

"I hear you, Minnie-Cora," he answered. "You come on out here and meet some nice folks."

"I don't reckon I can do that, Mr. John," the unseen Minnie-Cora answered, "seein' that I ain't got a stitch of clothes on. This hot weather and all I can't stand nothen to touch my body. You come on in here, Mr. John. I want to see you on some personal business between you and me."

Mr. John shook his head and smiled at Clay and Olivia. "I reckon it's about time I sprung a little surprise on you-all."

He caught sight of the shocked expression in Olivia's eyes and realized that it was well past time for him to spring his little surprise.

"You see, it gets kind of lonesome for an old man liven on here in the sticks by hisself. That boy of mine come over here whenever he want money and he don't do a blessed thing but sit and fidget the whole time he's here. And you know yourself, Mrs. Spencer, that an old man like me need somebody around to do the cooken and fixen. Why I could of died and laid over here for three or four weeks and nobody never would of known about it the way I was liven. So I didn't do nothen but up and get myself a little wife."

Clay was the first to recover from the news. "I'm glad to hear it, Mr. John," he said. "A man wasn't meant to live alone no matter how many years he's got on him."

"Mr. John, I'm waiten on you." Minnie-Cora's voice sounded plaintively from inside the house.

"It's what they call one of them May and December weddens," explained Mr. John in a pleased way.

"Then there has been a wedden?" asked Olivia and her voice was considerably relieved.

"Why of course there's been a wedden," answered Mr. John. "I'll tell you how it come about," he said, but Minnie-Cora's voice interrupted him.

"You tell 'em how it come about some other time. My Dr. Pepper's empty, and if I don't get a fresh one with some ice in it pretty soon I may just put on a piece or two of clothes and go on back over to my daddy's house."

"You be patient, honey," the old man said indulgently. "How it come about was like this. One day Percy Cook come down here looken for a bull of his that had got out of the pasture. Percy and me got to talken and I got to tellen him how scared I was that one day I'd pass on and lay over here for a week or more with nobody to go and fetch the undertakers. Percy agreed that it would be right smart of a shame and he claimed he had so many young ones around the place he'd never counted all of them and why didn't he send one over here to watch out for me. I said I'd be much obliged and the next day that gal in there showed up. Well, it didn't seem decent for a man and a woman to be liven as close as we was without benefit of preacher so one day we just got ourselves over to the preacher and we been man and wife ever since."

"We are not goen to be that way long if you don't haul yourself in here, Mr. John Pickett," called Minnie-Cora. "I have spoke my piece for the last time, and you can just like it or lump it."

"I reckon I better see what the little lady wants," said Mr. John. Using his cane to raise himself, he came slowly to his feet. "You-all excuse me a minute or two."

When he had gone in the house Olivia cast a disapproving look in Clay's direction, and when he saw it the delighted grin that had covered his face vanished. The children stood stiff and starched on the top step of the porch where Clay had arranged them. Clay called to them and said, "Y'all can go on down in the yard and play if you want to." But then Olivia said in a tight voice, "Stay where you are. We've been put here for collateral and we'll stay till we get an answer." The children remained where they were.

"Mr. Pickett, I'm still waiten in here," Minnie-Cora's voice came suddenly.

Mr. Pickett's voice floated down the long hall. "I'm on my way, sugar," he said. "I heard you say you was out of Dr. Pepper, and I went in there to the kitchen to get you a fresh one."

"I don't care nothen about no Dr. Pepper," said

Minnie-Cora, making no effort to keep her voice down. "I just wanted you in here so I could have a word with you."

"All right, sugar," Mr. John said. "What you want?"

"Them people are after money, ain't that it?"

"They come over here on a matter of business, that's right."

"Well, you tell them to take their business somewheres else."

"Sugar, I been thinken about letten Clay Spencer have the money. I knowed his Daddy and I know him and he's a man of his word. The money will come back to me in time."

"I'm tellen you not to let it go, Mr. John."

"Sugar," Mr. John's voice came floating out on the porch. "You are not the boss of me."

"I don't care about bein' no boss," said Minnie-Cora. "All I'm announcen to you is if you let any money out of this house I am setten my sails with it."

"Sugar, now you listen to me," Mr. John said, and then his voice became low and pleading and those on the porch could not hear what he said.

The next thing they heard was Minnie-Cora shouting, "I don't care. You said you'd name me in your will so it's already my money. Let 'em have it and you don't ever come messen around me again."

Olivia bristled. "I reckon that ain't fit talk for my children to hear," she said to Clay and rose. "We're goen back to the truck. You can stay here if you want to."

"Honey," said Clay, "he ain't said *no* yet. There's still a chance for us."

"Not much," said Olivia. "Come on, y'all," she said to the children. "We'll wait for your daddy in the truck." In a procession they marched to the truck and sat down looking back up at the old house.

Clay rose from his seat, went over and sat down on the porch swing. The creaking of the rusty old chain made a welcome sound, for all had fallen silent in the house. For a long time he waited. Once he heard a loud deliberate giggle come from somewhere in the house.

After a very long time Mr. John came shuffling past the door and looked out with pretended surprise when he saw Clay still sitting there.

"I didn't know you was still there, Clay Spencer," he said.

"I'm still waiten for an answer, Mr. John."

"Clay, I'd like to help you out, you know that, but I've got a little family of my own now that's got to be looked after."

"Mr. John," pleaded Clay, "you'd get that money back. I'll even give you interest if you ask for it."

Mr. Pickett made a helpless gesture with his hands, and Clay realized he had been given his final answer.

"Thank you all the same, sir," he said, and walked down the steps and out into the roadway. He did not speak when he got behind the wheel nor did Olivia. The children, sensing that something grave and disturbing had happened, sat still and quiet. The only sound that came from inside the cab of the truck came from one of the twins, who made an insane commentary of *ga-ga, ga-ga, ga-ga.* Finally, to end the noise, Olivia fed the child at her breast and they rode a long distance in silence.

Clay had been deeply hurt, and the hurt had come not entirely from Mr. John's refusal of the loan, but by his rejection of the collateral he had offered. It was Olivia who broke the silence.

"It is all the fault of that Minnie-Cora Cook. Oh, them *old* Cooks is trash and ought to be run out of the country on a pole. She's got that old man in a spell is what it is."

But Clay would not be comforted. As he drove he kept muttering aloud, "The son of a bitch. The mean old son of a bitch."

And for perhaps the first time in their lives together Olivia did not remonstrate with him for his profanity. Indeed, she wished she were a woman who swore. There were several words she would have liked to have used herself.

When they reached home Clay parked himself on the front porch and stared moodily off toward Spencer's Mountain. The children were sent to their rooms to change from their best clothes into clothes they might safely play in without ruining them and Olivia went into the kitchen to prepare the Sunday dinner. It was to have been a festive meal and she had even been extravagant the day before and used precious eggs and butter and sugar to make a chocolate cake. It was just as well she had made it, she reasoned now as she looked at it, proud and pretty there on the kitchen-cabinet shelf. The others would feel a little better for something sweet. It was a small thing, but it might help dispel the gloom that had overtaken the entire family.

When dinner was ready and on the table she called the children, who began trooping into the kitchen. When they were seated she went to the front porch to call Clay. He was gone.

She did not even bother to call him. She knew he had gone after whiskey. She knew that he would return, when he returned, crazed and mumbling old-dead hatreds and frustrations. Since it was Sunday and midday at that she knew it would be Tuesday before he could get back to work. He would miss a day from work and the money would be deducted from his pay-check. She blamed herself that he had gone away. He had been so cruelly hurt that she should have known, should have stayed with him until the hurt had ebbed away and he would not have needed to find solace in liquor.

She stood looking down at the empty road that ran in front of the house. The road led nowhere and every-where. Was Clay on it now, grinning and joking with anybody who came along who could offer him a ride to Miss Emma and Miss Etta's? Olivia looked at the little ribbon of road that threaded itself in front of the house and she hated it. It went nowhere. It was endless. All it did was circle back on itself. There was no Rich-mond, no college, no magic road that led out of New

Dominion. Why should she break her heart to send Clay-Boy down among a bunch of strangers and atheists? Why hadn't she and Clay known from the start that they were asking for too much? How could they have been such fools?

Clay-Boy had left the table, and when he came to the end of the hall, he saw his mother's figure outlined against the door to the front porch.

"Mama," he called.

She turned and he saw that her face was streaked with tears.

"What's the trouble, Mama?" he asked.

"I'll tell you what's the matter," she said angrily. "Just once we tried to do somethen in this world. Your daddy and me all our lives have been reachen out for somethen better for our children than we ever had for ourselves and what we got was a slap in the face and God forgive me, I can't find any excuse for it."

"Just don't cry, Mama," he begged. "Just please don't cry."

"I'll be all right in a minute," she said and began to dry her eyes.

She looked past Clay-Boy and saw that all the children had gathered there and that they too were near tears. She knelt down and held out her arms, and she was immediately covered with children and as she held them in her arms and felt their warm bodies pressing against her she regained her strength and led her children back into the kitchen where their meal was waiting.

• • •

The thought of Miss Emma's and Miss Etta's and the cool tin dipper of recipe had indeed crossed Clay's mind, but it was not where he headed when he left the house.

A half-formed thought was in his mind, and he had to be alone to work it out. He did not want to see any-body, and he was glad that this was the hour when most people were inside their homes enjoying their Sunday dinner. Earlier the front porches would have been pop-ulated by whole families who would sit and watch for someone to pass on the road, someone to talk to, someone to relieve the monotony that blanketed the place on a hot Sunday afternoon.

He walked down the hill and past the mill, dusty and silent now in the dreary waste of Sunday afternoon. At the mill he turned off the road and walked along the railroad track. This way he would not meet anyone and he could think quietly until he came to his destination. He walked five minutes until he came to Old Number Ten. This was one of the oldest quarries that had been opened, and the stone had been taken from it to a depth of more than three hundred feet. Clay had worked there on his first job with the company. He had been even younger than Clay-Boy was now, in his twelfth year, and his job had been to carry water to the men who were working down below. The quarry had been deserted for years now and had filled with water. Sometimes, if he had caught more fish than would be needed to feed his family, Clay had thrown them in the dark green water of Old Number Ten and they had flourished. As he watched he could see moving through the water the occasional dark shadow of a gigantic bass or carp.

Clay leaned over and tried to peer down through the dark deep green water and find some landmark his feet had touched as a child. Leaning over he experienced again the sickening feeling he had known when as a boy he had started to descend by ladder to the floor of the quarry. He had instinctively feared heights since birth and when he had taken the job he had been told simply that he was to be a water boy. Only when he reported to work did he find that the water was to be carried down into the quarry, that one hand would hold the bucket while the other hand managed his descent. As he lowered himself, step by step, there was on each step down one moment when he was supported only by his feet. Remembering it now made Clay involuntarily draw back from the edge of the drop.

"What's wrong with a man wanten somethen better for his babies than he had himself?" he asked the sullen empty August sky.

He walked back to the railroad track and continued on his way. When he came to the foot of Spencer's Mountain where the tracks turned off to follow the course of the small creek, he left the railroad bed and followed a path he remembered when as a boy he had come down to the creek to fish for minnows.

It always refreshed him to return to these woods. He had known them all his life and they held memories for him. He found an old tree which once held a great beehive. Often he had climbed up to the hive, his face protected by the mesh of an onion sack, his hands gloved, to smoke the bees out and then taken buckets of honey sweet with the scent of honeysuckle and wild grape and cherry blossom and rosebud. Now the tree had fallen and was rotting away into loam on the forest floor. Clay came to an ancient oak nearly strangled by a grapevine. When he was a boy Clay and his brothers had fashioned a swing of the grapevines and had swung far out over the side of the steep hill, closer to the sky—it seemed to him now—than he was ever to feel again. On his way up the mountain Clay came to the place where Clay-Boy had killed the white deer, and that mystical day returned to Clay's mind and Clay knew now that what had happened there in the snow on that cold November morning had been an omen and he knew now what the omen had been.

At the summit of the mountain, in the cleared place where he had worked in those leftover hours, where he had dreamed, had believed, had worked, he came to the place where the skeleton of the house was taking shape. Clay stood for a long time looking at it.

All around the framework of the house were piles of materials. To the casual observer these would seem to be pieces of junk, but to Clay they were precious pieces of a jigsaw puzzle and each of them had a place in the house he craved with all his heart to build. The neat pile of fieldstones he had lugged up on Sunday afternoons were someday to be the fire-place. The weathered two-by-fours were waiting for just the right place in the frame of the house. The old wagon wheel he was saving for Olivia to plant petu-nias in. The old automobile tire would be hung by a rope from one of the oak trees nearby and would be a fine swing for the children to play on. A roll of linoleum he had been given in payment for some odd job he had planned to use to cover the kitchen floor for Olivia. Now it lay weather-beaten and cracked with *age*.

In the heat of the dead August sun, Clay examined the house that had been his dream. But now for the first time as he looked at it there came in his mind no sounds. No shouts of children disturbed the imaginary lawn. No sound of singing came from the place where the kitchen might have been. No comfortable cluck of chickens or lowing of cows came from the unbuilt barn. There was utter silence on the motionless August air. It was August and everything had died.

Clay had known it for a long time and he would not tell it to himself, but now he knew with a wrenching wave of knowing, with a terrible sense of loss and bit-terness, that the jigsaw puzzle would never be put together. There were too many pieces lost. There would never be time or money enough to get them all together. There never had been. There had only been his insane hope and determination that the house would be built and what he had dreamed had only been a dream.

He rose and began to destroy that which was already dead. The horrible guttural cries of a man unaccustomed to tears forced their way through his throat, and tears and sweat rolled down his face together as he seized a sledge hammer and splintered each hand-hewn stud of the framework. Each blow he dealt the house fell as if on some living part of himself and Clay cried aloud with the pain.

When the studs and beams and joists were reduced to chips and splinters he turned to the treasures he had collected. He heaved the rotting linoleum high in the air and it fell into the hole with a dull thud. A roll of tin that was to have been part of the roof shattered the air with a shrill metallic scream. A piece of a cooking stove followed and then a shower of splintering glass as he heaved in some panes through which he had hoped one day to watch the falling snows of winter, the soft creeping green of spring's returning. When he was done with all that he could find to fill the hole he turned to the pile of fieldstone and with it covered all that remained of the place he had opened in the earth. When it was covered he walked away and did not look back on what he had done.

At the edge of the clearing he stopped and scooped up a handful of earth and then he went on down the mountain, carrying the earth in his hand.

CHAPTER 17

HALFWAY DOWN THE mountain Clay came out of the deep woods and into an open pasture. There at the edge of the pasture was the old Spencer graveyard. Overhead there was a ceiling of tall old pine trees and underfoot the periwinkle showed its little blue starflower. Many of the graves were marked by rude fieldstones that had simply been upended, and countless Spencers rested underneath them, but those who had died since the mill had opened had their names and dates neatly chiseled on soap-stone markers. And though Clay did not know many of the names of the dead, it was comforting to be among them and know that they were his own people and that someday he would join them under the pine and the periwinkle and the stone.

When he came to the stone which marked his father's grave, Clay knelt and tried to bring his father's face back into his mind. First he reconstructed the long prominent nose and then the white curling handlebar mustache and then the whole face took shape, the eyes with their brown merriment, the curve of his father's cheek, and the silken white neatly combed hair.

"How they treaten you down there, Papa?" Clay asked the empty air. "I hope you're haven yourself a time up there wherever it is. I reckon if they don't let no whiskey through the gates you'll find yourself a place to make some somehow.

"I reckon wherever you are you can see down here. If you really can see everything, like they say you can after you're dead, then I don't have to tell you what's goen on.

"Times is changen on this old earth, Papa, and it looks like we're goen to have to change right along with 'em. I don't mean me and Livy and Mama, but there's some kind of world out there waiten for my babies and I aim to see 'em get whatever they can out of it.

"I recken you know what's on my mind before I say it, Papa." Clay reached out the handful of earth and slowly let it fall through his fingers over his father's grave. "This is the last of the land. I'm sellen what's left of the mountain. I know what that land meant to you and only Old Master Jesus knows what it means to me. I tried hard to build that house on it for Livy and the babies, but I just never could get around to it. Somethen always got in the way. First the babies started comen along and the next thing you know I was putten in overtime tryen to make enough money to put food in their stomachs and clothes on their backs.

"Nights I'd get home from cutten rock all day and there'd be the cow to milk and the wood to split and the pigs to feed and then the old woman would have supper on the table. I'd get up from the supper table and think maybe I'll go and work on the house for thirty or forty minutes before it got dark, but I'd walk out of the door and find it was dark already. The sun goes down too soon for a poor man, Papa, and you know it yourself. There just ain't hours in a day to do

314

all a poor man's got to do."

Clay had spoken aloud, but now he fell silent and in silence he communed with his father's spirit. When he came to himself he realized that the sun had fallen beyond the horizon, the tree frogs had begun their evening chorus, and the chill of the graveyard had crept up out of the earth and through his body. The dappled green shadows in which he had sat earlier were gone and now the world had turned to a silver moonlit dusk and through it Clay walked thoughtfully, wondering how he might sell to the company those last remaining acres of the land of his ancestors.

While the decision was still fresh in his mind, before there was time for him to change his mind, he went to the one man he knew would buy his land on the mountain and the bargain was made.

When he came home Clay saw no lights in the children's rooms and he knew they must be asleep, and for the first time since he had left the house in the morning he had some sense of time. It must be late, he thought as he started up the walk. The only light in the house streamed out of the kitchen window and through it he could see Olivia bent over a washpan full of dishes.

When Clay opened the door he startled her. She glared at him angrily for a moment and then curiously when she realized that he was sober.

"Where've you been?" she asked, trying to sound cross.

"Walken around," Clay answered and sat at his place at the head of the table.

"You took yourself one long walk," said Olivia. "It's near bedtime."

The soapstone tub where Olivia washed her clothes, her dishes and the smaller children was old and chipped and worn. The walls of the room had not been painted in years and the white they had originally been had turned to gray in spite of the hard scrubbing Olivia gave them during spring and fall cleaning.

Olivia was moving from the sink to the kitchen cabinet, putting away the dishes she had washed and dried. Each time she tried to close the kitchen-cabinet door she had to work first with a hinge that had been unscrewed for months before she could make the door meet the latch which fastened it. It was an action she had repeated so often that it had become automatic and it no longer occurred to her to ask Clay to repair it.

As she pushed the broken hinge into place she was surprised to feel Clay's hand take hers and gently remove it from the faulty hinge. Then he reached in a drawer where he kept some tools and searched around until he found a screw and a screwdriver.

Olivia had been watching him in a puzzled way. Now she demanded, "What are you doen, you crazy old man?"

"I'm goen to fix this place up for you, honey," declared Clay. "I'm goen to fix this kitchen cabinet and I'm goen to get you a new sink and this time it won't be one from down at the mill. We'll go over there to Charlottesville to the Sears and Roebuck and buy one of them white porcelain ones. I'm goen to put some paint on these walls, too, and once I finish that I'm goen to screen in that back porch so we can sit out there of an evenen."

Olivia did not look pleased, only puzzled.

"I think the dog days have made you a little bit crazy," she said. "You been acten funny ever since you got home."

"Home is what this place is goen to be for as long as we got left on this earth, honey. Right here is where we're goen to live and die for the rest of our days."

What he told her Olivia already knew. She could not remember when, but at some point in their marriage, she had known that the house on the mountain would never be built, had only really gone along with his plans because men were foolish creatures and needed someone to believe that they could do the things they said they could. She had expected Clay to go to his grave waiting for that magical day when the money, the time and the materials would appear with which to build the house.

"This is not a bad house we're in," she said. "With a little fixen it could be real comfortable. Didn't you always say you thought you could build a basement under it?"

Clay nodded.

"And with all that lumber up there on the mountain I don't see why you couldn't add a couple of rooms onto it so the children can spread out a little bit."

"That lumber don't belong to me no more, honey," said Clay. "That's what I'm tryen to tell you."

"Clay, what you been up to all day long?"

"I went up there on the mountain and I thought it all out. Then I went over to see old Colonel Coleman and I sold him my land."

"I vow!" exclaimed Olivia.

"He didn't want to give me but a hundred and seventy-five dollars at first but I said I wouldn't let it go for a penny less than two hundred and thirty-five."

"Clay, I want him to go to Richmond bad as you do, but it wouldn't be fair to the other children to sacrifice everything just on Clay-Boy. They've got to be thought of too."

"I've put heart and mind to that already, honey," said Clay. "And I've decided we've still got to do it. The way I look at it, there's fine stuff in my babies. But it's like a river that's damned up. All we'll ever get to see is what little bit pours over the top of the dam unless somethen comes along that breaks the walls down and lets the river flow. Well, somethen has come along. Clay-Boy is goen to college. If he goes down there and makes good then he's goen to help Matt get a start in life, and Matt will help Becky and right on down the line. All they need is a little start and God knows they might turn out to be doctors and nurses and lawyers and salesmen or even presidents. I used to vision the most we could do for all of 'em was to get 'em through high school. I can see more than that now."

"It's putten a mighty responsibility on Clay-Boy."

"The boy will do it. It's in him. He's got heart and muscle and it looks like he's got brains too. All my babies is thoroughbred. There ain't a throwaway in the bunch."

"Lord," said Olivia, "you must be starved. Haven't had a thing to eat since breakfast."

"I was hungry," said Clay, "but I'm not any more. Hot in here. Let's sit on the porch."

For a long time they sat together, Olivia in the swing and Clay on the top step of the porch. It was dark but Olivia could see where Clay was from the red glow of his cigarette, and he could tell where she was from the soft creaking of the rusty chains that supported the porch swing.

A little breeze passed across the porch and carried on it the scent of honeysuckle. Clay rose and, going to the swing, took his wife by the hand.

"Come on," he said. "Let's go to bed."

CHAPTER 18

THE DULL AND HEAT-LADEN days of August, the endless leaden dog days, vanished in a rainstorm and September dawned bright and sparkling and sunny. The foliage began to turn and every hill and valley took on the subtle, delicate shades that by late September would be intense and blazing colors.

But the beauty of the autumn was wasted on Clay-Boy Spencer. He had become a nervous wreck who lived for two things, the morning and afternoon arrival of the mail at the post office. He would show up there as soon as the mail arrived and stand at the grillwork looking in while his Aunt Frances sorted through each sack.

If there were a letter she would bring it to him even before the rest of the mail was sorted, which was against the rules; if there were none she would be as despondent as Clay-Boy.

On the days that a letter did arrive he would slip it casually into his pocket and walk out of the post office with pretended indifference, only to tear open the envelope frantically once he was unobserved and scan quickly through the letter for the awful news he expected; then, not finding anything more than vague hints, he would reread each exasperating word.

His most recent, and by far the most cryptic, letter from Claris had also been the shortest:

Dear:
     Tremendous news! I cannot trust myself to write it. Will tell you in person. Meet me Friday after-noon at three o'clock at Friendship Corner.
                                        Always yours,
                                        Claris

He could guess now what the news was. She had never before visited her father twice during the summer and only one thing could prompt her return now. She was pregnant, and was coming to break the news to him.

Waves of shame and regret roiled in his mind.

"Damn her to hell. It was her idea to take our clothes off. All I did was go along with it." But no matter where he placed the blame he always came back to the realization that it rested squarely on his own shoulders.

He went through the remaining days like a sleepwalker. He would sit at the table with his family and the things they said to each other and to him would flow past him and through him, and he would not hear a word that was spoken.

Once his mother came to him, placed her hand on his forehead and said, "He's all flushed and hot. I got a good mind to send for the doctor."

And then Clay-Boy would push his mother's hand away and walk his sleeping walk up the stairs to the boys' room where he would throw himself on the bed and try to think of some way out of his dilemma and end up trying not to think of anything at all.

"He's lovesick," Clay ventured one night. "Lonesome for that little girl."

"It's worryen about leaven home," guessed Olivia. "He's not big enough to go so far from home."

"Honey," Clay reasoned, "all that's worryen that boy is will he get a letter from that little girl tomorrow or not. I know how a boy feels waiten around for some word from a little old girl. I was just as bad when I was sweet-talken you."

"And I hope we've seen the last of that one," observed Olivia. "She's got gland trouble or something, I figure. Anybody that can't think about nothen but sex all the time has got somethen wrong with their glands."

By Friday, armed with a plan of action, Clay-Boy had emerged from his coma. He was patient now with the children, polite and attentive when his parents spoke to him, courteous, correct, punctual. In a way this new pose was even more exasperating to Olivia. He reminded her of someone who had foreknowledge of his own death and was resigned to it.

A little bit before three that afternoon he left the house, saying he was going for a walk. Olivia stood looking after him. The strain of going away is too much for his mind, she thought. We've all pushed him into something he doesn't want to do and now it's too late for him to turn back.

She wanted to run after him and demand he tell her what was troubling him, but she decided that if he had not been able to unburden himself by now he probably never would.

Now the end of the world is coming, Clay-Boy told himself as he walked through the gold-and-russet autumn to meet Claris. He remembered a hundred sermons he had heard at the Baptist church, warning him against doing just what he had done, warning him too of the consequences his evil would bring upon him. He had heard the preacher's words but in the one important moment there on the mountain he had forgotten them.

He would marry her. He had made up his mind to

that. By marrying her he would be doing the manly thing. The baby would have his name and Claris would be saved from ruin. How he would support them he had no idea. He only knew that it would be in some place far from New Dominion and that they would have to run away to that place soon.

Friendship Corner was hidden by a massive mulberry tree. It had turned lemon-yellow in the autumn air and it had not yet begun to lose its leaves. It formed a glorious canopy over the old gray gabled building, and as he walked down the path, Clay-Boy wondered how such grim news could wait for him under so beautiful a ceiling.

Claris was sitting on the railing in such a lady-like pose that at first Clay-Boy hardly recognized her. The long dark braids were gone. Now her hair was parted in the middle and drawn back severely against the side of her head. What it did in the back he could not see. Her eyes, when they met his, seemed even larger than he had remembered, and to Clay-Boy they also seemed older and wiser.

Gone were the faded dungarees. In their place was a soft rose-colored sweater and a gray tweed skirt. Somehow she looked so much older than he had remembered her. It was the pregnancy, Clay-Boy supposed.

"Aren't you going to say anything?" she asked.

"You look different," he said.

"It's my hair," she said. "I didn't have anything else to do one night so I decided to lop it all off. I had to wear a beanie for a few weeks, but now there's enough for a French knot. Do you like it?"

"I don't know yet," he said. He glanced down at her stomach and back to her face again.

"What are you looking at?" she inquired. Her eyes danced with laughter, but her voice sounded reproachful.

"You," he said.

"You seem so nervous," she said. "I don't know if I like you this way or not."

"I'm not nervous," he insisted.

"Guilty, then?" she asked.

"What have I got to be guilty about?" he demanded.

"Oh, I don't know," she said. "Unless you've been taking other girls up to the top of the mountain."

"I haven't been back up there," he said angrily. "Alone or with anybody else. Look Claris, I came here prepared to do the right thing."

"And what is that?" she asked.

"I'm going to marry you. We'll have to find some place to go and we won't tell anybody where we are until it's all over. Then we'll let our people know and put their minds at rest, but we'll do whatever has to be done."

"You are the most confusing boy," she said. "What on earth are you talking about?"

"I'm talking about those letters you've been sending me. I'm talking about the baby."

"What baby?" she asked.

"Aren't you going to have a baby?"

"Whatever gave you that idea?" she asked innocently.

"Every letter you've sent me since you left," he replied.

"You really do have a guilty conscience, haven't you?" she said. "If you have such a guilty conscience later why do you take little girls off to the top of the mountain?"

Angered beyond words, he seized her by the arms and shook her violently.

"Are you going to have a baby or not?"

"No," she cried.

"That's all I want to know," he said. He released her, turned and walked away, but she ran in front of him and stopped him.

"I'm sorry I teased you. It was only because I had a wonderful surprise and I didn't want to tell you until I knew for sure."

"I've had enough of your surprises," he said and tried to push her aside.

"Will you just listen to what it is?" she asked.

He stood silent and waiting.

"The reason I went back to Washington early this summer was to talk Mother into letting me switch colleges. That was hard enough, but getting into the new school was harder still. But it's all settled now. I've been accepted at Westhampton."

"Where's that?"

"It's the girl's college at the University of Richmond. It's right across the lake from where you'll be. That's all I wanted to tell you."

Clay-Boy felt as if he had awakened from a dream in which he had been falling from some great height. The earth and all that surrounded him which had been so blurred and distant in his despair, returned to focus. He could hear the singing of birds again and see the trees and the earth and the eyes of the girl before him. The nightmare visions of the Colonel coming to confront him, of his father and all the family being turned out of their home, of the shame of betraying his father after he had sacrificed so much, all fell away with one shuddering surge of relief.

"Aren't you pleased?" he heard someone say and looked down into Claris' face. For the first time since he had known her she seemed shy and wordless.

"It's wonderful," he said.

"We won't have classes together, or anything like that but we could see each other once in a while."

"I won't have much money for dates," he said, "but you know that already."

"We could walk around the lake."

She stood looking up at him. She was not teasing him now. She was waiting for something, and then he realized that it was the same thing he wanted and bent and put his lips to hers. Their arms stole around each other and after a long time they walked out of the golden canopy of the mulberry tree into the brilliant September sun.

All during the last summer months Olivia had been

gathering a wardrobe for Clay-Boy to wear at college. She had mended every rip and tear in his existing clothing and she had gone through every article of his father's clothing to see if she could find something Clay-Boy might use.

Finally she had decided that the one thing he absolutely had to have was a good suit. Those she found at the commissary she decided were wrong. They all looked like something an old man might wear, and she wanted this suit to be exactly right.

One night after the children were in bed, she and Clay sat in the living room. Clay was lost in his Western story in a Zane Grey book Clay-Boy had brought to him from the library while Olivia studied the pictures of boys' suits in the Sears, Roebuck catalogue.

"I want it to be somethen like the rest of them boys will be wearen," said Olivia. "Somethen collegy."

"Honey, he's goen down there to get an education," said Clay. "It don't matter if he wear a burlap sack. It's what they're goen to put in his head that's important."

"Still, I don't want him to look countrified," she said. "He's goen to have to get used to so many newfangled things the least we can do is send him off dressed for it."

"Honey, it's goen to be the same as it was with me and that cow. Get all dressed up and your best friends will mistake you for a stranger."

"You are the ignorantest thing I ever heard talk," observed Olivia dryly.

"Honey," he said teasingly, "it's a mighty fine thing for you I never had the chance that boy is getten."

"How do you figure that, you crazy old thing?"

"Well, if I'd of gone to college I would of got myself one of them little college girls and where would you be today?"

"One thing's for sure. I wouldn't be sitten here talken to no fool now." Olivia returned to her perusal of the Sears, Roebuck catalogue. "Now here's what I kind of had in mind," she said and held out the catalogue so that Clay might see. "That one there," she pointed out.

"It's right pretty from the picture," said Clay.

"That one looks exactly like what I saw a boy wearen over in Charlottesville one time. I said to myself at the time how nice Clay-Boy would look in a suit like that." She read the description from the catalogue. "Green herringbone tweed. Comes with vest. Extra pants optional."

"How much they asken for it?" demanded Clay.

"Nineteen dollars and ninety-five cents."

"Methuselah's britches!" exclaimed Clay. "What's it made out of? Fourteen-carat gold?"

"It says this herringbone tweed is fifty per cent wool and fifty per cent cotton, long-lasting and keeps its crease. Clay, I know it's expensive and all, but I think he ought to have it. We could buy it out of that money his granddaddy left him, and he'd still have seventeen dollars in his pocket when he leaves."

"Honey, there ain't a thing wrong with that suit I was plannen to be buried in. I'll just put off dyen for a while and let him use that."

"Oh, he's goen to use it," Olivia said. "I've already taken in the britches so it fits him just fine, but that's goen to be his everyday suit. What I'm talken about here is somethen for when he dresses up."

"Two suits! Woman, you have lost your mind."

"Listen to me, you old hillbilly. I'll bet you some of them boys he'll be up against down there will have two or three of everything, and while we're on the subject I think he ought to have some more shirts."

"Give him that white one I was saven to be buried in," Clay offered again.

"I was already counten that one, but that still only makes four. I think I'll get him one more. A green one maybe to go with his new suit."

"Woman," he exploded, "whatever gave you the notion you married John D. Rockefeller?"

"I reckon it was the way you talked when you were courten me," she rejoined.

"Oh, I was John D. Rockefeller in them days. I had money to burn back then. Why, in them days I'd go out of an evening and spend five or six dollars and never think a thing about it. Then all of a sudden you come along swingen that pretty little tail in front of me and I knew my time was up. Now here I am with eleven kids to take care of, one of 'em goen to college, and nothen to be buried in if I die by accident. All my clothes will be strutten around down yonder at the University of Richmond."

They debated long into the night but the discussion

ended finally with Olivia making out the order, without the extra trousers, and sending it off in the morning mail. When the suit came she planned to keep it is a surprise for Clay-Boy and not give it to him until the time came for him to leave.

Eliza returned home unexpectedly. "Just wanted to get settled before winter time," she said. "Needed the feel of my own bed again. My own things around me."

Some of the pain had gone from her eyes, but the family knew that she would never completely stop grieving for the old man. They contrived to keep her busy. The girls went to her with happily granted requests for lessons in knitting and crocheting. Olivia brought out scraps she had been saving for a patch-work quilt and Eliza fitted them together, using her own Star of David pattern.

On Friday of the week end he was to leave, Clay-Boy stood in the doorway of the little library for one final look. He had read every book on the shelves and he felt better about leaving them now that he knew they would be left in loving hands—Miss Parker had per-suaded the Episcopalian minister and his wife to allow their daughter, Geraldine Boyd, to take Clay-Boy's place at the library. Clay-Boy locked the door, placed the key under the mat and hurried home.

Early Sunday morning Clay-Boy sat at the window of the boys' room and looked out into the crab apple orchard. He had not slept. In a few hours he would be leaving, and every sound that came to his ears filled him with pain and sadness.

The routine sounds of the house coming to life seemed more beautiful than he had ever imagined. He heard the clamor of his father's alarm clock, his father's long deep yawn and then Clay's muttered weather forecast for the day: "Goen to be a nice one." And then he heard the clank of the iron lid as his father filled the cooking range with wood, the whoosh of the fire up the chimney as Clay lighted the kerosene-soaked sticks, the squeak of the loose board in the hall as Clay came to the foot of the stairs to call Olivia—"Sweetheart."

"All right, I'm awake," her answer came.

At breakfast everyone was solemn. Olivia's eyes were swollen and red from weeping and she spoke hardly at all. The plate she served Clay-Boy was laden with ham and eggs and biscuits.

"Be a long time before you get good home cooken again," she said. "Eat hearty."

Once in a while Clay would think of some parting piece of advice for his son and would interrupt his eating long enough to say,

"Don't get mixed up with bad women if you can help it, boy. They'll ruin you."

Later he said, "Don't borrow money, play square with everybody and look 'em straight in the eye."

Clay-Boy promised gravely to follow his father's advice and the other children nodded their heads as if they too had heard and taken counsel from their father.

When everybody had been served, Olivia left the room and went up to the boys' room. Later when she came down she said, "I've laid your clothes out for you on your bed, son."

"I reckon it is about time I started getten ready," he said. He made his way up the stairs slowly. The first thing he saw when he walked into his room was the new green herringbone tweed suit.

All sound had stopped from down below. They were all waiting for some signal of his surprise, some cry of joy, but when none came everyone looked at each other uncomfortably. Finally Olivia came to the foot of the stairs.

"Son," she called.

When no answer came she called again, "Clay-Boy?"

"Yes ma'am," he answered, and his voice was thick with tears.

"You all right?" she called.

His footsteps sounded across the floor and when he came to the door of his room he was carrying the suit in his arms.

"You like it all right?" she asked.

"Oh Mama," he said. "I never in my life expected to have anything so pretty." He went down the stairs in a rush, embracing his mother and father and then was off to show his brothers and sisters, letting them feel it if their hands were clean.

When he tried the coat on, his father said, "Boy, you're goen to have to fight the women off when you wear that."

"I bet I will too, Daddy," he said, and then he went back upstairs to finish dressing.

His mother was waiting for him in the kitchen when he came back down. She was holding the envelope with the money in it that would pay for Clay-Boy's first semester of college.

"Can't I just put it in my wallet, Mama?" he asked.

"No," she said, "you'll lose it."

She slipped the envelope in the inner pocket of his suit and fastened it there with a safety pin.

"I've got it pinned there good and tight," she said. "Don't unpin it until you're ready to pay the college."

On the front porch, Clay-Boy found his Grand-mother Spencer waiting to say good-by. After they had kissed each other she held him at arm's length and said, "Don't take up fancy ways, boy. Trust in God and go to church."

Clay had borrowed a pickup truck to drive Clay-Boy to Hickory Creek, where he would catch the bus for Richmond. Clay was driving and Olivia, holding Franklin Delano and Eleanor, sat in the front seat. Clay-Boy and the other children rode in the body of the truck.

As the truck pulled out of the yard, Clay-Boy looked for as long as he could back at the house. He wished for one moment that the truck would turn around and take him back and that he could relive every moment he had known in that house, but then the house was gone in a turning of the road, and only the memory of the warmth and happiness and love he had known there remained in his mind.

When they reached Hickory Creek the Trailways bus was already lumbering down Route 29. Clay-Boy kissed each of the children good-by, then his mother, while his father flagged down the bus.

Be a good boy," said Olivia.

"I will," he promised.

"Give 'em hell, son," said Clay.

"Good-by, Daddy," he said, and held his father's strong rough hand in a quick handshake, and then the bus was there and he was on it.

For a few minutes after he reached his seat his eyes were clouded with tears, but when they were clear again he saw that the bus was nearing the top of a steep mountain road.

"Goen far, son?" asked an old farmer sitting next to him.

"Right far," the boy said, and watched as the bus arrived at the top of the mountain and went on into the beckoning world.

Center Point Publishing
600 Brooks Road • PO Box 1
Thorndike ME 04986-0001 USA

(207) 568-3717

US & Canada:
1 800 929-9108